RBIT — CALLOWAY MEMORIAL LIB
ESSA, DE

1-99

Y0-CUH-149

THE MAN I NEVER WANTED TO BE

BY

JOHN J. CLAYTON

THE PERMANENT PRESS
SAG HARBOR, NY 11963

Copyright © 1998 by John J. Clayton

Libary of Congress Cataloging-in-Publication Data

Clayton, John J.
    The Man I Never Wanted To Be / by John J. Clayton
      p. cm.
    ISBN 1-57962-014-0
    I. Title.
    PS3553.L3879M36   1998
    813'.54--dc21   97-36395
                                                                             CIP

THE PERMANENT PRESS
4170 Noyac Road
Sag Harbor, NY 11963

With love always for
Sharon, Aaron, Sasha, Josh, Laura, Jed, Lucie, Steve
Marilyn and George, Marlynn and Garry

One

My house at the edge of the woods looks back at me ironically. It's as if Pygmalion had dreamed and carved his Galatea and then was *stuck* with her, a *wife*, who kept him up late into the night. "Don't you love me anymore? I thought you were going to adore me forever! Didn't you beg Aphrodite?"—when all Pygmalion wanted was to get some sleep so he could sculpt the next day.

It was a house I built with a carpenter from unfinished lumber I bought cheap. Rough-made house with windows I picked up for a song at salvage yards, windows looking out on a small meadow south, where Nancy, Jeremy's mother, planted perennial gardens. Early autumn now, gardens turning dingy and raggedy. And anyway, these past two summers, Nancy gone, I've let them go to hell. Surrounded by a rise of pine and hemlock to the north, the house burrows into the steep hill against the winter. It's open to the south sun like a lover. Beyond the meadow, woods, mostly oak and maple, and beyond the woods a gradual rise to our mountain, what we call "our mountain," with a fire tower, tiny, at the top.

You come upon the house out of a small, new-growth woods to the east, and you know right away these people lived through the late sixties. The rough vertical boards aren't even stained; over the past twelve years they've grown heavily grained, gray or deep brown in the sun and rain, but they still keep out the weather. The rough lumber, the unskilled labor of friends, the inadequate flashing—because what did I know back then?—made it certain there'd be leaks. Inside, the walls are covered with old barnboard from a barn I tore down.

Jeremy and I drive up from the mailbox on the dirt road. A cherry-picker load of logs to the side of the driveway waits for me to chain saw it into about six cords, our winter heat. Be careful what you wish for, my mama used to say, lest it come true.

There's a note from my neighbor, Russell Warner, taped to a brown bag in front of my door: *Dave—Last tomatoes of the year. Syl figured you'd want some.* I do.

I still love this house. Jeremy's lived in it his whole life, eight years. I feel happy when I see him run from the gravel parking area, down the brick path he helped lay, to the front door. No lock on the door—nothing worth stealing. I follow, lugging my suitcase, and, putting it down, inspect the tomatoes Russ has left, the squash left in my own kitchen garden.

I see work ahead. Plus work upstairs, where two sets of compositions I should have corrected this weekend wait on my desk. And my article for *The Boston Globe* on community college teaching.

"Dad! Dad? Mom called, Mom wants you to call her back right away. And a couple of other messages. I didn't listen. Oh—and the rain leaked on my mattress again."

He's like me, needing to rush for messages. I sit down in the kitchen, walls of pine boards with family pictures nailed up, and call Nancy. Line's busy; suddenly, as I think for the hundredth time about how to fix that leak in Jeremy's room, I hear a long *shriek!—DISASTER! DISASTER!*—I race up the stairs to Jeremy's room —

"What!? WHAT?!"

"The card Gar gave me—"

I breathe again. "He gave you a baseball card?"

"He said not to tell you till later. It's a 1971 Carl Yastrzmeski, and you know how much it's worth? Mint it's worth over two hundred dollars, only it's not mint—but it's almost. It's my best card."

"Wow. That was real nice of him." I smile but in fact it pisses me off. Gar knows I could never give Jeremy a card like that.

We're back from a weekend in New York, first time he's ever been there. First time in years I've been back. Saturday morning we ran into Gar Stone in the sculpture courtyard at MOMA.

Jeremy slips the card into a plastic sleeve in his "best" album.

"So what did you think of Gar?"

"Nice. He talks loud."

"He does . . . . And what about Gabriella?"

"*Good.* She sat on the floor and talked with me."

It pleases me she sat with Jeremy at Gar's party, Park Avenue in the eighties, instead of working the well-heeled crowd for contributions and connections. Just seeing her in mind's eye, seeing Gabriella Rossi, pleases me. How we loved each other for awhile back then, just a few months, twenty years ago and then some—when we were lovers and political comrades. I see the way her thick black hair tumbled around us, under us, see me free-falling into its wildness.

All my life I've been a lover, all my life a fool about love. I've told myself, Why do you have to look at a woman and groan?—crossing the street, say, or two rows ahead at a lecture. I think it's the pain of knowing we'll probably never make love. No. More: knowing I'll never live forever and ever with this beautiful soul.

Surely, love warps my seeing. But intensifies it, too, as if my sex were an acute instrument of perception. I've loved women all my life, sometimes only for a few weeks, or a few days, or maybe, good grief, half an hour, but for that time I feel in touch with the secret heart of their heart, and often they feel it too and invite me in. Sometimes they're sorry and bewildered later, and so am I.

"We may—we may see Gabriella again," I say. "Okay?"

Jeremy starts twirling.

He started twirling some months ago, twirls when he's self-conscious or twirls out of sheer pleasure in movement. He holds the album of baseball cards over his head and twirls, head tilted back.

I put away my stuff, get Jeremy to pack for his mother's. He's always packing. The house stops looking unfamiliar—strange spaces of dark wood patched with sunlight, everywhere jobs needing to be done. It becomes our house.

While he packs, I listen to my other messages. Gabriella has called. I listen twice through, though she just asks me to call back, gives me her numbers. I try her at home first—in Brookline—but catch her at Sojourner House in Boston.

"We *do* need some help, David," she says as soon as she knows it's me. "I'll understand if you say no. There are other people we can fall back on. But you're far enough from Boston—and you're right near the shelter where she's going to be living for awhile."

"It's the woman you told me about?"

"She's very young, with a two-year-old. I don't say it'll be easy. But it'll be brief. She's an emotional addict, she keeps going back to the husband, and not just for support, she keeps getting beaten up, terrified, last time he picked up the little boy and held him in one hand over a stairwell. That did it for her; she came to us. When I talked to you the other night, I wasn't sure she'd be able to go through with it."

"For how long?"

"Oh, not long. A very few days. It seems a bad idea for us to take her here. The woman's husband comes from a Boston police family, and of course the police know where the shelter is. And his brother, the husband's brother, is a lawyer tied into political people. No, our shelter wouldn't be safe."

"I told you, I do want to help." I think, *Jeremy*—Jeremy goes to Nancy tonight, he'll be with her two weeks. That makes it possible. "I'd be kind of *honored*."

"There's space opening up in a shelter near you. In just a few days."

"Green River Women in Transition?"

"That's right. So it's just for now—because this husband is off the wall. I mean really *off the wall*. I'm afraid—she could be one of the murdered ones. David, we have women who are battered and leave—and are dragged back or seduced back with promises and their heads are split open or they're kicked in the uterus to pay them back for leaving or for getting pregnant. . . . You can't imagine. I can tell you about women who wake up in the middle of the night, night after night, with a gun to their mouths or a knife to their baby's throat. I've seen too much. I'm not easily scared. But this woman's situation scares me. So you *can* imagine."

"I can imagine."

Gabriella goes on. "I've never sent a woman this far from Boston before. We've got safe houses we can use for a few days, even for a month. But I'd really like her *way* out of the way. She's got a restraining order, but I wouldn't count on it. And until she's part of a shelter—well, I don't trust that she won't meet him, or that he won't follow her and she won't go back. Of course, finally, we can't rescue her; finally, she's got to rescue herself, but look—for the next few days—you think it would be possible, Dave?"

But a week can turn into a month, who knows? I say, "You don't think the guy would come out here after her?"

"Oh, I do. He would. If he knew where to come. But he won't."

"Let's hope."

"That mean you'll take it on? You're sure it'll be all right?"

"I'm sure."

"I've never done anything like this. Ordinarily, there are legal forms to fill out, we give training sessions, it's a pretty formal thing. But we don't have time. I'm taking it on my own authority. I'll drive her out myself, we can have pizza or something, I'll drive back. Is tonight possible?"

"What time?"

It's nearly nine o'clock before the lights from Gabriella's Taurus hit the walls and I step out onto the sagging front deck and wave, and Gabriella and a woman, child against her chest, walk down the brick path.

I was expecting a *black* woman and child. Why the hell *was* I? But she's white. So young, couldn't be more than eighteen, nineteen, long bleached hair, bouffant, big hair, uncombed, some of it pinned up on top, irregular bangs over her forehead. A little boy in her arms, a blanket in his hands, the kid twisting against her, two years old. I guess he's been sleeping in the car and now he's fussing at the lights and motion. Gabriella carries her pack.

"I've got his bed ready for him," I whisper, loving him at the first sign of the dangly legs and messy blonde hair and mouth like a little fish. I lead the way up the yellow-pine stairs with no risers, so it's like stairs in a dream, floating up through the living room to my bedroom and above that to the room I use when friends come. She puts the boy down on the foam mat I've covered with a comforter. As we walk back downstairs, the young woman looks suspicious, maybe because the house is so peculiar, maybe just because I'm a man. She keeps her eye on Gabriella. I'm like some German meeting a Jew and even though he was born long after Hitler and the camps were gone, the German feels implicated, ashamed, needs to show somehow that he's no Nazi.

"I'm Dave Rosen," I say, putting out a hand. She just nods.

"This is Kerry Latrice," Gabriella says.

"This is so crazy," Kerry says. "I mean it's *nowhere*."

"Isn't that the point?" Gabriella says. "That it's nowhere?"

Nowhere? That bothers me, the goddamn urbanism of it.

Kerry shrugs this off. She's wearing a sad old blouse and torn jeans. At first I don't see bruises; now I see the line of gray along her jaw line and the puffiness under her left eye. It's not as bad as I'd imagined. Neaten her up and she'd look like one of my students. But I see her as *off*, somehow, not exactly with it.

"This house of yours," Gabriella says, looking around. "It's like a relic of the early seventies. For awhile, I lived in a commune—we put up barn boards like this over the terrible old wallpaper. Did you build it?"

"With a carpenter." I notice again, as I did at Gar's party, Gabriella's sculpted face and high cheekbones that, even when we were in our twenties, in love, bespoke to me of *will*. I try to imagine, could I love a woman like that? God knows she's beautiful. Lines around the eyes and mouth, skin glow fading, a touch of flesh at the throat—but she has so much more character now. Her eyes in deep hollows over the strong cheek bones and still the dark, rich skin. The beginnings of lines in her face—who cares? I've never minded lines, only the makeup women use to hide them. Gabriella wears only a touch of eye liner. Reading glasses, like a pendant on a silver chain, hang around her neck, like a badge of having lived.

"It's nice," she says. "It's real nice. It's warm." She smiles into my eyes.

So I'm a little embarrassed. "Anyone want tea?" I ask. "And there's chicken sandwiches. *Good* bread."

"Thanks, no. And Jeremy—where's Jeremy?" Gabriella asks. "Asleep?"

"Gone. It's his time with Nancy."

"Oh." She's upset. "*Oh.* Why didn't you tell me?"

"You thought Jeremy lived me with full time?"

"I did. When you said your marriage was 'going down the tubes'— I took that to mean—that your marriage was *rocky*. I didn't understand. Oh, dear God. I feel so foolish."

"Separated for over a year now. I should have made it clear. But—we were at a party."

We're standing nowhere, not living room, not kitchen, a kind of non-space near the front door. I see Gabriella turning it over in her mind. "When I asked if it would be all right, I meant—I meant all right *with your wife* . . . " Now she turns. "Kerry—this isn't something we do at Sojourner House. But," she says, "I've known this guy a long time. You'll be safe here. All right, Kerry?"

"Yeah, sure. Whatever."

I walk Gabriella back to the car. "Not even your friends should know," she says. "That's part of the training you're not getting."

"I understand."

"Don't expect her to be an altogether wonderful person," she warns. "Most of the women who come to us, they *under*play their abuse. They say, 'Maybe it's my own fault, maybe it'll go away.' Kerry's almost flamboyant about her troubles. But she's really had it pretty hard. Give her time to loosen up. And David, *don't* let her get away with every thing, don't you do all the work."

"I understand. No. Well . . . it's real good to see *you*," I say. "You know that, don't you." And looking into her dark eyes in the dim light of the driveway, I can't make it out, how she moves me. Is it just the piece of me I lost or gave away—like a refugee in the forties meeting another refugee, someone who knew him in Poland and Germany, knew he was *somebody*, a person with a place?

Gabriella's hair, still long and curly, still black but even in the semi-dark I can see gray beginning. She's a woman who carries herself proudly as she always did, never trying to be a wisp, always a big-hipped lady with lovely, large breasts, and the contradiction of softly sculpted face like St. Anne's in the Leonardo painting, with strong jaw and big mouth. Something lets me see into the life she's lived through, though I don't know the details. Skin no longer so soft, eyes no longer attempting to project innocence—I see life hasn't been easy.

"You know what, Gabriella? You're more beautiful now," I tell her out of the blue. I figure it's okay to tell a woman of forty-five she's beautiful, because by then it's no gift, but her own doing.

She doesn't answer. As we crunch gravel under our feet, I catch a whiff of perfume or cologne. In the moonlight I notice for the first time the white lacy collar of her blouse. Blouse and perfume surprise me; I expect a woman, a political woman, doing the work she's doing, grim, purposeful, no-frills. It surprises me that she dares to be even a little soft. What do I mean *dares*? I mean it's a sign of open feelings. How can she keep an open heart? That moves me.

"You'll be coming back for her?"

Gabriella laughs. The old laugh instantly makes me feel we're intimate. It's a gesture of intimacy, her laugh, the tilt upwards to her chin, her eyes closing with pleasure, and I find my perineum and my thighs glowing, the boundary between Gabriella and the world grow strong, so that she seems etched and permanent—in a funny way enlarged, pulsing. "Don't worry," she says. "You won't get *left* with her. Someone from Women in Transition will pick her up."

"It's not that."

"*Oh*. I see. Well," and she smiles, "I'd like to see you, too. As a friend. I'd like that . . . . Dave? I never would have suggested this if I'd understood. A safe-house without a woman?"

"But what's the difference? I'm safe enough," I say.

"It's not that. You must see—it's just not done. When you said you lived in western Mass, I remembered WIT and Kerry and it all fit. I should have asked to speak with your wife." She stops. "But David, I *am* grateful."

"We'll be all right. We'll be fine."

"I hope. Well—let's get together. I'd like you to see Sojourner House. Maybe you'll write about it—who knows?"

I look into her eyes now and in my head formulate sentences I don't use. "Goodnight," I say, "drive safely." I touch her arm, hold it for a moment, as if the holding is merely part of my concern for her driving home.

Monday morning, gorgeous crisp day. I have to leave for my nine o'clock class without seeing Kerry; I write her a note: "Welcome. Food in the fridge. Make a list of what we need from the store. A hiking trail begins at the bottom of the meadow." The kid is crying behind their closed door. When I come back at four, he's crying again, or still—*still* is how I imagine it—and now the door is open, and there's Jeremy's old toys, there's half-eaten plates of food, and my kitchen tools strewn all over the living room. Kerry is lying on the sofa in a stained tee shirt and jeans, she's got the heat pumped up. I almost never turn it on, but I'd prefer to burn oil than have someone who doesn't know how to use a wood stove burn the house down. I'll make it a point to teach her.

I look her over. Half asleep, covered with an old comforter, she doesn't look very teachable. The kid is just sitting in the middle of Jeremy's collection of toy cars and howling, and she's hushing him from the sofa. He smells rank. She's pulled the TV out from the corner so she can watch it while lying down. As I stow my book bag, she half waves, half grunts hello—surly or am I wrong?—and I say to myself, Well, okay, I made a mistake. And the boy smells bad and looks sour and the love I felt for the half-sleeping angel last night has gotten crowded out by smell and mess.

Kerry sits up and straightens her pink cardigan, combs her puffy, ragged, hair with her fingers and kind of smiles. She puts on a cool expression, but I notice her baby-softness underneath. In daylight, the swelling of cheek and eye is more noticeable. It makes my stomach turn over. "I'm glad you're finally back," she says. "It's kind of spooky here, like there's just *nothing*."

"Nothing? But it's some beautiful day," I say. "Did you get out into the meadow?"

"Andrew wouldn't go," she shrugs. "Field's all so bumpy, and there's bugs, and he's used to sidewalks."

Right off, with our first words, we've set up a dynamic, me the encouraging poppa, she the sluggish, sour teen. I sigh. Not wanting just to walk away, I ask, "What're you watching?"

"Television. Is that okay?" She looks at me so blandly I can't tell whether she's making a joke or what.

She stretches, she reaches down into a huge shoulder bag for a brush and brushes out her hair, and the dry air makes it electric and it flies out towards the strokes of the brush, pretty hair, and I see her for the first time as woman, not just child. She's lean, punk-tough, angular, kind of pretty, but her eyes are glazed. It's not just that the tissue is swollen. They're glazed.

The little boy stops whining to stare. "Mommy hair," he says.

"I'm kind of watching Oprah," she says. "I dozed off."

"It must be hard for you, all day here, not knowing anybody. It must feel unreal. Just you and the boy . . . . What's his name? I just realized, I don't know his name."

"What's your name?" she asks him. He shrugs. "Tell the nice man your goddamn name." He shrugs. "Annnn . . . " she prompts. "Annnn . . . "

"Annn-drew," he says.

"Andrew love Mommy?" she says. "You love your Mommy?"

He runs to her and buries his face in her lap.

"There are times," she says quietly, calmly, over Andrew's back, "I want to wipe out the two of us." She puts her face against him. "Sweetie, sweetie."

I see him buried against her, his skinny legs sticking out. I can't stand to hear it. "Ahh, you'll get through this time," I say. "I don't know you, but you look pretty strong." It's a bald fucking lie. I *don't* know her, and I tend to invent people out of very little data, but she looks stuck together with children's paste.

"Hey, don't worry," she says, detaching herself from Andrew and starting to pick up toys, and carrying plates to the kitchen, says over her shoulder, "I'm not going to leave blood all over your bathtub or your towels or anything."

I ignore this. I say, "You'll be getting into a shelter near here—in about a week, Ms. Rossi tells me. It'll be the start of a whole new life."

"Sure. Hah! You can stop that shit. Okay?"

"You don't think it'll help you, the shelter?"

She sits down on the arm of the sofa and I want to say, Please, it was my mother's, don't—but I don't want to interrupt. "Let's say I had AIDS," she begins. "I don't, by the way, okay?—but it's like that. And you try to sugar it over, like 'Maybe they'll find a cure,' and—I don't know—it's like that, only it's worse, because maybe somebody *will* come up with a cure for AIDS."

I'm surprised, impressed by the analogy. "Okay, then. What's *your* AIDS? No money and a kid?"

"No! It's everything I am. There's no cure for that, is there? Not money. Money? If *you* were broke, it would be a different thing, wouldn't it?"

"But if you *know* that, know what your life is, then you're *not* it, you're *more*—you know what I'm saying, Kerry?"

"This talk is too fuckin' heavy for an afternoon."

I laugh, I see my laugh leaves her cold. "I mean, *knowing* it means you can step back from yourself, and that's like a vaccine."

It's what I'd say to my students. It's what I *do* say. I need to help, grope inside my self for the key to help, same as at the college. So many of my students, Green River Community College, have had a lousy start. Degrading experiences in high school, nobody—parents, counselors—to tell them that they can *do* anything, maybe with a child to take care of, maybe they're thirty and just getting started. It angers me, Kerry treating me as if I've lived rich and *with* the rich all my life.

"I've got to take care of Andrew," she says. "You want help with dinner, let me know." I leave her, she's sitting on the sofa, buttoning and unbuttoning her cardigan, buttoning and unbuttoning.

I correct student papers, check my E-Mail, pour a beer, turn on *All Things Considered* and start fixing a simple chicken sauté and rice. I'd rather cook alone than with this practically-child who wants to use me as the container for her bitterness. I think about calling the Warners over for coffee. But I feel somehow compromised.

All the same, I like having somebody to cook for and worry over. In my inner ear I hear Kerry's speech rhythms. A sixties edge. Maybe it's got nothing to do with the sixties—it's just youth. And as the beer mellows me out, I get into the rhythm of the moves—cutting, measuring, cooking. I squeeze a lemon through cheese cloth. A galley kitchen—it's like my playroom.

My friend Frank calls. Do I want to get out and see a movie tonight if he can get a sitter? I tell him no—I don't tell him about Kerry. While I flip the chicken pieces, I call Jeremy, ask how school went. Now a student calls, asks for an extension on a paper.

And I go back to my cooking.

I hear rock 'n roll from MTV and happy mother-and-child sounds from the living room, and I think, Hey, maybe she'll realize she doesn't have to be so defensive and things'll work out . . . and now, trying to listen to news about gang warfare in Washington D.C. over the music, I hear a howl of protest from Andrew and Kerry's angry yells and the kid's howls and *a slap, a slap, a slap,* and I pull the sauté off the burner and I'm in there, yelling, "Wait a minute, what's happening? Kerry?"

Kerry's holding Andrew in the air with one hand, he's dangling by the straps of his overalls, and with the other hand, she's swinging at him, smacking anywhere, his ass, his head, and when she sees me, she doesn't stop, she gets deeper into her task.

"NOT IN MY HOUSE! Cut it out now. Now! Get it together, Kerry."

"He was ruining your fuckin' floor, the little fuck, he was grinding food into your floor."

I try to take Andrew out of her hands, but he starts kicking at me and crying worse, and I pull back, I say, "Let's calm down. Come on. Come over to the sofa, please. Turn off the TV and let's sit, okay?" I'm a husband in some nightmare marriage.

"Look—" I start.

"Yeah, yeah, I got out of control." She plunks Andrew in her lap, and he nestles against her stiffly, and stiffly, not shaping her body to his, she pats him, says, "Okay, okay, okay." She looks up at me afraid, grins. "I don't smack him around all that often."

"You yourself, when you were little—you must have gotten smacked around?"

She rolls her eyes to the ceiling. "You *kid*ding?"

"So you went from parents smacking you around to husband the same."

"You mean Chuck? Yeah, and a couple of guys in between. I got a nasty mouth, they all say. I make it so tough on a guy, he starts going after me, you can't blame him. Not that they got a right, but—hey, look, no therapy, okay? Please will you cut this shit?"

"And Chuck beat up Andrew."

"Yeah. Hey, Andrew, get off, okay? Go play . . . okay? Chuck? That fuck can be one crazy animal. You don't have a woman with you?"

"Not now."

"When do we eat? He gets hungry, he's outa control."

"Five minutes. So what are you going to do to break the cycle? You want to turn Andrew into another guy like that animal?"

"Oh, come *on*. Come *on*."

I guess she understands what I mean. I say, "Sure. Enough. Dinner's in five minutes. Andrew like chicken?"

"You listen," she calls after me, pointing. "I'm not going to sit around here like your prisoner, like in some kind of jail."

I turn and smile. "Sorry. I don't mean it like that."

"You, you don't fuckin' ever yell at me like that again, you understand, or I'm out of here. I don't need another stepfather."

I've got a headache now, and my heart's beating crazy, but I stay icy calm. *It's her problem, this woman's problem.* "The rule is, no beating kids in this house. It's simple. Or else I call Ms. Rossi and she can take you back where you came from."

"I wasn't beating. I was smacking. You think that's beating you don't know shit. It's an entirely different thing."

"It looked like beating."

"Smacking. You got a rule against that?"

"Yes," I tell her. I stir-fry the veggies and I think, God, how smug I must sound to her. This is what it's like to bring up a child yourself, no money, no inner resources. In comparison, I've got it so easy. Still, I can't stand what I saw. I'm nauseated, tainted somehow.

Andrew comes in behind his mother and I chant, "Andrew, An-drew/ Here's some chicken just for yeww!"

So I play the fool and we get through dinner. It's like when I teach a bad class—one in which all the energy comes from me. I do magic—find peas in Andrew's ears so he'll eat the peas on his plate. I let him help cut the chicken with the sharp knife. I feel myself charming him, trying to make him—what? Be happy, little kid? Love me? How silly. As if I could give him enough love for the few days he'll be here to strengthen him for what he'll have to face— so clear, what he'll have to face, my God, and come through whole? How? Under my surface of magic, entertainment, energy pouring off me, I feel more and more despair every time I see Kerry's eyes, and I wonder if my eagerness to create life in this kitchen is counter-productive, turning her even more dead, self-hating, remote. How can she ever step off the bleak-go-round?

And if not Kerry, then *who*? Kerry and her child seem like representatives of the vast populace of Chaos, people brought up to feel lousy about themselves, beaten up or left alone, brought up by sour, angry parents, so many. Worse than suffering, they're in mid-air, in chaos. It's a tide of blood and here I am trying to stanch it with a phony smile.

After dinner, while I do the dishes, I hear her picking away at Jeremy's piano. Now Andrew starts banging. Family music, rhythm of a kid getting washed up and goofing around, into his sleeper. I say goodnight, I ask him for a hug and he hugs, and he wants a ride, so I hoist him to my shoulders and charge around the living room, both of us singing nothing. The faint smell of urine, the soft fuzz around my neck and ears, I remember Jeremy. I deposit Andrew in his mother's arms. I tell her I'll be out for awhile and don't say where. She shrugs. And now they're gone upstairs.

I drive through the dark hill towns of western Massachusetts, towns of old Yankees and turn of the century Polish-Americans and then the refugees from the sixties and early seventies.

I see them, the refugees, on the streets of the hill towns where they once lived in communes and later settled in single-family houses. Guys I maybe toked with or shared a jail cell with after a demonstration. Now they're lawyers or carpenters or whatever but there are little signs; maybe something about their hair . . . maybe a stupid little pony tail in hair almost all gray. Sometimes it's just in their eyes. They rode their youth dreams as far as they could, then they were stranded, beached. Maybe they can't figure out what went wrong, where they could have gone next.

There's my friend Frank's house; a contractor now, Frank's someone who, back in the seventies, wanted a simple country life. Now he's busting his hump to take care of his daughter—single parent to a nine-year-old, no mother nearby to share the job.

On the way out of the hills, dirt road to secondary to highway into Green River, I think about Kerry and Andrew and feel grateful to have such simple problems as tension with an ex-wife, a woman who, after all, wants the best for Jeremy, as I want the best.

Nancy is waiting for me at the Green River Cafe, as far from the baseball game on the bar TV as she can get. Sitting in dim light filtered through plants and colored by the old vinyl of the booth, she looks so young. It's like a first date. I slip into the booth, catch myself combing my hair with my fingers. The thing is, I don't know this young woman, young, too young, early thirties, fifteen years younger than me. Why did we break up? I can't remember. How did we get together in the first place? That, too, I can't remember. Except she has serious, honest eyes. She was never false. That I do remember. And she has long red hair that now she wears pinned up but used to wear loose or in a complicated braid that framed her head. And I remember how soft she was when we first met.

We order beers. I look past her into a wall mirror. Christ, I'm looking less a jock all the time. My hairline has retreated to the Bronx, and while I'm strong from chopping cordwood, I'm getting soft, there are scoops of sadness under my eyes. And was my nose always this conspicuous?

I tell her about Jeremy in New York. "We did a bunch of corny, touristy things. He just loved the show. We bumped into an old political friend of mine—not really a friend, we did some organizing together back then." It makes me laugh. "Actually, I never liked him. He was kind of what I was running from when I came here. Everything was political. Everything was a fight. You know? Anyway, he invited us to a party and we went. Park Avenue in the eighties. He had a real Edward Hopper on the wall . . . He gave Jeremy a great baseball card."

"Nice. Nice." She rubs her hand along the vinyl to soothe herself. "Peter and I are going to take him to Florida for a week in the winter."

"Hey, great." Only I'm thinking how fast we're moving towards divorce, sled out of control on a steep hill, how final it's getting to be. And I find this scenario waiting in my chest—that we'll look at one another across the table and suddenly it will all be over, this past year, we'll live together with Jeremy and he'll have his family whole again, and this year will be just a bad moment in a long life together. I think this and at the same time I think, *I don't know this woman. Did I ever love her? What's wrong with me that after all that talk and all that love making and child making, she can seem such a stranger?* I finger the beer ring on the shiny wood of the table between us, and say, "So you're doing okay with Peter?"

"Oh, yes. The truth is, that's why I wanted to talk."

Suddenly, I become very interested in the way the table feels under my wet forefinger. *It's okay,* I tell myself. *It's better for Jeremy.* "You mean you're getting married, you and Peter?"

"We're getting married next May. I hope you'll be there."

"I wouldn't miss it. And that's what you wanted to tell me?"

"Partly," she says.

Instantly, my stomach turns over; I know what she's going to say. "This is about Jeremy?"

"You've been just wonderful," she says. "As a father. I don't want to hurt your relationship, believe me, David. But this two-week, two-week, your house, my house—maybe we need to rethink that. Just think about it: maybe he'd be better off with Peter and me, a family? And he can see you a lot?"

I don't answer, because if I were to answer, I'd howl, I'd howl and rage at her, I'd scare the hell out of her, and Jesus, that's no good, so I half close my eyes and pretend to be thinking, to be considering carefully, when all I'm trying to do is cool down, and finally my breathing quiets, and I say, quietly, "Nancy, listen. Now listen, Nancy. You try to take away Jeremy and I'll take you to court so fast—"

"David! Oh, Davie!—"

"No, listen. Don't even *think* about it. You need other things, you want me to go out and rob banks or something, hey, *whatever*, you tell me, I'll consider, but not that—that I won't consider."

"David, you think I want to take Jeremy away?—"

"Nancy? Nancy? Just don't let's talk about it, okay?"

"I was just feeling you out, I'm not your enemy. Please."

I know I'm over-reacting. I crumple in the booth and sip my beer and say nothing.

"I won't be bullied. David, *you* listen. You better not try to use anger to negotiate with. I don't live with you anymore."

I wave her away. It's the old story, her feeling that I controlled her, this young woman, that I gave her no room to grow. One night, at the end of the marriage, we took a walk into the woods so we could talk without Jeremy around, and we were yelling at each other and she said, "You bastard, you treat me like a little girl, you want me to be this sweet little girl, and you, you know best about everything. And you think it's a wonder I want to leave you?"

I get quiet. "Just so we understand one another about Jeremy. He's . . . my life," I say. I'm embarrassed, sounding so corny. She rolls her eyes up to the ceiling, *Give me strength.* So I just say, "You want another beer?"

Home again, I listen for Andrew. He's quiet, asleep. I sit in my big poppa chair, once my own father's chair, under a good reading light and do some work, and Kerry sits across in the rocker—domestic scene—and pokes through a magazine, buttoning, unbuttoning, staring at me. Finally she asks, "What's that you're doing?" and I tell her it's student papers.

She tells me how much she hated high school. "I had to be stoned all the time just to sit through it."

"You can still get a G. E. D."

"Yeah, I know. When I figure things out. When I know what I'm gonna do. When I'm able to do it if I *do* know."

As a teacher, I'm somehow the butt of her anger, as if it's my fault she's in trouble. I should know better than to get pulled into her turmoil. But I say, "While you're here, if you want, I could get the materials for you, get you started on the G. E. D."

"Maybe."

"I mean—I won't do it unless you really want it."

"Thanks. For wanting to help . . . . But hey, what's the good, you got any brilliant ideas? You think I'd make a great doctor or something? Hey, I'm kidding. I mean, train, sure, but for what? Now, with a kid? Y'know, I liked school when I was little. My real father was around. That was a good time. Miss Rossi tell you about my stepfather?"

"He beat you up?"

"Yeah. With a belt. I'd have to bring him the belt. Yeah, when he wasn't coming into my bed at night. Sometimes both at once—fucking and beating. Old story. My mother worked —a night shift. I took a knife to him, night he got started on my sister. His pants were open, he was pulling at her hand, I took a knife and held it against his neck. Miss Rossi didn't tell you?"

"She wouldn't tell me."

"So he stopped. Later on, he grabbed me, he hurt me, said I was jealous. I told him, 'You fuck, I'm calling the cops.' You know something? My whole life, that's the only thing I'm proud of. I'm really proud of that. My sister didn't know shit. She was maybe ten, eleven."

"And your mother?"

"Oh, my mother—she kicked me outa the house. My mother? I didn't care."

"The things you've had to handle, Kerry—"

"Yeah-yeah-yeah-yeah."

I can't sleep. I lie in my bed, sometimes opening one eye to see the progress of the half-moon across my skylight. Panic that soon the moon will disappear and I'll still be awake and tomorrow my classes will be terrible and I'll wonder why I bother to teach. How does one ever fall asleep? I watch myself watching myself trying to sleep; how will the watched one, feeling watched, ever let go? I consider Valium. Instead, I sit at my desk, go to work on an article I've been writing for the Learning Pages of the *Boston Globe* on the good things that happen at community colleges, the education you can't explain in annual reports.

Now I hear a noise like a cat, I haven't got a cat. Is it Andrew?

Noise like a cat in heat. I get it now—I put on a robe over the long johns I wear to bed, and climb the stairs. The way an old broom "knows" the corners, my body knows this house. In the dark I walk like a blind man without faltering up the right number of steps without counting, over the stack of magazines on the landing without stopping, house an extension of my body. Knocking, I whisper, "Kerry? You okay? You sound awful. Anything I can do?"

She opens the door a crack. "Oh, yeah, I'm okay, I'm just fine, I want to fuckin' die but what's the big deal?" Now she opens all the way. She's wearing just a man's tee shirt. It covers her hips.

I back away. "I didn't mean to disturb you."

She brushes her hair and says, "You want to come in? Why not, only you got to be quiet. Don't want to wake up Andrew, do we?"

I get what she's saying. "I'll see you in the morning," I say. "Don't spook out, don't let the middle-of-the-night spooks get you."

"Then what'd you come up for? It's okay. I pay my way."

"Hey, I'm sorry, no, it's not like that, I just want to help," I mumble, and I fumble down the dark stairs, holding the wall of rough boards, half-tripping over the belt of my robe that's come undone. I sit up in bed with a book. Her words, *I pay my way*, keep going through my head, a bad commercial you can't get rid of.

It's quiet. I keep imagining her up there in her grief. Finally lying down again, I see her smothering the kid, over and over slicing open a vein, swallowing pills. I guess this keeps me from watching myself trying to sleep, because next thing, it's morning. I fake some yoga and come into the kitchen to make coffee.

Right away I smell the marijuana; the whole house stinks of it. "Kerry? Kerry?"

She's sitting at the kitchen table. Andrew is in the middle of a sea of Cheerios—bowl, table, floor. He's singing. He's sitting on a cushion from the couch, smelling of pee, babbling, tossing Cheerios with his spoon. Kerry's sitting and smoking.

"No way, Kerry. Not in this house. Hey—you hear me? I'm talking to you. And you've got a kid here."

Looking straight through me, she pretends she doesn't hear. Or maybe she doesn't hear, and that scares me. "Can you take care of him? Hey, Kerry!"

Now she smiles a stoned, mad-lady smile, and I get mad. "Don't fake that shit with me. You take care of this boy or I'm calling Sojourner House."

Still nothing. I make coffee. Andrew gets down, milk and cereal all over his sleeper, and eats Cheerios off the floor. I reach down to pick him up and he starts yelling, "Mommy! Mommy!"

"Mommy's not feeling well," I say. "It's you and me, kid."

He runs to her and bangs at her legs, and she starts to cry, to sob, slumping lower in her chair, and he's hitting and she's slipping and he's crying for real now, and I lift him kicking, I put him against my shoulder, he's hitting, hitting, but I carry him to the bathroom and undress him, his skinny legs kicking, his hips twisting, the kid making it hard as he can. And it's as I expected—worse—diapers soaked and shit-filled, his bottom and genitals red as if sun-burned. I immure myself to the noise and clean him down as gently as I can, dry him, let him go. Naked, he runs back to her, and now she plays crazy, hitting out at him, retreating into herself, hitting out, retreating into herself, a rock coming to life, slapping out, returning to rock. He puts his face in her lap, and she strokes, strokes, coos to him, "Pretty boy, Mommy's pretty boy . . . "

I leave them, head to my study and call my office. "I'm pretty sick," I say. "I won't be in today. Would you put up notes on my classroom doors?"

I call Gabriella, leave messages on both machines. As I come back downstairs for another bout, I hear a car bouncing down the gravel driveway. I figure it's Frank. Sometimes he stops for coffee on his way from lumber yard to job.

But the way the car scatters the gravel, squeals brakes, the way the door slams, I get scared—*not* Frank, somebody in a hurry, and before he's at the front door I have it bolted. I turn to Kerry, "You call someone? Kerry? Did you? You *did*, didn't you."

She blinks at me. "Just Chuck," she says, all innocent. "He's my *hus*band, all right?"

Just-Chuck is slamming a fist against the door. "Open up the fucking door!" he yells. A big guy, oh, a lot bigger than me, maybe half my age, and he's got an axe, my axe from the woodpile, in his hand, and he sees me through the window alongside the door and he yells, "Open up, you old fuck or I'll fuckin' smash your door in."

I rush for the phone, and he starts smashing the axe against the door. It's a solid wood door—my carpenter built it lovingly out of old barn boards, an oak frame, insulation, two layers of boards. Gonna take some time to get through that. I think, it's drama for him—if not, all he has to do is smash the glass and put his hand through, but he's after the door, he wants to murder that door. It gives me time to call. But it's the country, miles from town, emergency calls get picked up in Green River, sometimes no one answers, and before a cop comes —

The axe keeps smashing, I say, "Yeah, one minute, I'll open."

The police answer, finally, a dispatcher, and I yell my address and call for help, crazy guy with an axe!—and pick up my ten-inch chef's knife in my left hand, and with my right a poker from the woodstove and I yell, "Yeah, I'm opening!"

Andrew's crying, crying, Kerry's holding and rocking him, standing with her back against the kitchen wall as if she were watching a show. That's not just pot. What else has she taken? I'm scared. I see his mess of black hair tied up in a pony tail, and his mustache like some old bandito, I see his football shoulders. I've never been a fighter, and the guy is terrifying me so that my hands are shaking. Am I going to kill somebody? Maybe *be* killed? *Jeremy*—thank God Jeremy's safe.

The axe blade splinters the door, the blade shows through. Now I unlock and hard as I can *yank* it open, jerking the axe out of the guy's hands. "She has a restraining order," I yell in his face. "Yeah?" he laughs. He grabs for the axe and I slash out with the knife and there's blood across his hand. But I haven't touched him. The splinters cut him.

Behind me, Kerry is saying slowly, "It's just Chuck, he's okay, we had a misunderstanding."

"You keep out of my house!" I yell at him, and I find

I'm so pumped up with craziness now that I'm shaking but hardly afraid, I just feel rage and I'm gonna use the knife if he doesn't back off. Can I use a knife?

But Kerry has Andrew in one arm, her backpack over her shoulder, and she's out the door, wandering towards the car as if she and her husband had planned a picnic, and he slams his work boot into my shin and runs after her.

"He tried to rape me," she says. "Oh, Chuck, it was so crazy, I wanted . . . " and then I can't hear, they're in the car, spinning around and back out the driveway.

I find I can hardly walk, and the pain from the kick is shrieking through me. I hobble inside and sit, ice pack on my shin. Milk and Cheerios splattered around—I have to do something about that. I can see the front door, can see through the cracks. I wonder how bad it is. I can't get myself up to see.

Two

By now it's mid-morning. The swelling hasn't gone down; I've got it wrapped in ice. The leg doesn't much hurt except when I walk on it, but it throbs, and the throbbing fills the whole downstairs like music or a drug, it permeates the pine-board walls.

For my article on community college teaching, I take notes, remember Sherrill, the thirty-year-old clerical in a manufacturing plant who took a couple of evening classes and discovered how smart she was; she went from us to Smith College on a Comstock Fellowship for older women and from there to the Smith School of Social Work for an MSW. *But what it took out of her*, I write in my notebook. *Don't forget that part.* She paid with divorce, paid with a furious older son, and paid with a tightening-down, a hardening of character. She came into my office that first day like a religious convert, she'd discovered books! I wonder—would she have started if she'd known what it would cost? But had she a choice? She would have died.

For every person like Sherrill, a costly success, there are a hundred, three hundred, who simply go down the tubes. Like Kerry. I wince, seeing Kerry with her glazed eyes.

Gabriella calls. "Her husband," I tell her, "he came in like Achilles in wrath. They're gone. I couldn't stop her." She sighs, takes it in and sighs. "Every year, every month, some women go back who shouldn't. You lose them. But sometimes, Dave—you know—she thinks about it some more, a seed has been planted, and then the next time or the time after that, she comes back to herself. It takes courage. You can imagine."

"Why would she be with a bastard like that in the first place?"

"Bastards can be very sweet at first," she says. "I've heard women say that they knew the man was dangerous—

but the fact that this man was so dangerous yet so sweet with *her* was *flattering*. She felt special. And *then*," she says, and pauses, "dangerous people are seen as sexy. Danger is sexy. That's not a popular opinion in my world, I know, but it's true."

I can't help saying: "You ought to know, Gabriella." I'm thinking, of course, of her choice of leaving me for Gar, then the really mad choice of going underground with Gar.

He was like the king of some tribe—mostly women. They lived in a railroad flat on the lower East Side, and he fucked all of them. He was Dionysus, the liberator. He was Ajax, the fighter—six-three, two-ten, thick curly black hair down to his shoulders. One October morning he led his Bacchae on a crazy dance through the New York headquarters of IT&T, floor to floor, terrifying secretaries, tumbling cabinets, pouring cow's blood over files. The police caught a couple of the women; Gar escaped and went underground. And Gabriella Rossi gave up family, gave up her studies at Barnard. Gabriella went underground with him.

She chooses to ignore the reference. "Oh, but Dave," she says, "I'm so sorry. She should never have been sent out there, especially to a man's house."

"Oh—that's another thing," I tell her, squeezing the phone between shoulder and chin so I can straighten the ice pack. "As the guy took her away, I heard—I think I heard her telling him I tried to rape her."

"Oh, for godsakes, you don't need that. I'm really sorry."

"Of course you know I didn't touch her."

"Oh, *please*. Don't worry about it. Just words for her boyfriend—her husband. She needs to sacrifice you to him—show she's loyal to the bastard."

"Gabriella? The funny thing—I still feel bad for her. And the boy, Andrew. Sweet little kid—her chaos is his total reality."

"The husband—his name is Chuck Ahearn—he didn't do any damage?"

"Well, I've got a busted door and a banged-up shin."

It's got me laughing now. "He took an axe to the door. You should see it."

"Oh, God. How much will it cost to fix?"

"Me or the door? Forget it. Call it my contribution to the work you do."

"Well . . . . And your shin—not with the axe?"

"No, no! His boot. I'll be fine, and the door can be rebuilt. Gabriella? Gabriella? Why don't we get together on the weekend?"

Now there's a silence, and the silence is very exciting. It's in this silence that our real conversation begins.

"I'd like that. But not this weekend. I've got a conference."

And silence. It's warm, the silence, it's full of us. "Next weekend?"

And silence. "I'd like that," she says.

It isn't because we knew each other twenty years ago. In fact, I can hardly remember the Gabriella from 1970. It's this more complicated woman in the silence with me. Bruised shin, busted door. Small price.

We might as well be holding one another. Comfort for us both.

I'm in bed reading when Chuck Ahearn calls. Funny, because I've about calmed down, and the bruised leg is throbbing less, and I'm thinking to myself, Christ, am I lucky. The monster that in your heart you know, have always known, will one day appear, monster at the door, he knocked with his axe.

And Chuck calls.

Chuck calls and, without hello, first thing he says is, "Next time, Mr. Rosen, you won't get off so easy. You are one goddamn fortunate kike you didn't make it into her pants. You hear me?" He's threatening me, but he doesn't sound threatening, he sounds strangely mellow.

"I didn't do a *thing* to your wife, not a thing, she's just a child. She's a sad child."

"Yeah, right. That's right, Mr. Rosen." Now he adds, "You know, that is *right*. A sad fuckin' child."

"I tried to protect her, that's all I did."

"You couldn't protect shit," he laughs.

"*Hide* her, then. Keep her from another beating."

"You asshole. You come between a man and his wife. You take a son away from a father?"

"You're some father."

"I don't know you tried to jump her or what. *She* says so." He's probing; I can hear him probing.

"I didn't. I *didn't*." I'm more and more angry. At Chuck Ahearn, but also at myself—that I feel the need to absolve myself. To *this* guy, who comes at me with boots and axe?

"Those dykes, pimping her to you."

I don't answer. If he's saying all this, he isn't sure what's true.

"All they believe is how lousy the man is. My wife is a fucked-up bitch, know what I'm saying? Sad fuckin' child. She needs somebody who can handle her craziness."

"So that's why you beat her? That's why you beat your kid?"

"Beat, no way. That's not me. Maybe I smack her around once in awhile. Hey—she comes at me the same way. She tell you *that*? I'm supposed to take that shit? You know what she'd do to me if I let her get away with shit?"

"I saw her bruises."

"I don't say *never*. She drives me crazy. Times I got to put her in her place. Like, remind her. I'm an old-fashioned kind of man." This works him up with a sense of righteousness. "Listen, you old Jew fart, let me fuckin' tell you, you're just lucky we were out the door when she said you tried to do it to her. You got off real easy. Easy!"

"Easy! You kicked me with your boot."

"That was nothing. That was shit. You think you got kicked? Five minutes, I could've stomped you to death."

I don't know how to answer that.

Now he's calming down. Thoughtfully, almost pensively, quiet, as if he's talking to me in the back booth of a saloon, something we both understand, he says, huskily, quiet, like a secret we share, "Somebody's got to teach those dyke bitches a good lesson. They take a man's wife and son? See, that's fuckin' basic, that's like the Bible, it goes back and back forever, thou shalt not fucking take a man's son away. You—are you a father?"

I think about hanging up on him, but remember his rage.

"Hey—I asked you something."

"Yes. Sure. I am."

"How would you feel, somebody take your kid away?"

"Lousy," I say, my stomach turning over. "I'd feel lousy. But I don't smack my son around."

"Yeah, I get wild sometimes. But I'm basically a good father. You're trying to make me out like I'm a monster."

It shocks me: he's picked up my fantasy.

"I'm no monster. Maybe I used to be fucked up. Not now. You ask people. Now I'm a pretty reasonable guy. Drive anybody nuts to be with a wacko like my wife. But that's my fuckin' business. Nobody comes between us. Nobody comes between me and my kid. I'm just a guy who won't let anyone take away his son. That's all," he says gently. "That's all. And Kerry—" now he's whispering, so I know she's nearby—"she's no goddamn mother. There's your abuser. I'm up a fuckin' tree with that woman."

"Maybe you're both abusers."

"Wait a minute," he says, as if just hit by a bright idea. "Wait!" He calls out "Hey, Kerry? Kerry? Hey, baby!" Now there's a muffling over the phone, I figure it's his hand over the mouthpiece, and after a few seconds it's Kerry saying, "Oh, Mr. Rosen?"

"Kerry? Are you okay? Is Andrew okay?"

"Oh, sure, sure, we're fine," she says. "Chuck and me and Andrew are gonna be okay. Tough time, but we're okay."

"Why did you tell him a thing like that?"

"Tell him?"

"You told him I tried to rape you."

"Well? Maybe I was misinterpreting slightly."

"Misinterpreting!"

"But Chuck can be real sweet, we're stuck with each other, Mr. Rosen, so nobody better mess with us. Right, honey?"

Now Chuck takes back the phone. "I'm through talking. Okay? You're not off the hook. I've seen to that."

"What do you mean? What have you seen to?"

"But you're alive. Now look—I'm not warning you, I'm *promising*, you come between us again, you touch my wife, you take my kid away, and you're dead. Boom. Dead."

Now I just hang up. I'm glad I have a good book to see me through the next few hours.

Wednesday, I return from a day of teaching and tutoring to a message from Gabriella. She's still at her office when I call back.

"This situation with Kerry—it turns out it's something Sojourner House is going to have to deal with. David, can you come in and meet the members of my board?"

"The guy's making trouble?"

"I'm responsible to a board. Can you come in to see us? Please, Dave."

So Thursday afternoon I head for Boston. I wave to Russ Warner, who's painting the railing of his front porch. Stopping at the little general store a couple of miles down the road to buy a Coke for the drive, I get a big smile from Mr. Sikorsky. "That young man find your place the other day? He wasn't able to follow your directions or something."

"Oh, he found me all right," I tell him. I drive Route 2 to Boston, fast, on radar, slowing for potential speed traps. I'm annoyed. Gabriella leaving a crazy woman like Kerry with me.

I can't get it out of my head. Driving, I find myself explaining things to an imaginary board of angry, suspicious women. God, I hate politics, I hate ideology. Long before I reach Jamaica Plain, I've invented a tribunal of hostile, self-righteous feminists, refusing, simply because I'm a man, to believe any damned thing I say.

Jamaica Plain is not, as I'd expected, a run-down, tough area. It's largely working-class, but I don't know any area in Boston so mixed. There's a working-class clothing store and a second-hand store, but there are also hip cafes and right on Centre Street I pass a feminist bookshop, and I notice lots of Hispanics and blacks and a lot of gay men and women. If I were living in Boston, it's the kind of place I'd like to live, not fancy, not drab. I like the old back streets, every-which-way to one another, no grid, narrow winding streets going steeply up hill. Streets of triple deckers, brick or wood, with rippling bays, wrought iron balconies. There's hope here—I mean the way people have restored the substantial Victorian houses and articulated the architectural details by painting the trim a different color from the rest. In the middle of one block there's a battered house looking almost hopeless, ready to be torn down, but I have the feeling that a number of these houses were once like that and have been restored and gussied up with stained glass and balustrades.

I see why the center's offices and (somewhere nearby, secret) the shelter are located here: lots of housing for not-too-much money.

I pull the Honda up between two large Victorians, recently painted. One contains condos; the other—an elegant light beige with dark brown trim—has a small, hand-carved sign over the front door: *SOJOURNER HOUSE*; nothing else. *Sojourner:* a wayfarer. Someone residing for awhile in a foreign place. These women, sojourners. Biblical overtones. And echoes of Sojourner Truth, the nineteenth-century black woman who fought against slavery and for women's rights. *And ain't I a woman?* The sign small to promote good relations with their neighbors. No posters. Just a social agency. Well, and that's all it is, administrative and counseling offices; the actual shelter—where the women and children live—*elsewhere*, of course, secret.

I ring the bell, and a woman in her sixties opens, short hair, jeans, a work shirt. She's smiling, not simply politely but into my eyes. "Yes, can I help you?"

"Gabriella Rossi's expecting me. I'm David Rosen."

"Yes, you're meeting with us at four, I think. I'm Mary Adler." She shows me to an armchair, and beside it a pile of magazines. I could be wrong, but I feel I know her. She's all the good Quaker ladies I worked with on and off for years in the peace movement and later in Amnesty International. I say Quaker, it's just the tag I gave them—some may be Quakers, some Unitarians, some just decent people. They're sixty from the time they're thirty, and when they're really sixty they're still as committed and energetic as at thirty. Ask them to work, the work gets done, they don't get in the way, they don't want their names on letterheads, don't use words to decorate Self. They're the opposite of a Gar. They lack all analysis, all ideology; they simply care. Eros never gets in their way, though compassion might.

"You're on the board?" I ask.

She nods. "I'll be busy for the next few minutes. We should be pretty prompt." And she goes off. I'm left in the parlor, lovely high-detailed old room with ship-lap cherry wainscoting. It's a room too gracious to have heard all the stories it must have heard, beatings—worse. I can't even imagine. I look through the piles of pamphlets on somebody's old mahogany diningroom table: information on food stamps, on legal aid, on the psychology of abuse, on the network in Massachusetts of centers for battered women, on how to obtain a restraining order, on AIDS, on WIC and other forms of help for mothers and children.

The literature of grief and redress. I remember handing out leaflets at six A. M. to young guys up for their preinduction physical: Here are ways to keep from going off to Vietnam and coming back in a body bag. I wonder whether any of those young men, I mean the ones who went off to war—for very few of them took the leaflets seriously—became later on the men who beat up women, so that their women needed a Sojourner House. For a moment I half see an image of complex geometrical figures, all somehow interconnected.

A young African-American with a stack of papers held in her arms like a baby glances at me, walks on. The bell chimes and Mary Adler hurries to answer. A white woman—a girl, really, a pregnant girl—mumbles something, shows Mary a scrap of paper, and Mary directs her upstairs and presses a buzzer under her desk. Mary says, "There are other buzzers—under the desks—to set off an alarm, warn the house, they're connected with the police." She laughs. "I always worry I'm going to press the wrong one." She looks at me. "Gabriella and I—we've been together since Sojourner House got started. She's very wonderful. You know how hard things are for her."

No, no, I don't know.

Mary closes her eyes. "She's very wonderful. Mr. Rosen, will you follow me?"

Down a corridor to what must have once have been a guest room or library perhaps, room just big enough for a long table. Gabriella sits at the window end, outlined by the end-of-day light; smiling, she gets up and waves me to a chair. Slowly I become aware of the others. All women. A thick young woman, maybe thirty but hard to tell, tough looking, built like a wrestler gone to fat. She wears oversized chinos and an open shirt, and her breasts seem sunken, out of sight. I feel bad that she fits my imaginings so well. But then one beauty in her late twenties, romantically dressed in a colorful, woven North-African shirt, her long hair held by a wide band of leather.

As I'm telling my story, the door opens and a woman of Gabriella's age—early forties—walks in and hangs her belted wool sweater over her chair. She's African-American, with fine, sculpted features, and the skin of a child; she's cut her hair in a fashion I think of as African to follow the curves of her head. It's hard to turn away; if I saw her anywhere I'd want to stare: she's pretty magnificent. I notice her wedding ring, her simple beige skirt and blouse, the string of simple terra cotta beads. On the desk she places a beautiful leather attaché case, tan leather with the dark patina of a lot of use. It's the kind of case I've always loved, never given to myself. A lawyer? I wonder. A scholar? "Sorry," she says. "I'm Gail Kirkland." The others wait for her. "Please go on, Mr. Rosen."

I describe the few days with Kerry and her child. "That last night she was weeping, she was scared, I went up to her room to listen to her if she wanted that. I didn't even touch her."

"Of course not. The point is, Mr. Rosen," Gail Kirkland assures me with open palms, "you're under no threat—we're the ones being sued. And we don't believe you've done anything at all."

Mary Adler adds, "In fact, our job is to help one another."

"We don't even believe Kerry Latrice can win a suit," Gail Kirkland says. "But as you can imagine, our funding situation is delicate—United Fund, DSS, private contributions. Gabriella meant well, but I know you can understand—"

The young woman in the African shirt, Rosario, interrupts: "I really don't want to place blame, Gabriella, but it bothers me that you could put us all in jeopardy this way. Yesterday's column in the *Globe*—well, the writer is neanderthal, but dangerous. The problem is, Sojourner House is overly identified with one person. With you. Because of how you've suffered, Gabriella. I really don't mean this as an attack . . . "

This last seems not a statement but a question, and Gabriella nods her acceptance of the fiction that she isn't under attack. I wonder why she neglected to mention the column. And I wonder how Gabriella has suffered, what suffering Rosario means, what Mary meant. Looking hard at Gabriella, I see her now as *of course* a woman who's gone through a lot.

"The problem is," Rosario continues, "that if such a person messes up, well, it's hard to disclaim something she's done."

Nodding, Gabriella writes something in her small notebook.

I understand that there's an in-group battle going on, a

battle between Gabriella and some others. I pretend to think they're really interested in what transpired at my house. "Maybe," I say, "Kerry read my help as a sexual advance. It's likely that in her experience sex goes part-and-parcel with help from a man. In fact," I remember, "she herself made advances that night. Really sad. As if it were something she expected as the price of a room. But under that, oh, it was something else—it was real desperation."

The heavy young woman, the "wrestler," Kathy Edwards, drops the pencil she's been playing with. "Oh." She says it loud. Like a grunt. "*Oh*."

Gail Kirkland says, "Now it's a different story. Now, that's a very different story, Mr. Rosen."

"You think so? I mention it because I want to lay everything before you. I did nothing. You understand—I didn't touch the woman, I stayed away."

"But she may have thought you were going to do something."

"She may have thought a lot of things. She's pretty disturbed. She's a sad person, Kerry."

"Can't tell about madwomen," Rosario, the pretty young woman, laughs, and now I can sense there's a cabal here against not me but Gabriella—Rosario, Kathy, and the woman with the attaché case, Gail Kirkland. "You see, Mr. Rosen, it looks really bad when a shelter for battered women starts sheltering men who've been accused of abuse. I'm not saying you did anything, but you see the problem."

Gail Kirkland adds, "And calling a woman crazy, a woman who claims to be a rape victim, calling her crazy—well, that's what the courts hear every day."

"Of course," I agree. "But you're not saying—"

"*No*body's saying—" Rosario says. "Hey—I believe you."

"*I'm* not so sure," Kathy-in-the-work-shirt says. "What the hell do we *know* about this man? Why we being so fucking polite?"

I get the picture. It reminds me of political groups long time back. They're playing Kathy as the militant, more outrageous than the others—outrageous, courageous, on behalf of others. I fold my hands and wait to see what'll go down.

All this time, Gabriella has been sitting back from the table, taking notes in her small black book.

Now she looks up and smiles at everyone. She seems smaller than she is, soft, and I'm apprehensive for her. "I want to thank you all," she says, as if this were a tea party; I don't understand her calm. "I want to thank you, David, for driving all this way, and I want you, Rosario, and you, Kathy, and you, Mary, and you, Gail, to know how much I appreciate your support. You know, what political folks call 'damage control' is necessary—but situations like this aren't all negative; they hone an organization, temper its steel . . .

"I can imagine a center for helping battered women, a center like ours, I can imagine it wanting to disclaim any man at all, and it takes courage to say, No, we'll take people as we find them. I believe courage like that gets a good response. I can imagine a few people being cynical, but most people trust us—most people will say 'If even Sojourner House believes the woman is lying, is disturbed or scared and lying, then she *must* be.' Do you see Kerry Latrice as our enemy? I don't. I see her as more a victim than ever. Do you agree that our relation to her—in the press, in court, if it really comes to that—not be adversarial but sympathetic? Do you agree, Cath?"

And Kathy Edwards scratches at her jaw and mumbles, "Sure. It's her batterer we've got to fight."

"You did the intake on her yourself, didn't you, Rosario? You know what she's going through."

Rosario Cancion closes her eyes and nods.

"In fact," Mary Adler says, "Kerry Latrice needs our help."

"That's exactly right," Gabriella says. "What can we do about that, Gail? Is there a statement you can write? Should we call a news conference, and perhaps you and I field questions together? Gail, you're so good at that. And you'd lend us legitimacy."

"I suppose we have to. I'll draft up a statement and pass it by you."

"Really, Gail, I don't need to see it."

Now Gail turns to me. "And her little boy—did you feel she was able to keep things together for him most of the time?"

And so the focus is deflected from the challenge to Gabriella. Now the feeling around the table lightens, there are jokes, asides about an absent board member and yesterday's column from the *Globe*. "Can I see that?" I ask Rosario, and she passes it over. A columnist with a street-tough, man-of-the-people style tells about meeting this young mother who, in the middle of a dispute with her fiancée, went for counseling to Sojourner House, a shelter for battered women, and the shelter sent her to this guy's house. The columnist doesn't claim the guy *did* anything, but finds it pretty odd . . . .

I pass the column back with a shrug. Now they're discussing finances, a new TV for the shelter, an upcoming conference . . . .

Gabriella walks me back to my car. I say, "You couldn't have done that twenty years ago. I'm impressed."

She doesn't pretend not to understand. "Thanks." She stops me at the corner. "David. I want you to understand: Gail Kirkland has been my closest friend for ten years. She's simply brilliant, she's not my enemy—not now, not ever. We've always been a team, Gail and me. She's a lawyer, first-rate. Things have gone sour, but it's not just Gail."

"Why have things gone sour?"

She doesn't answer. "Until this quiets down," she says after awhile, "I think we'd be better off, you and me, not spending much time together."

"All right. I see that."

"But before you go back, I think we should meet with . . . our mutual friend. He's come up to Boston. I know he wants to talk with you. Can you spare another hour?"

"Gar Stone? Is here? Why?"

"He flew up this afternoon to help. Look—it's a long story."

"What's a long story?"

"You don't like Gar much, do you," she says.

"What do you think?"

"He's been a very good friend," Gabriella says simply.

"What's he doing with all this *money*? The duplex on Park. That glass-fronted wine cellar, the original Edward Hopper? I couldn't believe it."

"He comes from money. You didn't know?"

"I guess in the old days he didn't want to advertise. So that's how he got out of trouble? When you two went underground?"

"Oh!—I'll tell you about that some time."

My car follows hers to a back street in Brookline; I park behind her. A street of old, unassuming houses, a couple of four-story row houses, one small red-brick apartment building. Not the Brookline of turn-of-the-century houses, miniature estates, old money; just a middle-class suburb of Boston.

She hasn't fully moved in. She's still living out of boxes. There are open boxes of books, open boxes of dishes stacked along the wall of the foyer, paintings leaning against the walls. Heavy, old furniture—inherited, I suppose—makes the place seem substantial, charming; but I smell depression.

I find myself wondering, as I sit down in a wonderful, old cracking-leather lounge chair: What am I getting myself into? I see Gar coming out of the kitchen with a tray rattling—a pot of tea, cups, spoons, milk, sugar. Shouldn't I suddenly remember I've got a "parents' night"?

Tea?—so she must have called him from the office just as we were leaving. Some thing domestic about it bothers me. I see, not remember but in my mind's eye see, Gar coming out of his kitchen on the lower East Side, that day I visited Gabriella after she'd moved there, his hands full of bread or something, his bullhorn vitality filling the almost bare meeting room with its Salvation Army sofa and broken-down chairs, corners piled, spaces strewn, with pamphlets and books. I'm inventing Jim Morrison and Huey Newton posters on the wall. I imagine Gar with arms upraised, shouting, "Hey, hey, I got something for you . . . " but that's reconstruction. What comes back to me is Big Gar filling that room.

Different now. He still seems outsized, same football-end body, tall and rangy, long arms and big hands, but he's subdued, casual. He's wearing what he wore in New York—a very expensive, hand-tailored, pin-striped business suit, a modest tie, hair a little long but elegantly styled. Somehow, he looks more authoritative, more convincing, than he did twenty years ago. He runs his fingers through his thick hair. The old gesture—but now the hair is growing finer, silver in places. He grins, and the grin makes me remember everything. I think, *Gar, you prick, you were so important to me, you'll never know. You were the man I wanted never to become.*

He stops and grins hello, asks about the meeting, tells us his negotiations this afternoon, downtown Boston, went well. A Boston real estate deal. We have tea and talk, and I find myself disliking him as I've always disliked him—and yet interested, as I've always been interested.

He takes a clipboard from on top of the stereo. "Let me tell you what I've been up to. First *I'm* paying Sojourner's legal expenses—it's not a big deal—we have John Parker Goodwin on retainer."

"Gar—*no*! Sojourner House has good relations with a number of lawyers who work on a *pro bono* basis. You *know* that. Last thing in the world we need is a high-powered Boston law firm, a male lawyer. What are you thinking of?"

"How did you find out about this?" I ask.

"Small article on the suit in the *Times* yesterday. You didn't see it?"

"Christ. The *Times*? Really?"

"Gabriella, you don't have to have Goodwin represent Sojourner House. I do suggest a consultation. Will you go along with that?"

"*That's* possible. All right. But Gar, you're making too much of this. A young woman with problems. We're not particularly worried about the suit."

"Oh, I take that for granted. The suit is nothing. It's the taint, it's the stink. You remember that priest in New York accused of—What?—I can't even remember what, money, sex, it doesn't matter—his work was practically wrecked."

"Thanks Gar. I know you want to help, you've been really good. I don't mean to make it difficult for you. I'll see this Goodwin."

He smiles my way. "Let me take you both out to dinner—all right?"

"I've got to get back," I say.

"And Gar, I've got a lot of work," Gabriella says.

"What about calling in a pizza, then? There's things I want to talk to Dave about."

We call for a pizza. Gabriella goes off to change. To get away from Gar, I poke through the apartment. Boxes everywhere—except in one room, Gabriella's study, which is perfectly neat, papers in precise stacks on a five-foot by three-foot butcher-block work surface supported by file drawers.

Gar the businessman. Gar with family money. That knocks me out. I feel his eyes on me as I walk around. Finally, he says, quietly, "You don't know a lot about Gabriella, do you."

"No."

"You know how long she's lived in this apartment? Like this? Out of boxes?"

"No."

"Almost two years."

"Two years?"

"She didn't tell you about Sara—her daughter?" Gar says, dropping his voice.

"No."

"No, I figured. I want you to know."

"What *about* her daughter?" My stomach tightens against a blow.

"She got killed," Gar says simply. "Her younger daughter. She got murdered. A beautiful little kid, eight, nine, she used to come after school to the center. You don't remember reading about this? No? It was in all the papers. This guy came in, real crazy, hopped up on something, thinks the women's movement or something stole his woman, so when he can't find her, he starts spraying the place with semi-automatic fire. Everybody running and screaming—you know. He killed one woman, didn't care who he was killing, he killed Sara, then shot himself in the head, good-fucking-riddance. I wish I'd been there. I wish."

I can't say anything. Gar waves a hand in front of his face as if to clear the air of poison. "That was a couple of years back," he says. "It was so crazy to have her little girl down at a place like that, how could she be that fucking stupid?" I notice that Gar's eyes—Gar!—his eyes are brimming with tears. "I guess she knows that now," he says.

Gabriella comes back wearing a velour pullover top. Over beer and pizza we talk. I notice how seriously Gar takes Gabriella's work. They talk about the politics inside Sojourner House. I hardly care. I look around the unfinished apartment; now every box seems a memorial stone.

A dog starts barking in the alley behind the apartment building. Low bark, big damned dog. It puts me on edge. From upstairs, downstairs, next door, somewhere, a fight heats up, husband and wife, a buzz of noise, you can't hear the content, only the ejaculated "Now you listen to me . . ." of the man, and a shrill harangue, music without words, from the woman.

"Oh, I hate it," Gabriella says, her eyes glancing up through the ceiling to the fight. "They do that all the time. It's wearing. Not physically violent—no slaps, no screams—but it is violent, dear God, and boring—and so ugly to come home to after Sojourner House. It's like having tapes of my bad dreams playing . . . I think about moving, but—" she laughs, and the room lights up—"who has time to look for a place?"

She tells us about the women who need Sojourner House "More and more. We tell people, abuse doesn't know *class*. Still, in hard times, abuse goes up."

Gar puts down his beer and sits back, looks up at the ceiling for what he wants to say. "See—your work is like the needle of a geiger counter. But what's it *mean*? The radiation is being emitted anyway—whatever you do. You're a terrific person, Gabriella, you're helping women, helping their kids, who could knock it? But from a larger perspective, say you helped every woman make a new life, say you helped every man to change his life, the larger situation wouldn't be touched. All right? Here's how I see it." He spreads his hands out, palms down, as if clearing and preparing a playing field on his lap. I see the radical analyst of twenty years ago. Was this what he wanted me here for—to be his audience again? I remember a night we spent together in a jail in Washington, remember the brilliant, endless harangue.

"The line is that we were in an 'economic downturn' followed by full employment. They called it 'Recession'—that was bullshit. So is 'recovery.' It's masking what's happening—and what's going to keep happening for the next fifty years. We used to talk about the working poor as *exploited*. Well, that doesn't wash anymore. Here's what's going down. People are still exploited, sure—there's this huge cesspool of the unemployed all over the world in case workers complain. But it's worst for the deep poor—they're not exploited. They're *useless*." Gar pauses.

"Superfluous," he goes on. "Economically irrelevant. The jobs created in the next decade can't *use* these people. We're stuck—here, England the same, Germany—with an unnecessary work force. So conservatives say, 'It's their fault. Cut welfare and they won't be able to sit on their asses.' That's blaming the victim, right? They pretend the problem is the immorality of the poor. Exactly like in the nineteenth century! But where're the great jobs the poor aren't taking? Cleaning toilets? Serving hamburgers? And who are the poor? Mostly mothers—the people you try to help, Gabriella. They're taking care of their kids. It's a pathetic joke.

"And liberals—they're just as self-deceiving. They say, 'Spend funds to retrain them.' But that's deluded. '*Retrain*.' You think you can take twenty, thirty-year-old men with a lousy education and retrain them for hi-tech careers? Not to mention the young mothers! It's a big lie. Fifteen-year-olds? How about them? Nah—already too late. *Six*-year-olds, *six*—yes. But that's not happening. So we'll lose them, too. I'm talking inner-city black people, sure, but they're just the shock troops, the ones who always get hit first and hardest. Blacks, Hispanics—then the less-educated whites, and more and more. Ever see the movie *Bladerunner*? You remember that terrifying gray, wet L. A. with the polyglot poor everywhere and a few wealthy as hell in high-tech safety?"

I get up, irritated, to go to the bathroom. "What I don't understand," I say, standing above his chair, "is why—if it's all so hopeless—why do you feel so goddamn pleased talking about it?"

"Pleased? Not me, Dave. It's depressing. I don't see much anyone can do. The system can use people who can put chips onto boards, sure, but the economy is international, and wages will tend to level out for people like that, they'll decline towards the lowest available wage. Koreans? Indonesians? And the rich—people like me, okay?—the rich will get richer. And you—you teach in a community college, you feel righteous, you offer hope, but in the long run, that hope is an illusion."

"I've got stories, people whose lives we've helped change—if you want to hear. But Gar, I think *it turns you on*, the separation of classes, you dig it because you can *analyze* it. You haven't changed," I say. "You still outflank us to the left. But it seemed more authentic years back—before you were rich—before I *knew* you were rich."

"You slay me," he says. "You're still such a moral idealist. Gabriella, Gabriella, you remember I used to call this guy the Great Reconciler? You remember one time he steps right between a line of cops and a bunch of yelling clowns like me? He holds up his hands and says, loud as he can, 'These aren't your enemies.' Profound! He says this to *us*—" Gar laughs. "—just before they came at us with the tear gas and the clubs."

"I could never see the point. You call people pigs, they become pigs—they become worse."

"They become worse *anyway*!" Gar laughs.

Gabriella says, "Gar, *my* question is, if there's no hope, then why help Sojourner House?"

"Oh, you know as well as I do. Frankly, Gabriella," he says, serious now, "you're why. You are."

"I do know. All right. But really—you're so inconsistent," she says. "What about your business? What about your development? Gar's family," she says to me, "builds in New York."

Gar laughs. "You could say that."

"All right. You see, Gar's laughing because he builds not just one building but many. Gar, what I don't understand is—how can you believe what you do and build luxury apartment buildings?"

"I've got my eyes open. I say, 'This is the way things are. People are going to have to live in cities—not just New York—the way the rich live in South America. Bullet proof cars, buildings with great security, gated perimeters with dogs and guards."

"I don't understand," I say. "You *support* that kind of life? *You*?"

"It's not a choice, man—support, critique—it's like, given the realities, what do we do about it? I can't retrain millions of poor bastards for non-existent work."

"It's not that bad," I say. "The new jobs you talk about, sure, it's true, are going to be unavailable to a lot of people. But there are traditional jobs in the meantime—"

"What planet are you living on? Right now, I'm going through a shitstorm in New York, dealing with the Housing Board, liberal critics, nobody wants to let on what's coming down. And I want to build moderate-income housing, not just luxury, the papers don't give me credit, but I want to gate the whole area, block off the streets. No go. 'Undemocratic.' I mean, think about it: it's like you turn people into garbage and then you don't own up to the result. I own up. It stinks, but I'm putting in a private police force."

"Can you imagine," I ask, "if someone said that to you twenty years ago?"

"Oh, sure, I'd have called him a fascist bastard. But now we're older, and there are kids involved, and suppose your little boy were living in New York. You telling me you'd rather give the angry ones, the ones left out, you'd rather they had democratic rights, free access to the streets, and your son might get mugged? I don't think so."

Beyond words, unable to look at Gabriella now that I know about Sara, I go off to the bathroom. On a shelf beside the sink I find a man's shaving kit, shaving brush sticking up. You don't bring a shaving kit for an afternoon visit.

So driving through Boston after a cool goodbye to Gabriella and Gar, I'm not feeling so hot. I keep hearing Gar's analysis and I can't answer it. And I want to answer it, or else what am I doing teaching? I see as if in a scene from a helicopter, street after street of broken buildings, people sitting on stoops, litter. Dead bodies in a playground.

But that scene's in my head. What I'm actually driving through is Brighton streets of the working poor, out towards Route 2, and it's still rush hour, and suddenly traffic stops. If I imagine gridlock, I think of New York or L.A., but *this* is gridlock, cars backed up through the intersection, and the honking starts, a couple beeps, a long, enraged steady whine of one horn, another, and some good-humored rhythmic beeps to keep the others company; and then just ahead of me, honking in three-second bursts, an old Chevy—short man with a thick neck—makes its move, up onto the sidewalk, to a gaggle of honks, and the Chevy sideswipes a brand-new Lexus and doesn't stop, driver of the Lexus gets out and yells after the Chevy, but the Chevy keeps on, and cars try to move over for him, and from up ahead I hear more metal on metal, now he's gone, and the traffic opens up ahead and we pass through and from somewhere I hear a police siren but what happens after that I don't know.

And I think how close we are to violence all the time, I think of Sojourner House, and for a few moments I enter the body of that crazy man with an assault rifle. He must have seen the place as the castle of a monster, Womanpower, holding his woman in thrall. But no—no, because then he would have felt like a hero; and a hero doesn't need to suck on a gun barrel and blow his skull apart. No, somehow he must have felt that *he* was the monster, he was serving his rage as if his rage were a god and he the servant of the god.

I think about Sara. Gar's private police force doesn't seem like such a terrible idea.

The light on my answer machine glows red in the dark kitchen. Frank Polidori has called. Frank wants to know, do I have Jeremy this weekend, because he's taking Nora to the foliage fair in one of the hill towns.

I jot down a note to call him back.

The next message is from Nancy.

David? Pick up if you're there.... David, what's this about a young woman in your house, woman and a child, what's going on...?

By now I'm down a well somewhere, scratching the brick walls, I hear the tension in her voice, hear how much she's holding back. Did somebody call her? I only half-hear the next message—my department chair, Leonard Noble, droning a precisely articulated non-message, *strange allegations... If it would be convenient....* Now I'm certain—*somebody called them*—called Nancy, called Leonard. Must have called. My name wasn't in the Globe column.

Leonard can wait. I call Nancy, she's not in, I slam down the phone and fix myself a drink. The house is so dark. I go around turning on lights, blasting an old Dizzy Gillespie record, so old I can't think of the music without the scratches. I call, Nancy's not in. I organize papers on my desk, even write a calm letter of recommendation for a student. I call, she's there, back from an early movie with Jeremy. "Nancy? Somebody call you?"

"David, what's going *on*, David?"

"Listen, here's the whole thing: a woman needed shelter from her husband, he'd been beating the hell out of her, she has a kid, I was asked—I took her in a few days. That's it. That's all. She turned out to be pretty flaky. Who called you? The husband?"

"David, you and I talked about Jeremy the other night. I can't have something like this craziness, suppose Jeremy had been there . . . . Whoever the man was, he scared me."

"Must have been a guy named Chuck. He called? What did he say?"

"He *scared* me. And there *was* a story in the *Globe*, wasn't there?"

"How did he scare you? What did he say?"

"It wasn't what he said."

"Listen—he scared *me*. He's dangerous. Thank God Jeremy wasn't there."

"Look, David, I won't have Jeremy living in the middle of crazy people. If you want to be alone, then you have a perfect right—"

"Do I make a practice of hanging out with crazy people?"

"You did once, David. I don't know. No. I'm just saying—"

"Can't you trust me a little, Nancy? You think I could rape anyone?"

"Rape? You think I think *that*?" Her voice has calmed down now, she laughs, and I realize the steel rod through my shoulders doesn't need to be there. "Oh, this man was screaming 'rape' at me, he was, but I never even considered . . . . It's the getting involved with people like that, that's what worries me."

"Oh, I'm not *involved*," I tell her. I'm sitting at my oak roll-top desk and I'm stroking my shin, black and blue, painful to the touch. "Really. It's all over."

Three

Friday afternoon. I pick up Jeremy at school, take his beaten-up, back-and-forth duffel from the teacher's closet, say hi to the kids, go off with Jeremy as with a prize. He's babbling, he always babbles when I first pick him up, and I do too, and we get through it. It's bringing not just him but me to that other planet of the-two-of-us. Gravity is different there. It's a little strange, you have to learn your footing. We don't talk abut the strangeness. On our way home we try to blur past it with words, I hear about the fish in the aquarium at school, about a new kid nobody likes, about the Walkman that he got for a present . . . but nothing about who gave him the Walkman. Peter, I suppose—his stepfather-to-be. And nothing about his room at his mother's. And nothing about his mother. What's the cost of his diplomacy?

I listen, but I'm preoccupied; Leonard Noble asked me to stop by "for a chat" this afternoon. I told him I'd have Jeremy with me. "Ohh, I don't think we'll bruise his sweet young ears," he drawls in his William Buckley patrician voice that must have begun as parody but through long use has fallen into simple affectation.

"I've got to talk to my chairman," I tell Jeremy. "Not my idea of fun for a Friday afternoon, but I'll make it up to you."

"That's okay."

"Did your mom tell you what's up? No?" I tell him about Kerry, about Andrew, even about Chuck and the door, because he's gonna see it anyway. "So Kerry's with this tough guy, and Gabriella asked me to help her, and Chuck got her to say I'd been mean to her, but it's a lie— and he must have called Professor Noble. It's all so stupid. Wait till you see our door."

Green River Community College is set back a quarter-mile on farm land, flat land, ten minutes outside town.

From the secondary road it's a sixties style concrete and glass factory, even a modern prison, but the curving entrance road is thickly landscaped and the trees have grown up these twenty years so that the place has the pastoral pomp that the architects must have sold the Department of Education on in the preliminary sketches.

The rough facade is horizontally ribbed, as if someone ran a giant comb through the wet concrete. Jeremy runs up the poured-concrete steps, fingers the ribbing, then jumps down, down, down, feet together, pretending to parallel-ski a slalom. Now he twirls. He likes it when I take him here; it's a giant's playground. Inside are fifty-foot-wide marble stairs to jump up, two at a time. He'll call out to me just to hear his cry echo from the stone. "Watch—watch, Dad!" He slides his bookbag along a step—he's bowling. "Strike!" He raises his hands, jiggles his knees, a victory dance.

Only a couple of students still around, late Friday afternoon. *If* they're students. You can't tell, at a community college, students from staff from repair workers. Everyone in chinos or jeans, work shirts, people of all ages. This semester in my American literature class I'm teaching a woman in her forties, a pregnant woman of eighteen, a man—a carpenter—about thirty. That's part of what I like about teaching here. It feels real to me. And most of those who are here care a lot, have dreams that fuel their study.

We go up to the second floor and down the hall to Leonard Noble's office; sign on his door:
Prof Leonard Noble
Chairperson, English
There are at least twenty doors along this corridor. It's like any unpretentious state office building. But when we rap and walk in, we're inside an imported metaphor—a large, carpeted panelled room lined with bookcases, some glass-fronted. On the circular table in the center is a stack of literary journals with boring covers. Leonard is alone, he's been listening to music and reading in a leather easy chair in the corner, and as he stands up and looks at us over

his half-glasses, I want to giggle, the fantasy is so complete—the man's pretending he's at Princeton! At least. Oxford, perhaps.

He turns off the music, waves me into a lacquered black armchair with a college crest embossed, says, "Jeremy, m'lad," and offers Jeremy a clipboard, blank paper, and markers. "Now, then—a little Friday afternoon delight, shall we?" And he tiptoes to the closet, stage-secretive, and takes a wood-and-leather tray from the shelf—two different sherries, two glasses. "Ahh, Jeremy, my boy, 'fraid I haven't a thing for *you*. There's a soda machine down the hall —" He reaches for his wallet but Jeremy says, "No, thanks. Really."

"Well, then." Leonard turns to me. "You've been busy-poo, it would appear. I had no *idea* we had a Samaritan on staff."

I shrug. I shrug too often. "Well, hardly," I laugh, sharing his mode of droll casualness. *Casual* or *casualty* feel like my choices.

He sinks into his leather chair, hoists leg over knee, I see calf-high ribbed black socks. Two gentlemen at college. His wavy hair, graying, is well groomed; the fullness in back, where it curls, like a musician's, is a conscious bohemian touch, a touch of looseness, like the worn Harris tweed with leather patches on the elbows. Behind him, over his desk, I notice his credentials, *Universitatis Yalesnis*—his B. A.—and his Doctorate from Brown. Like a physician in the provinces establishing his credentials.

I try to bury my resentment—the man's been decent to me always. Why resent his defenses, meant to disguise the basic fact of his professional life: that he went to first-rate schools, was denied tenure at Harvard—hardly unusual, absolutely to-be-expected—and that instead of finding a tenure-track job at a lesser school and pounding out the research, took an easy berth, the Chair here, early seventies when the school grew, and has hidden himself away ever since, doing a couple of gentlemen's essays on Dryden, nothing else. An easy *berth*—I think of indolent captains in the China Sea in Conrad's stories. And now the final stage—he plays out the joke that this is a traditional upper-class institution—Yale, say, or Williams. *No.* It's inaccurate to say he's pretending it's Yale. The constant underlying gag is, God knows it's *not* Yale, but let's pretend, hmm? His style expresses a constant put-down of what he thinks of as a third-rate school. And in his terms, it is. It's camp. Maybe the real object of satire is his own inadequacy.

"Yesterday, a not-very-nice man called. You understand," he murmurs, "I'm not taking his idiotic charges seriously. I've known you too damned long."

Meaning he really wants reassurance; I offer it. "He's a violent, pretty terrifying guy, this Chuck. In a moment of weakness the woman went back to him; he's after revenge."

"I don't want to hear what happened."

"I'm happy to *tell* you what happened."

"I'm not interested in what you did or didn't do. Good lord! I'm protecting my community of scholars, that's my concern."

"What I *did*? What I did was nothing at all."

"Of course, of course. Anyway, this . . . Chuck . . . got the ear of that fool columnist at the *Globe*, and the *Globe* is in Boston and it's read by the delightful bureaucrats and legislators who provide us our meager sustenance. You see my drift. Now, your name wasn't mentioned in the paper, David, my dear, but the name of this institution *was*, and I've already been on the phone fending off inquiries with charm." Suddenly, he calls over to Jeremy, "Child, are you content over there?"

Jeremy nods, as if he's been in his own world all this time and hasn't heard a thing.

"So you can imagine my little problem—a *little* problem at this moment, but filled with promises of splendid complications. My job is to protect us all, my boy. Including you, because you're what I call in my reports a 'credit to this institution.' But please understand—the less brouhaha the better."

"I expect no more brouhaha at all."

"Good. Avoid brouhaha. There are so many crazy people running about. It *is* best to keep them at a distance, don't you think?"

"I don't expect to take any more women and children into my home, if that's what you mean, Leonard."

"I'm sure. I know you're a marvelous father, I know you're a sensible man, even though you *don't* see Dryden as the definitive English poet. But it makes me happy to hear you say it. Frankly, I need to cover our collective ass, so to speak."

I share a smile, sip my sherry, share the joke of sherry in a sherry glass in a well-appointed office—inside a factory. Playing in his theater, in this play of his, I feel, as always when I talk to Leonard, as if I'm betraying my work, my students, my hope for them. Every time I leave his office, the belief I go on, keep going on, mostly unstated, that I'm doing something that matters, that belief gets a little more tarnished, more dim, more frayed.

"What did he mean, 'brouhaha'?" Jeremy asks, holding my hand and walking almost primly down the steps. No twirling.

"*Noise, a mess*—see, there was an article in the newspaper, it doesn't mention me by name, but it says I didn't protect this young woman as I should have."

"But you *did*?"

"No. I guess I didn't. I couldn't protect her. She called this lousy husband to come and get her. That's the worst thing in the whole world she could have done. Well, I couldn't protect her from him. But that's not what the paper is saying."

"Oh."

"It says I wasn't *nice* to her. But I was."

"Why don't you call the newspaper?"

"Maybe—maybe that's a good idea, honey, but I don't know. All I've got to do is keep low. Hey—but you don't worry, okay? Okay? You let me tell you what I've got planned for tomorrow."

On the way home we stop at the town library and I find the *New York Times* from day before yesterday, looking for the story Gar saw. As I suspect, there *is* no story. So Gabriella called him—must have—and I suppose Gar came up that evening. The shaving kit.

"Come on, Jeremy, let's go find a video." I shape dinner in my mind the way you would a poem or painting. *Adventurers' Stew*, I decide. Which is just my mother's old chicken fricassee. When chickens are cheap I buy four or five and in a huge restaurant pot make stock out of everything but the breasts, which I freeze separately and use for fricassee the way she made it but in a huge, heavy, stainless-steel restaurant pot, with the tops of celery bunches, the stalks of parsley, carrots and onions, herbs; I freeze it in half pint containers, squirrel it away for nights like this.

It grows dark and the phone rings; I let the answer machine pick up. My stomach grows tense, like a high-pitched cello string off-key. I'm right, it's Gabriella, her voice flat, uncertain. My body feels her unease.

"Aren't you gonna pick up, Dad?"

"Let's ignore them all," I say, grandly, as if above such things as phone calls, but the cello string is working away in there. I chop each breast in two with a cleaver.

It soothes me; and Jeremy is my *sous-chef*, we're a team; it grows dark outside, and the kitchen is a small sailboat in the darkness, the whole world is in this kitchen. We chop onions and listen to *Alexander's Feast*; Jeremy tells me about soccer. I braise the breasts with onions and garlic—"like *this*, Jeremy, see?"—and, in some of the defrosted stock, stew chicken with mushrooms, pearl onions, a bay leaf, herbs; it sweetens the kitchen. Handel's music warms this space, fills it with light. I ask, "What d'you think? More salt?" Oh, this can't last; in a few years, I know, he'll want to hang out with his friends on a Friday night. But for now it works.

How am I so different from my chairman— from Leonard Noble? This has been my life for years now, this sweet hiding. Staying safe. My marriage to Nancy was a dream of pastoral retreat. My involvement in the bigger world, the political life at the cusp of the seventies, was long gone by then. Even hope for a revolution of the heart, gone. Nancy was a young girl when we met at the end of the seventies, barely out of college. As she stood on the porch of the falling-down farmhouse where she lived with friends, under a full moon I remember, so gentle and yielding, I imagined sharing a kind of traditional, simple life with her. We'd can tomatoes and cut cordwood for heat, make our own Christmas decorations and craft our own stained glass to separate open spaces in the house I'd built. If we can't make a new community, at least we can make our private lives like a work of art. We'd have a child and watch him grow, and that would be our world and enough.

I finish our fricassee with flour to thicken, cream to enrich. The machine takes another call from Gabriella, a call from Gar, a call from Frank. We pretend, Jeremy and I, that we're such important people we can't possibly be bothered. Let the butler take our calls. "So? What d'you think? You like our Adventurers' Stew?"

"Except for the bones," Jeremy says.

After dinner, Jeremy goes back to the front door to stare at Chuck's work—the deep grooves in the vertical oak boards a really good carpenter put together into an insulated frame door. He fingers the splintered edges, and I say, "Be careful."

"He was real mad."

"Oh, he was." I realize he's imagining himself inside, hearing the pounding and crunching. I say, "He never had a chance against a door like that."

"You're lucky," he says.

I nod, solemnly. "You're right. Lucky."

Nancy calls while we're watching Danny Kaye in *The Court Jester*—watching it for our second time. I tell her I'll call back. Basil Rathbone snaps his fingers and the hero slips into hypnotic trance in which he is the greatest swordsman in the world. Another snap and he is just himself, cowering before the evil Rathbone. After, we dance around the living room, imaginary swords in hand, snapping each other into spells of courage. We circle the swing that hangs from a twenty-foot crossbeam. It's what everyone who comes here remembers about this house—that swing. Escaping Jeremy's sword, I pull back on the polished yellow-pine seat and fly through an arc of almost thirty feet. "Ha! The masked Nogoodnik will never be caught!" But because it's after ten and time for bed, the Caped Avenger manages to unseat me and take away my magic powers. And so to bed. We talk about the day past and the day to come. Alone, I sit in my reading chair under a standing light, the room dark all around, a glass of wine in hand, and I gather myself and calm myself so I can call Nancy. She picks up on the first ring.

"That man called again," Nancy says.

"I'm sorry. You don't need that."

"He wants to make trouble. Listen, David, I know it's not your fault."

"Thanks. It makes me feel good, hearing you say that."

"Although . . . if you didn't go around taking in crazy people, none of this would have happened."

"Look, I told you—"

"I want you to know, I don't intend to *use* this against you. Do you understand, David? I think you think I'm unscrupulous—"

"—No, no!—"

"Well, maybe I *am* when it comes to Jeremy. But don't worry."

"I'm not worrying. But thanks."

"But please, you *will* avoid unnecessary entanglements?"

"Nancy, I already told you—"

"Because my lawyer tells me that a thing like this—"

"Your lawyer! Oh. What does your lawyer tell you?"

"The point is, David, I just want the best for Jeremy."

"You think I don't? Don't worry," I say.

"*I* have nothing to worry about. Do have a good weekend."

Her *lawyer*. I pour a little more wine; with only me drinking, it takes me a few nights to work my way though a bottle. It's getting sour. I put on a CD of Bach suites for keyboard and violin, programming only the sweet largo and andante movements. I let them fill the empty space with their atmosphere so I can breathe a little. Breathing sadness is better than not breathing. My grandfather hummed synagogue melodies to himself, murmuring the Hebrew with the heavy *ch* sounds that breathe out suffering. Bach's music fills my synagogue.

In this room that I hammered and nailed together, two stories high, the old barn boards absorb light so completely I can barely see at all beyond the circle of lamplight surrounding this old chair, red wing-backed chair I carted up here when my mother died. Glints off the nickel fixtures of the woodstove, off a hanging terrarium, off an inside window from the bedroom that looks down onto this room: that's all. In the dark I'm oriented to Jeremy in his bed, to my kitchen, to my study; I know where I am.

My synagogue? I'm more like a gloomy Calvinist in solitary retreat. My grandfather had a community—a congregation of old men, all out of place in New York; some, survivors of the camps, all survivors of the war against the Jews. By the time I was in college, mid-sixties, the synagogue seemed a place to hide from history. Old men like these had been spun off by history; I was entering it. I felt sorry for the old men as if their synagogue were a nursing home. I was out to make a new world. We were a new species, not just a begotten and begetting generation—Abraham begat who begat who begat. A whole new species we were making of ourselves; generating ourselves out of nothing.

The last Bach largo ends. I'm just sitting. I don't even realize I've been considering, deciding: I reach for the phone and dial Gabriella's number, which, it turns out, I've memorized. Dialing it, I find I've been saying it inside, like a prayer.

The next two weeks, before she comes to see me, I imagine different scenarios with Gabriella; I rehearse questions, speeches. Friday night, Jeremy and I have dinner with Frank Polidori and Nora, and after dinner, while the kids watch a video, Frank and I shoot pool in the basement.

A big guy, though not nearly as big as Gar, Frank is solid from pumping weights now that he's not personally hefting two-by-fours, now that he has a crew for that. He's got a heavy, bulbous face with a big jaw and bushy brows. I've thought of Rodin's bust of Balzac; a sculptor ought to love all the thick, craggy planes of his skull.

"You got something on your mind?" Frank says after he misses a shot. "I can *hear* you got something on your mind. I can't play pool like this."

"What?" I say, innocent, palms open.

"I see you moving your lips. No kidding. Like this." He demonstrates. "When I'm shooting." He puts up his stick on the rack and sits in the easy chair with the broken springs. I sit on the edge of the table, then, embarrassed at my lack of consideration, slip off and sit beside him on a rattan porch chair past retirement age.

"Well," I say, "I keep thinking about the woman—"

"—You kidding? A young kid like that?"

"No. No. The woman who sent her to me. I knew her twenty years back. My old lover, as a matter of fact. I keep thinking about her." The rattan pokes me along my back. "I worry she's lying to me, and we don't even have anything going. There's a guy we both knew back then . . . and I don't know what's going on. You see?"

Frank grins. I recognize that grin. It says, *Let ol' Poppa Frank Polidori tell you about the real world, about which you know not a goddamn thing.* He likes to play the practical guy who gets his hands dirty with the work of the world. I let him. I like it. I talk ideas, he pops a beer can and belches. That wouldn't be much of a relationship, but there's more. For when his heart is sore, when he's ragged over cash flow or like the night he found Nora crying, a little album of her mother's pictures on her pillow, or when he's confused about how to handle some guy who works for him and has a drug problem, then he comes to me, shuffles around, but clearly wants my help.

"Let's play some pool," I say. "I'll keep my lips closed."

"No—tell me."

I tell Frank about Gabriella, about Gar. Is she sleeping with Gar—after all this time? What's going on? "It's really crazy how much I rehearse what I'm going to say when she comes. . . . "

But when Gabriella drives up on Saturday late morning—Jeremy gone to his mother the day before—I don't say anything, not a thing. She carries her canvas overnight bag, her laptop. She touches the scars of the front door and shuts her eyes for a moment. "I've been meaning to fix that," I tell her. In the kitchen I set in front of her a bowl of the lentil and sausage soup I've cooked. We share a baguette. "You must be tired, end of a long week?" I say.

She nods. "This is *your* soup, isn't it? You made this. It's just wonderful, Dave. Real comfort food."

"Good. Watch out for the bay leaf. Jeremy and I put it together. Oh—and the peppercorns. I should make a sachet in a cheesecloth bag, but I'm out of cheesecloth."

"You amaze me."

It's these little amazements, affirmations of my life—that let me think she understands things we're not saying. After lunch we go for a hike in the woods. I strap on a day pack filled with fruit and nuts and cider. It's the first weekend in October; it should be peak season, but down in the valley, it's not. I stand in front of the house and point up at the tiny fire tower on our mountain. "See up there? That's where we're headed." We climb through hemlock and pine to a meadow fringed by old apple and maple trees, and from this height on, the color *has* peaked, the gold and red, then a stand of oak, the red just beginning to glow through the murky greens of earlier fall. I find I'm letting the colors *in* today. I peel open my rib cage and feel them through lungs and heart. Someone's lit a woodstove around these hills; the musky smoke is faint enough, strong enough, to be delicious.

We're both silent; like a much younger man, someone seventeen, I want to take Gabriella's hand, but I can't until I ask her things, and, like someone seventeen, I'm afraid to bring things up. Instead, I say, "Gabriella, these woods remind me— did *we* ever do psychedelics? You and me?"

"I don't think so. No . . . . One time," she adds, "I did acid with Gar."

"With *Gar*."

She laughs, I guess at something in my voice. She stops, leans against a tree and closes her eyes so that she looks a little drunk, the way we imagine a child, unguarded, and she hoots. It's a long bout of laughter. She holds her belly. At once, believing in the laughter, somehow I'm relieved. She slides her back down the trunk and sits cross-legged at the foot of the little birch, and I want to tell her that the seat of her jeans is going to be full of twigs and dead leaves. Now I'm above her, awkward, holding my bones upright, the balancing act we do all our lives so that it's stopped amazing us; I'm gawky, looking down at the wavy, curly mass of her black hair, gray-flecked, and I think of the gray as battle stripes—then what about my own?—and I see the two of us not as woods children but, God knows, as ragged adults who don't belong to the woods, beaten by time, by our choices meant to keep us safe. Each of us has travelled complicated, tortuous paths to this place. Do I want to go back? It would be humiliating to pretend that we hadn't broken and scarred along the way. Here I am, wearing my choices.

Hearing the kindness in her laugh, I sit down cross-legged in front of her. "*What*? What are you laughing at?"

"Oh, *you*—you funny man. You want to know about Gar, what you want to know is, *are we sleeping together.*

Look how old we are and here we are worrying about such things—it's so funny. Old Gar! Well, we *were* together, but not for the past few years, not that way. Gar's been good to me, good to Sojourner House. He stays with me when he comes up to Boston on business. He keeps a car in Boston. When he flies up, we get together. But lovers?—No, David. Now," she says, "can we just have a happy couple of days away from things?"

"Away, huh? You brought your computer, I noticed."

"Oh, I carry it wherever I go. I'm afraid of leaving it in the apartment and having it stolen. I bring my back-up disks, too."

"It's okay with me, you want to get a little work done."

"Maybe." She thinks a moment. "I have my journal with me. I keep a journal. I've put a lot of different things into it. Clippings, poems, copies of letters. Letters I'll never mail. I'll show you sometime."

I lead her up a blazed trail to a switchback path up the south side of a small mountain. We rest halfway on an outcropping, digging the keyhole view through the woods: the whole valley. "The strange thing is," she says as if we'd been talking about Kerry and Chuck the whole time, "we've heard nothing about the lawsuit since the day you came to Sojourner House. Nothing at all. We're pretty sure it'll be dropped."

We're up into the trees now, seeing nothing else. At our feet the path is yellow with beautiful, pointed beech leaves. There's a stream sometimes on our left, sometimes to our right, we keep crossing it over buried ribbed culverts. Not much life in it now; just a little flow. "You should see this in spring," I tell her. We're guerrillas climbing over a border into freedom. "Just another mile, we'll be at the lookout tower." I unfold the topographical map, but I've forgotten my reading glasses. Gabriella hands me hers; they're dangling from the silver chain. A silver chain! I laugh that she wears them even in the woods. They work for my eyes, and I point out on the map the trail to the lookout and hand the glasses back.

Gabriella sighs. "The old days," she says, "it was a *joint* we used to pass."

As we start to climb again, I tell her, "I know about your child."

"I knew Gar would tell you about Sara."

"I'm really sorry."

Saying "Sara" quiets Gabriella. There's no more laughter in her. "David," she says . . . with nothing to follow. We are both fingering pieces of bark, the long tree roots above ground. "You wonder about Gar. But I think you understand. Because of you and Jeremy, you understand. What it's been like. I've not been sleeping with *anyone*, David. Not anyone. I've been celibate. I've been incommunicado . . . . I have good women friends. But I hardly see even them. I hardly see Gail. Gail has been my closest friend, my ally, and I'm turning her into an enemy. Even *Jenny*."

"Jenny's your older daughter?"

"After Sara—Jenny went to her father, and I moved to my little apartment."

"You've been living there—out of boxes like that—*two years*?"

"Jenny . . . went to her father. He demanded that. No—not *demanded*. I mean, his child—our child—was killed in *my* care, because of *my* work."

"So you've lost everything."

A little further and the trail intersects an old logging road, stones piled along the sides in fallen rock walls so that it's clear that the loggers followed a disused country road. We stop and feel the cold in our faces. "I want to show you something." I lead Gabriella up the old road, so steep it's hard to imagine that there were houses here a hundred years ago. But there were. I point out the line of maples and rock walls and the stones of old cellar holes. In a couple of the cellar holes, the foundations of huge stone fireplaces have survived from disintegrated farmhouses.

Grass like rough carpet, foundation walls rising above eye level. Jesus, the work put into its making: clearing giant trees and ripping their stumps out of the ground; lugging rocks for the walls and fireplaces. The work of clearing fields. Then carting up this hill milling machinery for the felled trees. And, slowly, somebody built a house.

Without words, I invent for Gabriella a gaunt, strong man placing stone on stone. He's no hero but he lifts the stones because he has to, has to build in order to live somewhere, to survive and raise a family. To do that he had to carry these stones. I imagine she understands. I lift a giant flat stone from the grass and heft it onto the crumpled foundation wall.

She nods. For the moment, perhaps we both have a sort of mournful courage. For the moment, this is our house. I lead Gabriella back to the trail towards the fire tower, from which you can see your relation to everywhere; Mount Monadnock to the northeast, Stratton to the northwest, the Holyoke range to the south. We're breathing hard. Now we share a look and I take her hand for the climb up the tower.

The tower, like an Erector-set construction with a tiny house on top, trembles and whines in the wind and the iron stairs shiver and clang under our boots. Knocking at the ranger's trap door, we come in from the cold wind. The ranger lets us look through his field glasses and aligns the view to the maps on his desk. He's a young man. Is this his first job out of college, is he taking a semester off? Is he lonely up here? Jack Kerouac worked as lookout in a forest tower in order to escape his persona, to dry out, to meditate; he became lonely. We talk about the danger of fire this week, dry as it is in the woods. There's a stand of maple on the next rise, maple and oak coming into color, that looks as if it's already burning.

I notice that Gabriella isn't happy; she's closed in on herself, brooding, hardly noticing the hills full of color. Right away I find a panic rising in me, the old need to assuage, heal, make things right. It's leftovers from home, something my mother handed me, a CARE package. It's my mother standing in the middle of the kitchen, stoned with grief, rocking, nodding, lighting *yortzeit* candles.

I put an arm over Gabriella's shoulder, not asking. I

thank the ranger and we leave through the trap door, down the quivering stairs. I have a crazy worry Gabriella could decide to jump. I find myself watching her, though there's no justification; she doesn't even stop on the way down.

We're silent a long way through the woods until we pass the old road and further, the outcropping that overlooks the valley south. She sits at the edge. "It's beautiful, David." And then she says, "You know, don't you—did Gar tell you?—I tried to kill myself after Sara, after Sara was killed. He didn't? I tried to arrange an accident with a car. I didn't want Jenny to have to go through her life knowing her mother died on purpose. At the last second I jerked the wheel. And then—then I stopped caring about whether Jenny knew, and I took pills but they turned out to be the wrong ones. I could have drowned on my own vomit but I didn't. Nice thing to talk about on a day like this—but you need to know about me."

Now that she can talk about it, my heart stops being afraid. I trade anxiety for sorrow, and sorrow I can live with. The fact that she said I "need to know" settles in me like whiskey. I take her hand; the rest of the descent into the valley is gentle.

We're home just before the sun goes down. Gabriella helps me build a fire in the woodstove. We share a bottle of wine while we cut up vegetables. She belongs here—as if there was never a time I didn't know her. Am I still making her up? The thought scares me. Neither of us have the time to fool around we once thought we had.

We talk, old married couple, sitting in the kitchen while the chicken and vegetables bake—about my teaching and a couple of my articles, about Sojourner House, finally about her older girl, Jenny.

"I do see Jenny," Gabriella says. "Not often. She's at school—boarding school—right near here. I'm going to stop in Sunday night as a matter of fact. We talk on the phone . . . we don't talk. I don't tell her what I'm feeling, she doesn't tell me. We never talk about what happened. After the pills, what happened with the pills, her father had every right. We both felt Jenny had to go to him—'until I felt stronger'; that was the cover story, but I knew that once she settled . . . He's got . . . a comfortable home. Anyway, she's away from both of us, really. It's a good school. She'll be off to college next year. She does *like* me, David. I'm hoping now we can get together more."

"You seem so heavy sometimes."

"It's a lot of things. It's not only Sara."

"No."

"It's my work." She gets up from the table, puts on her reading glasses and takes a black leather-bound book from her bag. "I put things in my journal. I told you. Here."

A clipping is taped in at the open page.

> . . . *man arraigned in Superior Court for second degree homicide. According to police accounts, he has confessed to anally raping his girlfriend's five-year-old daughter. To keep her from screaming he pressed the child's face into a pillow until she suffocated.*

"And this is the kind of thing you put in your journal?"

"Oh, David, not only this. Good things, too. But I want you to understand what I have to deal with every day."

I'm scared for her. I also need to pull back. Has she handed me this journal so that I *will* pull back?

I take out the stew, lay on breadcrumbs and slivers of cheese and a sprinkle of cayenne and put it back to bake uncovered. So the night comes on. We play old, scratchy Beatles records, Miles Davis, we even dance. "Remember . . .?" one of us asks. When it gets late, she tells me, "You show me where to sleep. Or if you want, we can sleep in the same bed—just sleep. All right, Dave?"

I shrug. I get her towels, she changes into a flannel nightgown, and we slip into the same bed. She turns to me for a hug. I look at her hands, the deep lines along her knuckles—mine too. We lie together with the residues of twenty years between us like a board. Here we are, the woman an Italian-Irish Catholic, the man a Jew, here we are practicing the American Puritan tradition of bundling. I'm about to make the joke, when she pulls away and begins to speak almost in a whisper, as if this were a confessional, begins to say what she's been waiting to say all this day or longer.

"I want to tell you about the afternoon Sara was killed."

Please—is this just to tell me why we're not sleeping together? To say that that would be a slap in the face. I listen.

"Of course I should never have let her near the place— Sojourner House. Her father warned me. But I wanted to expose her to . . . people. And it didn't seem dangerous. The worst I could have imagined was an angry man coming in and yelling."

"Expose her—to suffering, you mean?"

"No, *not* just suffering. To people who came *through* suffering. I know you'd be amazed at some of these women, Dave."

"And *you*."

"Me, what?"

"Coming through. I mean you're one of them, aren't you?"

"No," she says, flatly. She sighs. "She used to get dropped off by the school bus, she was a sweet little girl, everybody loved her. But that doesn't matter," she says fiercely. "That's not the point.

"We'd touch base now and then during the afternoon. Sometimes she'd help out, take care of little kids while their mother was interviewed. She was good with little kids. Or she'd fuss around the kitchen or draw at a desk. Or she'd stop by the library on the way and be carrying a huge pile of books, so heavy.

"The afternoon this man came in, she was talking to one of the counselors near the front desk—it just happened that way. And this little man came in, in boots, thick long hair, everybody's nightmare husband we used to joke about except he was so small and wearing a sports jacket and a dirty white shirt—he'd just been to court—and he had a machine pistol, and he was screaming for his wife. He wanted his wife back. I heard him from upstairs and I pressed the buzzer connected to the police and ran to the staircase and said in Spanish—I don't know, something like, 'She's not here, your wife, you put that down and we can talk about her, I'll call her, you can talk to her.'

"I don't know if he heard me. He was standing in the middle of the entrance room, cursing us. And maybe I could have come down the stairs slowly and made him hand me the gun, but I didn't. Women were slipping away. And then Sara got scared and ran up the stairs to me, and he started howling like an animal and spraying the stairs and the women running and by the time I reached her, her white blouse was full of blood and I could feel her chest ripped open so that under the wet skin she was *loose*.

"And then I didn't care, I just held her together, and then he turned the gun on himself, but I didn't see that. That was when my life ended. Sara passed out, and I kept thinking 'So this is the end of my life.' It was as if we were dying together, and I just held her against me. I think I had the fantasy we would just die that way together."

Now Gabriella is silent a minute, two, and I stroke her forehead. I imagine she's crying, but when I turn to look, in the light of the moon coming in the window I can see she's not. I say, finally: "But you *didn't* die."

She says, "I did. I'm not being theatrical. I've thought about it a great deal. My life *did* end. My work kept going but my life was over."

This is sorrow I can't absorb or succor. I take her hand and we lie on two sides of the story and try to fall asleep in the bed I made.

Four

I want my heart to open. It's like the moment when an ophthalmologist, about to hit my pupil with a puff of air, says *Try to keep open, Mr. Rosen,* and I try to force my eye to stay open, yet it closes, and I'm the one closing it.

It used to be easy.

For instance, with Gabriella in the late sixties. We met on a chartered bus from Columbia University to a march on Washington. I read her dark eyes and thick black hair as richness of soul, sensual fire. Back from Washington, we squirreled ourselves away in her room in a student apartment, making love, going down for pizza, back upstairs to make love again. We shared a hash pipe and a bottle of cheap wine, talked politics and made love. It was days before I knew a thing about her. I fell in love with her deep quiet and with her moral passion.

We dovetailed our record collections, our books. We went to political meetings together, were arrested together. Then I lost her to Gar.

But I'm saying how *easily* we took up residency in one another's hearts, because each of us was still unformed; how easily—at least for the time being—our lives seemed to fit together like the hooks and loops of velcro. It's as if back then, young, we had sufficient loops, sufficient hooks, unclaimed.

It's so different now. The hooks and loops are torn or taken, so little left. I've never *not* fallen in love with one woman or another. I walk down a hallway full of students and inwardly I groan at one, the radiance of some young person. But I'm not dumb enough to make anything of it. My groaning is a tribute. I see a woman at a concert and I imagine the richness of her heart, and her eyes seem to tell me of her inner architecture of spirit. But that's not the same. I want my heart to open and let the future in.

We become set in our ways. Me, I live with music going on behind my doings—Renaissance, baroque, classical, romantic, modern; I hover over my stacks of cassettes and CDs until one calls out to me, and that's the one, ah, satisfying like a drug, just that Pergolesi choral sound or the chromatic tug at my skin of a madrigal by Gesualdo. Mozart! Mozart!—or a mass by Stravinsky or *La Boheme*. Or sometimes it's cool jazz, old Pacific coast jazz, Gerry Mulligan, Chet Baker. I let Jeremy play his "classic" rock music, knowing much worse is to come when he hits his teens. But could I passionately love a woman who fell asleep over classical music? Back then—ah, sure. Now?—no way. Could I be the lover of a woman who smokes cigarettes? Or somebody who watches David Letterman? Oh, I'm getting cranky-peculiar. I exercise when I wake up, thirty minutes, don't talk to me, okay?

Gabriella, on the other hand, she starts her Sunday cross-legged in meditation, no music godforbid, and then coffee, and she sits at her laptop and types fiercely for half an hour and just when I've had my coffee and am sitting down with student papers, she wants to talk. She likes the heat pumped up; I keep the house cool and wear layers of clothing.

But that's nothing, or it's a joke, two prima donnas negotiating the choreography of their dance. More difficult is the battle of schedules. Tomorrow, I go off to teach, while Gabriella will be at an all-day meeting in Hartford for social agencies in New England; Tuesday she's back at her desk, but Wednesday she flies to Chicago to a conference of mayors. On the weekend she needs to pour herself into a grant application for private funding, while I have to work on my article for the *Globe* on the value of community college teaching. When can we get together? Thursday evening, we decide, halfway to Boston, dinner at an inn.

We're each full of our own busy selves—Gabriella, me, all of us after youth is finished. The mutual enfolding, the illusion of utter intimacy, the fusing of souls—no more. We're drier, shrewder, cooler, we'll each stay who we individually are. We get more and more idiosyncratic; others more and more annoy us with their otherness. Is it possible to give ourselves in love? For now it means loving a fully created person. Young, we have sweet flesh and young eyes. We are succulent to one another, we love the glow that shimmers off the skin of the other. But now, our skin no longer gives off light, we own the wrinkles not just of age but of anger and smugness, lines of defense against too much pain. I wasn't lying to Gabriella when I said she was *more* beautiful now; she is. But to love a man or woman for the beauty they've made of themselves is a hard thing.

What substitutes for the easy love of our youth? What might let us restore the naiveté of youth, let us peel open our shirts and our chests and *say* our hearts? It's the fantasy of reparations, the fantasy that with this person, who's been through so much, maybe I can do it right this time. We might reclaim a generosity of spirit, more real, less triggered by the spectacular curve of a breast, the firmness of a thigh. We might be able to love the particular flesh and soul of this other person.

I come through this weekend brushed by hope again. After failures in marriage, after my smaller suffering and her greater, maybe our hearts can open again. Maybe after children and the loss of children and the loss of the changed America we hoped to share, after hopelessness, we can still live with such intensity, at such depths, with such caring. I hope for it.

Chuck Ahearn calls again, early afternoon. I hold my hand over the mouthpiece and whisper to Gabriella, "It's Kerry's husband, it's Chuck." I sit at the kitchen table. "What do you want this time? You've been calling everybody—my wife, my chairman—now you listen to me—nobody is paying attention. Why don't you stop?"

"No, no, listen, Rosen—I'm calling to apologize to you. That lying bitch, that crazy wife of mine! You never tried to rape her, okay, I know now. I apologize I fucked up your door. That's all. That's all I wanted to say."

"Forget it."

"You see what I've got to put up with? The fuckin' liar. Jesus, is she messed up. She messes my head. You know what I mean? She messes my head. I mean . . . I *used* to be a bad motherfucker."

"I know."

"No. You *don't* know. Anyway, hey—*that's not me*. Not now. I've got a kid now. You see what I'm saying? I swear to God I try to be a good father. But that bitch *does* it to me. You just don't know. I found out last night. I worked it out of her, she was lying, plain lying. After I put the screws on her, she stuck it in my face, like, What are you gonna do, asshole? But hey! She's *my* problem. I can handle Kerry. I'm just letting you know I know I was wrong about the rape. You're not the type."

"No. I'm *not* the type."

"No. Frankly, you haven't got the balls." He laughs, sharply. "Anyway, you try something, she'd have cut you." When I don't say anything, he adds, meditatively, "I know, I ought to get rid of her. But that's my son. *Andrew*," he says, he half-sobs, with tenderness. "Andrew, he's my son. Get what I'm saying?"

"She loves him," I say.

"Love! She's crazy. Love! She's kissing him all over the place or shoving him away, no in-between. She's no goddamn mother."

"I'm sorry."

"Sometime, you come into Boston, you come see me, I'd like to buy you a drink, no hard feelings. I want to tell you what I've been through with that crazy woman."

"I'm sorry," I say again. And I am—sorry for them both.

"I've got a short fuse. But I'm trying, honest to God. She knows just how to make me crazy. You come in to Boston, my brother and I, we want to take you out to dinner, no hard feelings. Okay?"

"Sure," I say. "You take it easy, man. Good luck to both of you. To all of you." Hanging up, I look at Gabriella, who's looking at me with big eyes, and I shake my head. "I guess you don't have to worry about that law suit," I say.

This afternoon, Sunday, we both feel the end of the weekend coming. "Tell me about the women who come to Sojourner House," I say. We're sitting at the kitchen table. There's a sonata for piano and violin by Mozart playing low.

She tells me terrible stories. The woman who walked in last week, face cut deeply in maybe ten long wounds, each needing stitches. "He took his time," Gabriella says. "That's what she told her counselor. He was teaching her 'a lesson she'd never forget,' he told her. She never will," Gabriella says.

"And Kerry Latrice," she says. I didn't want to talk about it, it was confidential, but now it doesn't matter. Her husband—of course he wants to feel like a victim. They all want to feel like victims. That little boy for instance . . . . This Chuck Ahearn took it into his head that the boy caused the fights, and say Kerry talked back to him, or she went out with some other guy, the boy—"

"—Andrew—"

"—Andrew—got the brunt of it. Andrew was like a hostage. You shut your mouth or I'll smash the kid. He saw everything as disrespect. If Kerry was bad-mouthing him and things got loud and Andrew got scared and cried for his Mommy, Chuck would pick him up and shake him until she acquiesced."

"How do you know all this?"

"Well, that's right, it's just Kerry's word. But I believe her for the *most* part. She's no angel. We've filed an official complaint to DSS on behalf of the boy."

"I couldn't do what you do."

"You keep saying that. Mostly, in fact," she says, "I'm so involved with administration, with meetings of the board and the staff and fund-raising and attending conferences, I'm less and less involved in the lives of the women who need the shelter. I'm sorry about that. But I have to work where I'm needed."

"Sometimes," I say out of the blue, "I think of you as a nun." What I *mean* to mean is her dedication, not for herself (she's told me she 'died,' and the word hovers over her all this day, she's a religious woman who's died to the world); what I mean to mean is the frugal simplicity of her life. I mean it as a word of respect. But she looks up at me sharply—we're having a cup of tea before she has to drive back to Boston—and at once I know there *was* something else, something hostile in what I've said. She takes it as a dig, meaning she can't make love, that she's buried her heart out of guilt at having survived her daughter's death. Maybe she's right.

"I'm no nun," she says flatly.

Years back, I would have gone off at the mouth trying to cover over my stupidity; now I'm silent. The silence lets me listen down into her life. She enters me, I sense what her life has been; I close my eyes for a moment just to bear it.

We rise from the table and I take her in my arms, and she lets herself sink against my shoulder. It's a slow sinking, like a child fighting sleep then giving way, and the slowness, the hesitance, makes it terribly intimate. Can I support her like this? I stroke the back of her neck. We stand and stand like that. Finally, she stands up straight, touches my nose with the tip of her finger, laughs, picks up her laptop, and easily we kiss goodbye. She's off to have dinner with Jenny at school before heading home.

So there's a window open in my life; I can smell the sea. Future enters the only way it can, wrapped in the pain of the past.

We've made plans: I'll visit Gabriella in Boston, this time with Jeremy. A little giddy, I call Jeremy, purportedly to ask about his weekend, and after we talk, Nancy gets on and tells me about plans for her "trip" next May—she won't call it a honeymoon—with Peter, and would I mind keeping Jeremy an extra week and then let him go to them for three? I say, *Sure, sure, of course*, because I'm full, not hungry, tonight. And like old friends we find ourselves gossiping about a couple we know divorcing after twenty years, the woman off with another woman. Typical Valley story.

I finish a lesson plan and a set of papers while a violin sonata by Shostakovich and a fire in the woodstove warm the big room. By now, I suppose, nine o'clock, Gabriella is home, working. I imagine we're in the same room, a room large enough to be on two opposite sides of Massachusetts. And a car pulls up in the driveway, its lights arc across the walls—who the hell at this hour?—and there's a knocking at the door, and it's Kerry, Kerry and the boy, Andrew, and he's just waking up and blinking, and there's dried blood on his face. So how can I not let them in? The driver calls out, "This the place, all right? I'll be getting home, then." And he's gone.

"It took just three rides," Kerry says, pleased. She slips the bag from her shoulder, shifts Andrew to the other hip, and covers up her embarrassment by smiling and blabbing. "No problemo. Real nice guys. This guy brought me like miles out of his way."

"Don't you have *friends* to go to?"

"Yeah. Friends. Where you think Chuck is gonna go looking?"

I wave her to follow me into the bathroom, and I wash Andrew's face gently with cotton balls. He's howling. I can see the abrasions on the cheek and temple, they're not bad. I look into his eyes and they're focusing. So thank God.

Kerry rocks him, sings to him, "There, there, you little turd . . . ." I wish Gabriella were here. I'm beginning to feel panic. Should I call Frank? No—another single man, and anyway, Frank can't leave his daughter. What about Sylvia and Russell Warner from down the road?

All this time, Kerry's babbling about Chuck, how I ought to see her ribs where he fucking kicked her, how she called Sojourner House but "those dykes were real snotty because of Chuck, and Christ, I said, 'You think it was *me* laid that lawsuit on you? It wasn't me,' I said. But they said I had to wait till tomorrow, and the cops, they do shit.

So...." She shrugs and hands me Andrew so she can get her coat off. Shrieking, he reaches for his mother and she walks him through the house. I stay in the bathroom and panic.

And now I hunt for them. Carrying antiseptic ointment, I follow the smell and the whining and find them in the kitchen. She's poured him a glass of milk.

I rehearse: *You think I'm gonna let you stay here? No damn way, Kerry.* But I look at her sleepy little boy having a tough time keeping his head off the table, and his abrasions get to me and my stomach turns over. "Can I put on some medicine?" I bend over his chair; he doesn't respond. I look up at Kerry. Vaguely I make note that she's wearing a tee-shirt with a fancy logos from a rock band, her bra shows through, and this is October, a chilly night.

"Uncle Dave has got some nice medicine," she says, "for where Daddy Chuck smacked you. Okay, kid?"

"*Mommy*," he says.

She says, "Andrew, You want Mommy to put on the medicine?"

"*Mommy.*"

I hand her the tube and cotton. She smears the ointment on his cheek.

"And his temple," I say.

So she does it—for me.

"What about family? What about your mother?"

"You shitting me? My mother! I called her a couple of days back, told her I had to get out of that prison, Chuck was watching me, he was looking for a chance to belt me again. This time I shut up, I got scared, real scared. This time he said he was going to go all the way, and I called first chance I got...."

"Your mother?"

"My fuckin' mother. Yeah. She said she doesn't want shit to do with me. She says, 'Leave the kid somewhere and you can come home for a few days.' Fuck her. Anyway, she's living with the same guy who got into me four, five years ago. Yeah, my mother. So? You gonna let me stay here?"

I take the phone from the wall and call Sylvia and Russell Warner. Russell's retired, Syl works as a nurse at the hospital in Green River. They're neighbors, not close friends. When it snows, Russell drives his tractor over to plow my driveway. Sylvia calls me over for cookies when she goes into a baking frenzy. When they go off to visit their daughter, I watch their dog and their house, make sure the pipes don't freeze.

"Syl, this is Dave Rosen. Would you do me a favor? Would you come over here for a few minutes? I've got a serious problem."

I haven't got a plan. I know I want a witness; I don't want to be accused of rape this time. And Syl's a nurse. And then what? There's no way Kerry and the child should be dumped on Syl and Russell. But when Syl hears the tone of my voice and says, simply, "Of course. We'll be right over . . . . Russell . . . ?" I breathe easier.

Sometimes I realize that I do my best thinking with my body, with my fingers. Like when you get to a door with your arms full of packages, you don't need to think out a plan. The point is to use your *body's* mind; if you do, it's amazing how well your body knows how to shift weight to one hip, balance groceries on your belt buckle, press with your whole body as you turn the door handle, your body knows, knows the peculiarities of this particular door, knows how many seconds before the bag will slip, knows which bag to place on the counter first. All that, known without thought. Now, putting the phone down, I let myself fall into that consciousness.

I don't plan anything. I get on one knee by Andrew's chair: "How would you like something delicious?" Reaching into the cupboard for semi-sweet baking chocolate, I break off a nice bite. He doesn't say a thing but huddles over the chocolate as if to take it into his chest; protecting it, he eats, he's happy.

"So what's happening, Kerry? what's happening? Tell me." I put up water for tea and sit down to listen.

"What d'you want to know?"

I look up to the ceiling for an invisible friend to witness this craziness. "Hey. You're the one who came for help."

"Well, the bastard came after me and Andrew with a knife. He was spooky-quiet. I can take it he smacks me sometimes, people get crazy, I give him a hard time, he says I drive him nuts, I guess I do, the kid hears us yelling and it always sets him off, and Chuck freaks when Andrew starts screaming. You know? But this is different. I got scared for both of us this time . . . .

"This time I got so fucking scared I couldn't see straight, so I tell Chuck I got to give the kid a bath, I carry our clothes in, I turn on the water and put on a rock tape loud and we slip out the window onto the back porch and down the stairs. That's all."

She chuckles, how she foxed him. "He's gonna be so crazy-pissed, and I figure, shit, first thing he'll do is go after Cheryl, she's my best friend, so I call her from a pay phone to get her boyfriend in to protect her, and he's one crazy fuck, he's got a gun, he won't take shit from Chuck. Anyway, Chuck won't try anything. He sees we're not there, I figure he'll go nuts, but he won't know where. You tell me. What could I do? They wouldn't let us come to over to the shelter, they wouldn't even tell us where it *is*."

"So there's Chuck with a knife."

"Yeah. Maybe a gun. But he can't do anything."

Still not knowing what *I* was going to do, still deciding nothing, I turn away and call Gabriella.

She picks it up on the first ring. "Oh, David," she says right away, "something's happened."

I say, "I know."

But before I can tell her about Kerry, she says, "David—Kerry's run off, and Chuck came to Sojourner House. I had my finger on the Police button, but he wasn't violent. But his restraint was terrifying. He wanted to know where she was, he talked about our 'brainwashing' and 'kidnapping,' her. You be careful."

"—She's *here*. She's here, she's in my kitchen."

"In your kitchen? Kerry's in your kitchen? How did she get out there?"

"I've got neighbors coming. I guess you better call the Boston Police. Chuck might figure it out. Who knows what he'll do? Andrew's face is bloody." I turn to Kerry. "What's Cheryl's address?"

Kerry just shrugs. I yell at her, "Listen, you want me to dump you in the center of the goddamn town? You tell me and *now!*" I'm shocked at myself, getting so loud. But Kerry tells me, she gives me the number, I tell Gabriella.

"Dave—take it easy . . . . We could have gone with her to a judge, we could have gotten a 209 A—a restraining order on him. Why did she run out *there*? I'll call you right back," she says. "You take it easy, Dave. And Dave—there's no way you ought to take her in. Not even for a night. Please. Think if there turns out to be a lawsuit. Bad for Sojourner House, *terrible* for you."

"There's no lawsuit now. And if she came out here, who'll believe a rape charge?"

"Don't get involved, David. Look—I'll call you soon."

I wave Kerry into a chair. "Tell me. How can you come here to me, how did you have the gall to come to me after what you said?"

"*What?*"

"What? You said I tried to *rape* you."

"Oh, *that*—that was Chuck."

"No. That was *you*. I heard you tell him on the way out." And then I remember: "'I pay my way,' you said that night. When I came up to see you. You were crying. 'I pay my way.' What did that mean?"

"I don't know—hey, you're not my *fa*ther, I don't have to answer these questions."

"You thought I was coming on to you—you thought I was making a move on you."

"How do you know what I thought?"

"Well, didn't you?"

"You?" she sneers. "You're the age of my Uncle Jack."

"So?"

"So . . . maybe I thought that. I don't remember."

"You remember telling Chuck—"

"—Yeah, but that was bullshit. That was for Chuck—so he didn't beat the shit out of me for splitting on him. And—I was kind of a wreck."

"And you're not now? *How am I supposed to trust you?*" She doesn't answer. Why do I *want* an answer, why do I want to trust her? This is crazy, get rid of her. It's like inviting a bomb into your house. But the little boy—there he is, head bobbing as if he's in a tiny boat, he's being rocked by sleep but his eyes are half open. I dim the lights in the kitchen. I say again, quietly, "You tell me. Why should I trust you, Kerry?"

There's a knock on the door and I stand up, guilty as if Kerry were my lover and I didn't want it discovered. Through the window alongside the kitchen door I see Sylvia and Russell and they smile as if this were a social call.

I've known the Warners for the twelve years I've lived in my house. In summer, taking a walk with his collie, Russ Warner will see me sitting on the front deck listening to music. So he pokes fun at my "highbrow musical tastes." He enjoys having the differences to kid about. Sometimes I walk with him and Rascal through the woods and he tells me what it was like around here seventy years ago—dirt roads, few telephones, a one-room school. He tells me about getting out of school to put in crops or hunt for deer. He speaks with a funny lilt I now understand is from Polish. He's a tall, skinny man in suspenders, with a small belly bulging over his pants. He's balding, a tonsured priest.

Funny—I see him as old rural America, but Russ, he's bitter about the way his father and mother were treated when they came to America, came to this valley, just before the turn of the century. They were outsiders, seen as ignorant aliens. They changed their name to Warner; it didn't help. Sometimes I try to make the connection for him between his parents and the new immigrants from Central and South America and the Caribbean—he complains a lot about foreigners on welfare—but he doesn't see it, and I don't push. I often wonder how he feels about Jews, but I don't ask. He treats me with respect.

So does Sylvia. She's a lean woman, strong, with short-cropped gray hair and a frank look. She's the head of the nursing staff at Green River Hospital—next year her retirement year. She and I have a separate relationship—a relationship of heart and cooking. We tell each other stories, I bring her a quart of lentil soup with sausage and she tells me about her mother's soups. When I wedged a bad splinter in my hand, she removed it, dressed the hand, and healed me with strong coffee. Sylvia likes the fact that I'm a teacher; I'm the only one she knows she can talk to about her extensive reading.

Russell and I never talk politics, we don't talk about hunting, we don't talk about anything that will trouble our relationship. He kids me that I won't take his extra gun and come hunting with him. A couple of times Frank Polidori has gone out hunting for quail with him. Russell probably thinks of me as a fuzzy intellectual; he's never read my articles and it's just as well. I wonder what he thinks about his daughter, who teaches history at Yale. Different as she is, I imagine she's gotten there *because of*, not *in spite of* her parents. I think of the Warners as decent, intelligent, energetic people. They're not really friends; but sometimes I think of them as aunt and uncle, the only family I've got left.

Russell and Sylvia bang their shoes clean on the mat and bring in with them the smell of crushed leaves and the cold, and I introduce them to Kerry and Andrew, who reaches for his mother; she picks him up and right away starts talking non-stop while I'm trying to explain.

"I've got a tough situation, look at this little kid. This is Andrew, this is Kerry, Kerry, this is Mr. and Mrs. Warner. Mrs. Warner's a nurse. Okay? Syl, what do you think? He's okay, it's just abrasions? I looked into his eyes, what do *you* think?

"Hey, he didn't have to drag you people out, Jesus, the kid's okay, you'll just scare him. What right you got to go dragging people in? This is embarrassing," she says, "I didn't have anyplace to go, y'see? So this guy is doing me a favor—the kid's

She looks, and Andrew clutches his mom and Kerry tries to get free so she can light a cigarette and I say, "No smoking in here, pay attention to your kid," and she's talking, talking at us. okay, no, really. I'm grateful to you for coming but you don't need—Jesus, Andrew!—lay off. He's tired, it's a long way out, this place is the middle of nowhere. Hey, will you *listen*? Will you *listen, goddamnit*?"

Sylvia is rubbing Andrew's head and he's letting her; in fact, he's moving his head towards the stroking the way a cat will do. I say, "Kerry, please, let me just explain to them—" but now it hits me I'm talking to the Warners as if she's not there. I'd be pissed, too. I back off. "Kerry, I'm sorry. Please, these people are great. You need help. Explain, *you* explain, okay?"

She rambles. Andrew. Then Chuck. Then her stepfather. Andrew. All over the place. Finally, *me*. "This is a guy I can *trust*," she says.

"Well, of course you can trust Mr. Rosen," Sylvia says simply. "But what do you expect him to *do*? You have this terrible man to deal with. Don't you need to talk to the police, dear?"

I break in. "Why didn't you call the Green River Women's Center—what's it called?—Green River Women in Transition? That's where you were going in the first place. They'd take you on an emergency basis."

"Last time I was here," Kerry says to Sylvia, ignoring me, "this guy was real decent to me. He said he'd help me get my G.E.D. Maybe I could even do some college where he teaches. So this was the first place I thought of. He's okay. I didn't mean to make things hard for him. That was Chuck's doing."

Not understanding any of this, Sylvia looks at me. I shrug.

"We've got to call the police," I say. "And the shelter in Green River."

Kerry begins to cry, she's gulping air like water, and her cryings sound like the cry of a sea animal. How much she's on the edge. My heart sinks. Andrew, sitting on her lap now, is petting her face, saying "Mommy, Mommy," his little face worried but completely concentrated and—curious.

Sylvia strokes her hair and gestures Russell and me out of the kitchen. I'm only too happy to go. "You want a drink?" I ask. No, he doesn't want a drink, so we go into the living room and he sits on the couch while I sit on the swing for comfort; we glance at one another as we hear Kerry's crying and Syl's voice murmuring. Russ is getting old; to cross his legs, he has to lift one over the other, and he's embarrassed about it, so I shrug. "It's late," I say.

"Dave, you be good and careful," he says. "Now Dave. You've been kind of protected—no, listen, you know I'm your friend—you don't know what the world is like. You don't know what people can do to you. You got your own little boy to watch out for."

"I've been thinking about that."

"Hell, *I'd* take them in, but I don't know as we have the . . ." He couldn't say what it was they didn't have. I nod.

"Well, I'm not asking. I wouldn't *want* that."

"You think we might call our minister?"

I can hear a delicacy in his tone. I guess it's that he knows I'm a Jew and worries I might feel uncomfortable. "Good idea," I say. "Sure. *Good* idea. But listen, Russ, I want to go call Frank Polidori. I'll be right back."

Up in my study, I don't call Frank. I sit in the dark, listening down into my own blood thumping. It's so strange to me that I still want to help her. It's Andrew, of course, but not just Andrew. The old hunger in me—to *rescue*. When she said that about the G.E.D.—the high school equivalency certificate that might be the beginning of turning her around—did she know how it got to me? Oh, there's something shrewd about her, she's dumb as hell but . . . not so dumb.

And listening down, I understand—my God—I'm going to try to do something for Kerry. Get her some place to stay, at least that.

I call the hotline at Green River Women in Transition. I

explain, hang up, Ronnie Gordon calls back. They'll have space for her, opening up in about a week. Can I find a place for her in the meantime? I'll try, I say. If it's life and death, they say, we can try to find something temporary. I'll try first, I say. An idea has begun to take form in me.

Now I call Frank.

"You know when Barbara's getting back to town—Barbara Johnson?"

"I don't know," he says. "End of the semester? Or is she away the whole year? I don't know."

"Frank, you got her number in Boulder? I lost it. I think her house may be empty. I think I remember her saying that."

"What are you getting into?"

"Remember the woman with the kid, the guy who beat her up?"

"Yeah . . . . You're getting involved in that again?"

"She needs a place and she can't stay here. You want me to send her back, let this guy kill her and the boy?"

"For Christsakes." But he goes for the number. I grope around the messy desk for a blank sheet of paper. Andrew's crying down in the kitchen. Now, Gabriella gets me on Call Waiting. I tell her to hold on, I take Barb's number, say, "Goodnight, Frank. I do appreciate your worry. It's good we worry about each other, you and me."

He grumphs, I laugh and call Gabriella.

"Chuck Ahearn is in custody," she says. "They found him outside this woman Cheryl's apartment building. And Dave?—he had a tire iron on him—no knife, but a tire iron—they put him in custody. He said he was afraid of his wife's friends."

"You be careful."

"You, too. Don't think of taking her in, Dave."

I leave a message on Barbara Johnson's answering machine in Boulder, and go into the kitchen, where Kerry is telling Sylvia her story. I half-listen to her talk about her mother's boyfriend molesting her. Is that someone different from her stepfather, another abuser? Or is it the same person, and *stepfather* just meant someone living with her mother? Or is she a liar—and if she's lying about this, what else has she been lying about?

Andrew is asleep on his mother's lap. And then there's this: is Kerry a good, loving mother who gets overwhelmed sometimes? Or is she a sick, destructive mother, and am I keeping the kid from help? Am I a fool for trying to save Kerry, help her get an education? It's so impossibly late. It's twenty years ago, before she was born, that the help needed to be given. Or fifteen years at least, when she must have already taken inside her sense of worthlessness and started covering it over with sugar. Give it up, it's too late. Like seeing on the news the films of starving kids in some village, sitting empty-eyed, covered with flies, and I'm thinking of saving them, and knowing how impossible it is and wishing that the village, all the villages, be obliterated so the suffering can be obliterated, and knowing it's my own selfish suffering I'm concerned with, needing to block out so much pain—like the time I hit a squirrel on the road and in the rear-view mirror saw it twitching in pain of dying, and turned the car to run it over again and end its pain.

I think of my grandfather in New York, his recipe for peace by mourning in advance. He mourned not just his wife's death, nor the loss of so much of his family in the Holocaust, but all the deaths that hadn't yet occurred: his own, his daughter's, and, I suppose, my death, too. And accepted all other losses in advance, since everything was finally to be lost. He was someone whose bronchia were constantly singing of death, advertising death.

Walking through Central Park with my hand in his, I hushed inside, and although my grandfather, stroking his beard to soothe himself, breathed in all the city's pain and, processing it in his heart, breathed out thick sorrow after sorrow, yet I rested sweetly in his hand and the significant world came in—the world worthy of being mourned.

With another part of me, I felt the comedy, the anachronism, of this old man, himself arthritic, asthmatic, ignoring his own sufferings yet taking it on faith that the burdened woman boarding a bus suffered her burdens. Probably the woman, obese, feet swollen out of her shoes, half moons of sweat in the armpits of her dress, had routinized her effort of lugging herself and her groceries onto the bus. Still, his sighs made her real to me.

I turn back to Kerry with different eyes. I just see someone who's holding a sleeping kid in her lap. Someone who must be exhausted. I see a young girl looking helpless in a tee shirt torn at the neck, the logos faded. It's late. I'm tired, too. "Kerry? You want some warm milk and honey?"

For the night, Sylvia and Russell take in mother-and-child. I don't argue too hard. What are my alternatives? By next afternoon, after I finish teaching, I've got the key to Barbara's place, a sunny apartment full of books in Green River. It's the whole upper floor of a Victorian house; the walls have been broken through and the windows enlarged to make big sunny areas. Barbara has found pretty, old pieces at auction, nothing fancy but warm. We've been friends for years, me and Barbara. I've spent many evenings here the last couple of years with Barbara and her partner, a young woman, a flutist. They're both off in Boulder, but their spirit is here, the prints, the plants, the books.

Barbara teaches music at the University. We're both on the board of a regional music series. Like a rental agent, I show Kerry around and make her promise to take care of things. Andrew clings to her pants; I smell urine. Kerry half-listens; I bet the stereo and the TV excite her, it's as if she's won a contest on television. We don't look into one another's face.

I look around for things Andrew might break, and a couple of vases, a couple of knick-knacks I move to higher shelves. "I hope you're happy here," I tell her. "It's just for a week or two. Now look. I hear about any problems," I add, "you're back in Boston the same day. Barbara's my friend. Okay?"

At the upstairs neighbor's, I make calls, find out how to

get her food stamps and welfare transferred, put her in touch with community services, tell her about the family daycare at the Congregational Church. "Don't let's get ahead of ourselves," I say, "but look: if you stay with it, I'll keep helping. Okay? Green River Community College might be a good second step. You get into the shelter—or even," I say, full of sudden tenderness, "even staying here at Barbara's if it works out. Staying here but getting some help from the resources at the Center. I'll stick with you. Anything is possible. Good luck. Be strong. Take care of that nice little kid."

When I'm finally out of there, I take a deep breath and feel the impossibility of what I've just told her was so possible. I feel false, I'm the one needing rescue. Strange that it's coming home from Barbara's, because it was just a month ago, coming home from saying goodbye—just before Barbara and her partner left—I experienced this falseness; as if I'd done it all wrong—as if I should have been a musician, was it that?—or as if I hadn't learned to savor my life.

Messages on my answering machine: Kerry already!—*How the hell you supposed to turn on the gas?* The first of many calls, I figure.

Next, Jeremy—*Hi, Dad. Are you coming tonight to the sing at the school*? I'm coming, I say to myself, though God knows I'd rather flop into a hot bath and then get some work done.

Finally, Gabriella, a message from Gabriella. First "David?" and then a silence. Then: *David? I keep getting funny calls. No one on the other end.... And the last couple of hours, I look out the window and I think I see someone out there. A man across the street. Then he's gone. So I don't know. It's probably nothing at all. But I'm afraid to go out, I'm afraid to stay here. The police are sending someone, so it's okay; I just feel like talking. Please give me a call when you get in. Oh—Gar is flying up, so don't worry about me. But I'd like it if you gave me a call.*

Twenty minutes later, I'm back on Route 2, sandwich

and soda in a paper bag. Driving, I'm already kicking myself for the waste of time. I've got to be back in the morning to teach. What am I doing to myself? And Jeremy's got a school sing and I won't be there.

I drive in silence, while words, like ants, dig tunnels through my head.

Five

Hiss of wind, hum of tires. I'm just going to stay with Gabriella. I can't protect her, but I can hold her. I see myself holding her through the night. I know it's because Gar is coming that I need to be there.

Galahad in a gray Honda? Well, I'm used to the role.

Last week in a composition class, my only evening class, the students were talking about education. They're a mixed group: young people who maybe didn't do well in high school and never imagined they could go to college—but some have the ability; plus older students, mostly women, starting or returning to college after years of raising children. Could education, I asked, give them better lives? John had written an essay; Look, it said, I need credentials to get a job that will pay me better and bore me less. Period. The rest is "bullshit." Students argued, but were secretly thrilled at John's cutting through idealistic verbiage.

I needed to tell them how differently I saw things. John's argument, I said, was the way big-shot administrators like Clark Kerr at Berkeley justified education back in the sixties. Those guys were our *enemy*. That wasn't education, we argued, that was training—fitting people into niches. *Real* education helped individuals fulfill themselves, express themselves, find themselves, make themselves ready to liberate others and live as members of a liberated community. I'm doing work I like, I said, so it's easy for me to talk. But it disturbs me, you let them take away your birthright.

The chairman, Leonard Noble, makes his pitch to the dean on behalf of the English department, the dean to the higher-ups, on the same phony basis: that the "jobs out there" require literacy—the ability to understand texts and write them.

Is that what I'm doing as a teacher?

I don't think so. While my students *tell me* they're interested in better jobs, I think that secretly they hope to *broaden*, to *deepen*—all the things you do to open a channel to sea traffic. They don't admit it, but they want to live more fully.

Take Kerry. She needs an education. To get work so she can raise her child? Sure, of *course*. Money for day care, a job to be proud of. But more: she needs an education so she can see what's been done to her and how she can take charge of herself.

It's just about dark by the time I drive up Gabriella's street in Brookline. I pass her squat, red-brick apartment building cruising slowly, looking for a man in the shadows. Nobody there. I park around the corner. What good I can do against a young man as big and crazy as Chuck? I'll just hold her.

No one around. I buzz, say hello into the speaker, get buzzed in. Gar is waiting for me at Gabriella's door.

He looks more like the old Gar, Gar of twenty years back; he's wearing a flight jacket and jeans, and there's something in his eyes I recognize from demonstrations; he's digging this. I meet him with a deadpan expression. But privately—there's something else. *Working with Gar after all these years.* My plan to stay with Gabriella, to hold her, it suddenly dissolves. I have to go with him. It comforts me that he's six-three and weighs two-twenty and makes daily use of a personal gym.

I hear the clicking of computer keys from the next room. He thumbs over his shoulder—"Yeah, that's our Gabriella. You can't keep a good woman down."

"How'd you get up here so fast?"

He ignores this. We find Gabriella at the keyboard; standing up, she finishes her sentence and saves a document, takes down her glasses, lets them dangle against her blouse, smiles. "Thanks. You know you didn't need to drive all that way. But really thanks, David. Can I fix you something?"

"He's not still out there?" I ask. "I didn't see anyone."

Gar beckons me to the window; there's a shade drawn; he turns out the desk light behind us, pulls aside the shade a crack. "Look up on the roof. Across the alley."

Between chimneys and TV antennas, half-hidden in the shadow of a stairway bulkhead, one floor up on the flat-roofed building across a narrow street is—someone. A shadow. I'm not even sure I see anything, but just as I'm turning to ask Gar something, the shadow moves.

"We don't know it's Chuck, do we?"

Gar ignores this, too. "I've been trying to imagine what he's waiting for. I don't get it—does he know I'm here? I don't think so. I doubt it. Maybe he's waiting for her to leave? Or sleep?"

I look around at Gabriella. Typical for Gar to talk *about* Gabriella instead of *to* her. I say to Gabriella, "I thought he was in custody."

Gar answers. "I guess they couldn't hold him. And then it turns out his brother is—my sources tell me—some kind of pol, or friend of pols, a downtown lawyer, one of the boys. He's behind the original suit against Sojourner House. My legal people up here put a detective on this—an ex-cop who knows the score. Guy named Bill Akavian—you'll meet him later. This Chuck is the Ahearn black sheep, Akavian says, but the family is sticking with him."

"Gar," I say, "who the hell *is* this guy?

"His father is some kind of small-time liquor distributor. They're not poor. His brother, as I say, he's a lawyer. Chuck works for his father, but it seems to my people he lives too well for a guy who sells beer to package stores. Who knows? Cocaine? Heroin? That's my guess."

"Remember," I say, "when you were talking about poverty and abuse? Here's someone who doesn't fit."

"Hey! That was Gabriella," Gar says. "Anyway, I was talking about people who don't fit in the new world of work. This guy, all he can do is sell shit and beat up people. Does he fit?"

"Gar, what about a gun? You haven't seen anything that looks like a gun?"

Gabriella says, "That's a good question. Gar? Suppose he has a gun. Can't we just call the police again now that we know he's there?" She turns to me: "The police came by an hour ago, but there was nothing to see."

Gar says, "He sees one flashing blue light or funny-looking car, he's out of there. No. This is the way it goes down. Down at the corner, Bill Akavian is waiting, out of sight. I call Bill on the cellular phone, I go up on the roof. Now that you're here, Dave, you get up on the next roof—see that doorway over there?—meet me at the top, we hold the guy and call the cops, bust the son of a bitch on a harassment charge. My legal people say we won't get our ass sued—not after he was arrested yesterday with a tire iron. If he slips away, my detective friend will follow." Now he takes a small canvas bag from the table. "Here. I've prepared this for you."

I'm surprised at the weight of what he hands me. A cloth bag from a Crown Royal bottle.

"It's a bag of nails, screws, whatever Gabriella had around—something to swing."

"Oh, Christ, Gar. You love this kind of emergency, don't you."

"If the cops come, just empty the bag and like magic it's not a weapon anymore."

I laugh and empty the bag onto a chair. "It's not a weapon anymore."

"Asshole!" He laughs and pushes *redial* on the phone.

We zip up our coats, we're down the stairs and one at a time we walk easy in opposite directions, cross over down at the corner, hug the buildings, climb adjoining stoops, walk into the alcoves. I'm about to press all the buttons when I see a woman coming down the stairs. I pretend to fumble for my keys, she lets me in, I smile, I walk up five flights—what if the door to the roof is locked? It's not, only bolted against entrance from the roof. I climb a little ladder bolted to the inside of the bulkhead, and open slowly, just enough to slip out.

Coming out of the light, I can't see a thing but silhouettes. Now my eyes begin to adjust, I see plumbing ducts and roof fans, bulkheads and chimneys—no movement. He must be on the other side of the next bulkhead.

A shaft of light as the bulkhead door crashes open, now there's a shout, a smashing, I'm running, hands spread like a defensive back, running low like Groucho in case he's got a gun. There's Gar on the ground, twisting away from a boot. I yell "Get the fuck away from him!" Maybe Chuck is startled—suddenly he's down, they're rolling around on the roof and I can't get in a blow.

Gar is yelling, and Chuck stands up, he's holding a knife and I'm hoping Gar isn't cut. I'm ready to swing, but I'm shoved away before I can even pull my arm back and my head hits something, I'm on the ground and now Gar is helping me up. "You hurt?"

"No. No. You? He cut you?"

"Cut me? Did he have a knife? Shit!"

"Yeah."

"No. I'm an asshole. He caught me, elbow in the throat. C'mon. I'll kill that prick." Now Gar is bent over, hunting the phone. "There! Not broken, I think." He pushes the redial button. "He's coming down the same stairs where I went up!" he yells into the phone, and we run after him.

Bill Akavian has him at the bottom. Akavian is a little guy, much older, but Chuck didn't expect anyone, and Akavian comes out of the shadows and hits or trips Chuck, and Chuck is down. By the time I'm on the street they've grabbed Chuck, he's kicking, and Gar lets go a full boot to his shin as if his shin were a football. Chuck screams and he's down again, something metal clatters on the walk. I hear someone down the street shouting from a window, and I know the cops will be here soon one way or the other.

Gabriella rushes out of her building and across the street. "Stop. Stop this. Please!"

"Call the cops again," I call to Gabriella.

Gabriella takes the phone and calls. There's Chuck on the ground and rocking to ease the pain. "You lousy fuck!"

"Yeah," Gar says. "Right." Now Akavian yanks Chuck up from the ground, twisting one arm behind his back, and Gar kicks up into his jaw. Akavian lets him crumple, and Gar boots him in the gut, again in the chest, and Chuck can't do anything but cover up. "Listen," Gar says, out of breath, shaking him on the ground, "I want you to know who you're dealing with. You hear me?"

Chuck mumbles a curse or something.

"You *tell* me you hear."

He doesn't answer. Chuck's mouth is all bloody. His moustache is full of blood. It makes me sick to see, but— I'm *with* it.

"Now you listen, you *piece of shit*. You try anything again, I'll tell some guys I know, they'll bust your kneecaps—you hear what I'm saying? I'll have you put away in the fucking ground you try anything. And anything—*anything* happens to my friend, no *way* you can run fast enough, I'll have you found, I've got the money, you're a dead man, I'll track you down and have you killed, you understand, you piece of shit?—I said you hear me?" He reaches down and grabs a hank of the guy's long hair. "*Do you hear me!*"

Chuck nods, but that's not good enough. Gar boots him hard in the stomach. Chuck writhes as if hit by electric shock. "I said —"

"You lousy fuck!" Chuck Ahearn shrieks, and he's twisting on the ground, trying to shake off the pain, when the flashing lights appear and we're hit by spotlights and headlights.

As I turn, I catch sight of Gabriella. She's holding the mobile phone, she's got her hand over her mouth and she's shaking, and I go over to her and put my arm around her shoulders and she leans into my chest, I feel her sobbing, though there are no tears on her face when I touch it, and I say, "He was just scaring him, he's not killing anybody. He just goes overboard, Gar."

"*No*. He's as crazy as he ever was," she says.

"You're shaking, honey. It's okay. Don't be scared."

"Scared? I'm not scared. It's *not* okay, David. It's the *same thing*. You understand? The same thing."

"I understand what you're saying. But it was you he was protecting."

"No. He wasn't protecting anybody. My God—and I was married to that man."

"Married? You were married?"

Two police cars. Their radios were squawking. Slowly, three cops walked up the driveway towards us. "I want to see your palms open in front of you. Stand still, all of you, put your hands in the air. I want to see your palms. What's going on here?"

"Married, Gabriella—to *Gar*? When?"

"A long time ago. I don't want to talk about it."

"Gabriella?"

Irritated, she says, "He's the father, Jenny's father. He was Sara's."

Now we're sucked into the cop's routine, and I listen to Gar explaining in a cultured, calm voice; the detective shows his credentials and Gabriella tells them about Chuck Ahearn and Kerry and last night at this woman Cheryl's house where he was found with a crowbar, and they take it down, and I tell about Kerry and the knife; and Chuck, mouth bloody and tongue thick, says, "That's full of shit, my wife, she's the one with the knife, she had a knife on *me*, I took it away. That bitch, you don't think I'll get her? I'll get my kid back from that bitch!" He looks into my face with a wish for my destruction. He wipes a hand across his moustache. "And this piece of shit here. You ask him. He must have her somewhere."

The cops shut him up, turn to Gabriella. "You holding his wife?" the older cop asks.

"*Holding*? You mean sheltering? You mean, is she at our *shelter*, officer?" She waits, and he has to grunt agreement. "No. But she came to us once before, he's been beating her up, beating the boy—"

"All right. All right. And you—" the cop says "— *you* got his wife?"

"No. I haven't got anybody."

"Tomorrow morning, Miss," the cops says to Gabriella, "you can ask for a clerk's hearing, take out an application for criminal complaint. You, too," he says to Chuck. All right. For now, my call on this is we calm down, we go down to the station, and we'll need everybody to follow." I expect them to put Chuck in handcuffs. But they don't. He's allowed to get into his own car.

Gabriella turns to me. "Will you come with us?"

"It seems I'll have to," I say curtly. "I'm at least a witness." But walking back to Gabriella's Taurus, I hunker into myself, wish myself on the road again. I feel like a sucker. I don't want to hear her explanations.

I sit behind them in back. My shoulder aches like hell, I must have wrenched it when I went down. "You went way overboard," I say to Gar. "But now we've got a problem. I want you to do something for us. This Akavian, this detective, I want you to put him onto Ahearn, see if he can dig up Ahearn's record. This isn't a one-shot, a guy this crazy. Let's see what we're dealing with. Can he do that, Akavian?"

"I'll go for it. A few hundred dollars, sure, he can find out. Public record, mostly."

He tries talking to Gabriella. I don't think Gar knew when we got to the car, but he knows now that something's very wrong between himself and Gabriella. She's dead silent. She follows the police car slowly through Brookline.

"That crazy bastard needed to be scared off," he tells her. Still she's silent. "And I meant what I said," he says, defiantly. "There are ways, Gabriella. And there are times . . . ."

Gabriella says, "Let me tell you how we surfaced back then. Gar and me. You asked, David."

"Oh, Christ," he says.

"He got caught stealing underwear. The big radical. Really—*underwear*. We were up in Brattleboro, Vermont, an army-navy store. I told him not to be foolish, but of course Gar couldn't use a check and we had no money, and he was used to getting what he wanted."

"She's getting back at me, Dave. I got a little rough back there."

"I kept the salespeople distracted while he put on layers of long winter underwear and sweaters over that and a parka shell under his own coat and walked out fast. We were on our way back to the van when a cop car pulled up. And that was that. Then he used his family connections."

"Be better if I went to prison on a felony?"

"Yes. Maybe it would, Gar."

"Christ, you're not fair to me."

I stay out of it. Let it be a family affair between them.

Finally, she says quietly, "I let David know we were married, Gar."

"Listen to this! Fine. Your call," he shrugs. "Hey—her call in the first place, Dave, the secrecy. She figured it wouldn't go down well with the women, ever being married to a man like me."

"That's not it, Gar."

It's starting to drizzle. I lean my head against the car window, think about my classes for tomorrow. To hell with this.

"She didn't want anybody to know—but she takes my money. I've been the secret partner all along," he says to me. "She couldn't let the women know she was taking funding from a New York real estate man. I've been the dirty secret behind Sojourner House."

"That's nonsense," she says flatly. We keep close to the police car. Hardly any cars—it's nearly eleven. Now Gabriella looks at me over her shoulder for a moment. "I should have told you on the weekend, David."

"You should have told me from the beginning," I say quietly. "We were old comrades, Gabriella. You could have trusted me."

"It's hard to explain," she says.

Gar turns in his seat to look at me. "It may seem weird to you, funding Sojourner House after Sara was killed there. My own little girl. Ahh, she was such a wonderful kid. I'd been warning Gabriella. Warning—but helping. I should've put my foot down. The thing is, I respect the work she does. There were no hard feelings between us. Isn't that right, Gabriella?—All the hard feelings came before. I got rich, she couldn't take it."

"Why don't you just be still?" she says.

"What are you so angry about? What? I knocked that bastard around a little? Is that it? Is that the problem? So what? I know what you're feeling. 'Male violence.' Well, there's a difference."

"Not 'male violence.' *Your* violence. You were being Gar, that's all."

"I only wish I'd been around the day Sara got killed. You'd have seen male violence, lady."

I can't wait for this to be over. Did I ever want to be with this woman? I'm deeply tired, I'm all bruised, and now I realize—my cheek is lacerated. It's stinging. I must look a wreck. I can't imagine how I'll go in and teach tomorrow.

I sit back, arms folded. Gabriella says to Gar, "Let's do what we can to keep David out of it."

Now I begin to worry—*yes*: what happens if this gets back to Leonard Noble? To Nancy? Now I begin to really worry.

Waiting for a light to change, Gabriella turns and puts a hand on my stinging cheek. "I had no idea, David, I mean when we met again, no idea we might become friends again, you and I. You see, I've kept it from almost everyone."

"Why?"

"I wanted to put away that part of my life. It was nobody's business. They knew I'd been married. They didn't have to know who. Some people knew," she adds. "Gail knows. You remember Gail Kirkland?"

I nod. "I thought you were fighting each other."

"I told you. She's my closest friend. That's a separate thing. And the others don't have to know."

"Then Gar is right—they would have been suspicious of him. Something about Gar? Something bad?"

"Not exactly."

I stop asking. More secrets. We pull in to the parking lot of the station house. We sit in the car while Chuck gets out of his car and follows a policeman across the lot into the side door. "Personally," I say coldly, precisely, wanting my words to hurt, "I'd have been happy to see Gar kick that son of a bitch to death."

One by one we go into a room with the detective, and a typist takes down our statements. I wish I didn't have to wait for a lift, but I do. Waiting, I think about James Baldwin's "Sonny's Blues," the story I'm teaching in my first morning class.

It's three-thirty in the morning before I'm back in Western Mass, back in Green River. I drive through the stunningly silent town, past a police car standing guard by a closed-up Burger King, to a secondary road into the hills and home.

Waking, I find my shoulder is aching worse than I'd imagined; my body feels stiff and pained as if I'd been in a car accident. I need strong coffee, I need Motrin and the Tylenol with codeine I've been hoarding. I'm surprised when my body eases and class goes well. More coffee, my office hours, another class. It's only after lunch, when I rest in the big, old, torn-cushion easy chair in my office, that I let myself remember last night.

My own body feels Gar's blows. Chuck's face. It might have turned into murder. I want to put it all behind me—cut my losses, take care of my child, work at this college, write. *Gabriella may have her reasons*, I say for maybe the tenth time. And add: *Let her keep her fucking reasons to herself, let her keep herself to herself.* Remembering Kerry, remembering that she's still a loose end, I say aloud to the concrete block walls, "All right. That I can handle. I can handle that." But not Gabriella, not love. "Fuck love!" I yell—and shut up: students might be passing my door.

I doze off. It's okay—next class in an hour. But I'm awakened after a few minutes by a sharp, loud rap at the door. "Just a minute." I finger-comb my hair and settle myself in my desk chair and reach over to unlock and open the door.

Someone I don't know, a man in his thirties in a pin-striped, Italian-styled business suit, a lean, good-looking man, comes in. *Too well dressed for a publisher's traveller or a student.* Nobody in the whole valley wears a suit like this. Coming to me out of my near-sleep, he seems like a dream figure—especially in those clothes.

"I'm Patrick Ahearn," he says, smiling so broadly it makes me squirm. He hands me his card; I shake hands automatically, now I realize who this must be. "Chuck Ahearn's brother, Professor," he says, taking the seat by the desk.

"Yes." I pocket the card. I wonder if "Professor" is ironic.

We're aware of so much at once. Reality pours in on us rich in meanings. I see at once that Patrick Ahearn's suit is putting me off, putting me down. I'm wearing gray corduroy pants, crumpled, a blue denim work shirt, a tweed jacket that's seen better days. These clothes are right for my students. Still, I feel judged by that suit. I'm aware of the seedy old Turkish carpet I bought to cover the linoleum floor, the cracked lamp that gives me warm light in this drab room, a desk whose imitation veneer is peeling off the sides, the chair next to my desk, the vinyl of its arm rests lying cracked under Patrick Ahearn's gabardine, the foam rubber disintegrating.

Yet at the same time I see this man himself as also somehow seedy, not classy, not professional. Partly, of course, it's his younger brother; I associate him with Chuck. But also, something about his attempt at elegance fails. Because it can be read *as* an attempt. He's shaved badly, for one thing; I notice patches of stubble at the jawline. His face, a little florid, seems the face of a drinker—eyes glassy, bags heavy for a man in his thirties. I have a friend who meditates daily; his eyes have a focused quality that is the exact opposite of this emptiness.

I sense vulgarity, seediness. I "know" how this man's apartment must be decorated. I "know" what he reads—or doesn't read. I "know" his relation to women. And I'm aware at the same time of how much I'm inventing and aware of the nature of my own criteria. I'm a snob. The working-class Boston accent, is that part of it?—he expresses a lack of "class" that fits with his brother Chuck. *Class!*—God! We're almost as class-conscious here in America as in England. Me, I'm almost as tainted as Leonard Noble. If he came in with the panache of culture, of old respected family, I know I'd trust him more *and* fear him more.

"You've got some brother, Mr. Ahearn. Not your fault, I don't mean that. I suppose you know what he was up to last night?"

He laughs. "Chuck was up to no good, I know," he says, then, more darkly, " . . . and he suffered for it pretty badly. I saw him this morning, and I was shocked. My brother is such a big fellow. Your friend Mr. Stone must be some fighter. Of course, he had help, didn't he? My brother may file a criminal complaint."

"You know he had a knife? You know he'd been watching Gabriella Rossi's apartment?"

"Chuck said you were imagining things. He was simply trying to frighten her so he could get his wife's address." He sighs. "But who knows?" Patrick Ahearn throws open his hands. "In any event, I know he went a little crazy when his wife ran off with his son. Don't think we support his craziness. The family does what it can to straighten him out. We've been encouraging him to get into therapy, as a matter of fact. Well, you know, he has his good points," Patrick Ahearn laughs again, "but common sense isn't one of them. You can imagine how the family feels. I don't blame you— I heard he went after your door with an axe. We hope you'll let us take care of that door. My brother certainly does fly off the handle." He grins a grin appropriate for contemplating a mischievous teenager.

"I saw Andrew the last time your brother went off the handle."

"Well, Professor Rosen, now, you don't know the whole story there. Perhaps you oughtn't interfere when you hear only one side."

"I've seen Andrew's face. That's the only side I care about."

"But aren't you making assumptions? Are you so sure who it was damaged Andrew's face? She's the abuser in the family—I expect you don't know that, but it's true."

I shrug, but I see her smacking Andrew around that night. Do I really know? I say, "But what is it you drove out here for? I'm not intending to file charges, if that's your worry."

"*I'm* not worried, Mr. Rosen. I'm your *ally*."

"You drove all the way out here to apologize?"

He's laughing again, broadly, his head tossed back, and I imagine him laughing with a group of men. The laugh represents a way of being I've always wondered at, maybe envied. "Not exactly, not exactly, although indeed, on behalf of the family . . . No. I need to speak to Kerry Latrice Ahearn; I'm representing my brother as his attorney. His wife has disappeared with his child. He believes you know where he is. Whatever the facts of the case—well, that's up to a court to decide. But I need to speak to her. I've driven out here to get her address and to talk with her. That's all. We hope to convince her—or the court—to place the child in our custody. In my *sister's* custody. Frankly, neither my brother nor the boy's mother—"

"—Andrew—"

"— Andrew's mother—is fit to be a parent. No. Not at this time. Don't you agree with me? You're a perceptive man. If you've spent any time at all with the woman, you know that about her. Don't you?"

He speaks as if he were on a stage or in front of a court. He's using this quality of speech, using his deep baritone and his charm, as armor over his shabbiness. Oh, I can feel his charm. He's a man used to winning people over.

I try to smash that armor. My breach of discourse is my weapon against him. "Look, Patrick," I say, "you've got a problem, your family's got a problem, and I sympathize. And *Andrew* has a problem, he sure does. But I'm not disclosing a goddamn thing about Kerry. I'll take your message to her. Then it's up to her. I wouldn't dare tell you where she is. Think about it. He could kill her. He could kill them both."

Patrick Ahearn folds his hands and places them between us on my desk. He smiles, he frowns, it's all theater. "Mr. Rosen, David, now, that's not credible. She can get a 209A, she goes to court and asks for a restraining order, she's had one before, and if Chuck breaks it, he's letting himself in for a year in jail. Do you think he's crazy enough to take a chance on a year in jail?"

"Oh, yes. Sure. He's pretty crazy. I can't take the risk."

"Mr. Rosen, I can get a court order requiring that she appear; if I have to, I will. You'll be served with a summons, and you'll be in contempt if you refuse to reveal her whereabouts so she can be served. You're not a priest, as far as I know. Not with a name like Rosen. Sojourner House may have certain rights of confidentiality—you do not."

"'Not with a name like Rosen,' huh?"

"Now, now . . . . "

A rap at my door. "Just a minute." It's one of my favorite students, a young man with an earring and hair that falls to his shoulders. Steve is the kid of a family from one of the hill towns, father a woodworker, mother a weaver, a couple who met on a commune in Vermont in the early seventies. Though by now his mother and father are straight, Steve goofed and smoked dope more than studied in high school, and only now, at twenty-two, has he begun to find his brain. He often turns up during my office hours in cowboy boots and a braided leather thong at his neck, wanting to talk about God knows what—Nietzsche, the Holocaust, slave ships, his own poetry.

He looks in, says, "You're busy."

"I'm afraid so. Sorry," I say. "A few minutes."

Unseen by Patrick, Steve fingers an imaginary collar

and tie and grins. I nod. "See you later, Herr Professor," he says. Usually, he calls me David. He knows me well enough to gesture with his head and wrinkle his face—like, *who's that?* I wave him off.

"I'm not keeping you," Patrick Ahearn says.

"No, no. It's all right."

"Frankly, I'm interested in forming an alliance with you. We were talking about your laudable desire to protect a woman. Well, I tell you, you don't know her. If you knew her, you'd ask for my *help* for Andrew. But the fact of the matter is this, Mr. Rosen." (He's speaking calmly, sweetly even.) "If you put me to the effort of getting a court order, I promise I'll make things difficult for you. I don't smash doors with axes, I have all sorts of sensible strategies when aroused. It's a trait of the Ahearn family. We don't stop."

"I noticed that last night. Please cut the crap, Mr. Ahearn, I'm not telling you a thing, don't you know I'm not?—stop threatening. Do what you need to do. Hey, look," I tell him, spreading out my hands in innocence, "I'm not even involved. I hardly know the woman. I found her a place for a few days. That's all."

"Ah, but that's plenty. You're sheltering her, you're letting her be her vicious, druggie self with that child. Tell me, how do you feel about the rights of a child? You see, I think you're essentially on my side, Mr. Rosen. Let me take you out for a drink this afternoon—I've got some stories will curl your hair."

"I think you might be right about Kerry as a mother, your brother Chuck as a father. Maybe they're neither of them fit. Maybe your family *ought* to take the child. But can't you see? I tell you where she is, your brother finds out and goes on another rampage —" I'm beginning to plead, and I hate it.

"And what if I promise you he won't find out?" he asks. "What if I give you my word?" He crosses one leg over the other and tilts his head to one side, as if we're at the point of coming to terms. "I'll give you my word, Mr. Rosen. *I can't trust my brother.*"

"But I don't know the value of your word. I'll call and let her decide. If she wants to see you, I'll take you over there. Or if she doesn't, you can talk to her over the phone." I reach for the phone. "Maybe she'll be there, maybe she won't."

"No. She hears it's an Ahearn, she'll just hang up. I've been through it with her over the phone. That's not good enough."

I take a deep breath, sit back, and taking up a pencil from the desk, twiddle it between forefingers the way I do when a student comes in to argue about the grade on a paper. "The thing I'm trying to decide about you is this, Mr. Ahearn: which is it?"— I number the possibilities on my fingers—"Are you in this with your brother, I mean do you know that he threatened Miss Rossi, that he was harassing her and was holding a knife—and you're still behind him? *Or* do you believe what he tells you? I guess I'm asking, Are you promoting violence or are you naive?"

"I'm *protecting* my brother. I always have protected him. I didn't say anything about believing."

"No. But you're representing him." My head is buzzing with energy. I've regained strength. Yet I'm aware, too, of belly pangs of fear. At the same moment the drained but florid face of Patrick Ahearn takes on a sinister, surreal, nightmare quality, I'm seeing not a misguided brother or threatening lawyer, I'm seeing something really evil, and out of the blue I worry: *Jeremy.*

"I've got a class in a few minutes," I say. "Shall I phone? You want me to ask Kerry about whether she'll speak with you?"

"I tell you it won't do any good," Patrick Ahearn says, standing up. "I tell you I've tried that. It won't do a bit of good. Now look—will you credit the possibility that Kerry Ahearn might be the really dangerous one? That he might—my brother might—be wilder but that she's the parent who's likely to severely damage Andrew? Maybe kill him? How would you feel then? You ask whether I'm in this with Chuck. I'm in this with our mother and father, and especially with my sister in Mattapan—she's the one we want to have take Andrew. You say you're after the best interests of the boy. Well, we are, too. How about it, Mr. Rosen?"

I don't reply. But I'm bewildered. I do credit what he says. Suppose he's simply right? Suppose he's really the one protecting Andrew? I fuss over the papers on my desk.

"You have my card," he says. "I do hope you call. For the boy's sake."

I don't turn around until he's out the door.

Six

I sit a few minutes after Patrick Ahearn is gone. Just before I have to leave for class, I call the Green River Center for Women in Transition.

I ask for Ronnie Gordon; we know each other a little. I tell her Kerry's story; fill her in on Chuck's mad attacks in Boston, on Chuck's lawyer brother. "Here's the thing, Ronnie. If a court order comes to me, I can't protect Kerry. You can claim confidentiality, I can't. I want you to take her and to take her *now*, Kerry and Andrew. I don't even want to know where she's been taken. I may have to tell the court that I've passed her on to you, but that's what you're there for. You handle this sort of thing."

I expect her to claim that the shelter is full up, that we'll have to wait; I expect an argument. But all she asks for is address and telephone.

"You'll go get her?"

"No. We'll talk. There's so much to go over."

"Of course. And look: you do need to be careful," I say. "Make sure she takes out a restraining order. The husband is really dangerous."

"Oh, of course. She'll have an advocate, the advocate will refer her to a local lawyer. I'd love to see this husband put away for a year. Let him try to get near her."

I have to add: "Best if he didn't try. The husband—the husband is terrifying. But . . . I'm not saying this woman is an angel. You understand? She's pretty lost."

"Is she on drugs?"

"She smokes dope, but it doesn't seem to be her major problem."

"We'll let her know—if she does drugs—even alcohol—she's out. That's our policy. Do you think she can handle that?"

"I hardly know her myself. Look—I'll call and let her

know—assuming she's home. If she's not there, I'll get back to you."

Kerry's there. She sounds stoned or half asleep, and my stomach turns over. She doesn't like the move to the shelter, she starts grumbling. "Jesus, I just got settled. Andrew likes the TV."

"Look," I tell her, "it's either that or I might be subpoenaed to give the court your location. Then you might lose custody of Andrew—temporarily, at any rate."

"All right. Jesus. You're something."

I tell her, Look, Ronnie Gordon will take good care of you, and maybe this should have been a women's thing from the start, and she says, "Yeah, yeah, well, thanks for everything."

"I'm *sorry*, Kerry. But you're getting help, you're getting a place to live for awhile. And if things work out, I'll be around to help with your education." I can hear in my own voice I'm brushing her off.

In the background, Andrew is howling for his mommy.

"They'll be calling pretty soon," I tell her.

Hanging up, I feel the tension drain from me. Collecting my books and walking down the hall towards my class, waving to a couple of last semester's students, I think about a hot bath, I think about getting to bed early. I think about never seeing any one of them again. Not Kerry. Not Gabriella. Not Gar. Not Patrick Ahearn. Not Chuck.

After class, I call Patrick Ahearn's number from my office. I want to finish up with him. He's not there, but when I tell his secretary who I am, she says she can reach him in his car, can I wait where I am? And in a few minutes, Ahearn calls back.

"I want you to know I've taken seriously what you said . . ."

"Well, *good*. I'm glad," he says, his Southie accent less obvious over the phone. "As I say, we have the same interests at heart."

"I've just taken myself out of the picture. I want you to know. I no longer *know* where Kerry is. There's a shelter for women out here."

"The Green River Center. I know about it. The dykes."
He wants to shock me; I don't bite.

"They've taken her in. I have no idea where they've taken her. I don't *want* to know. And you'll have no way of finding out."

"Oh, you're wrong about that, if that's what we want to do. The police know, every taxi driver knows. You think—seriously—I can't find out?"

"And she'll be taking your free legal advice about a restraining order."

"Look, Mr. Rosen, I don't believe a thing you say. I don't believe the Center has moved her so fast, I don't believe you've stopped knowing. This changes nothing. Let me put it this way. I'm a busy man, I hate to waste this drive. You get me to her, I turn around right now and try to make a deal with her—I'm talking about money, and I do think I can get her to listen when I show her money, Mr. Rosen."

"Sorry."

"Let me spell out the alternative. All right? I said I'd make things *difficult* for you. I mean with your chairman, Dr. Noble, I mean with your wife, and certainly I mean with the local press. You'll look just terrible in your community, and it's a small community, and *you will look just terrible.* 'Difficult' isn't really what I mean. I *mean*," Patrick Ahearn says, as pleasantly as if we were talking about football, "I'll ruin your life, it's as simple as that. Now, don't you think I might turn around? I can be back in Green River in an hour."

I'm not heroic. In demonstrations I was the guy on the periphery, away from tear gas and clubs, and when the cops came out from their buses, the plastic shields on their riot helmets down, I strolled away slowly, just a bystander.

If I had known beforehand what Patrick Ahearn was threatening, I might have shrugged and given him Kerry's address. To put this much of my life at stake—and over a woman I don't respect, don't trust—no, I'm not at all sure I would have held out. Especially with Gabriella out of the picture, as Gabriella *is*. It's as if I've been acting in a play for her benefit; as if she were director and audience. That play is canceled.

But only now, too late, do I see what I'm letting myself in for with Patrick Ahearn. And I find I can't cave in. Not to this slimy, charming lawyer, I can't. "I'm sorry," I told him on his car phone a few minutes ago. "I really wish I could make things easier for me. I can't." He hung up on me. It's not like me, but I find I can't back down now. Even with my life with Jeremy at stake? Even then, and even with my job on the line, even not knowing whether this mother, or that father, is worse for Andrew.

An hour ago, to get involved with Kerry seemed melodramatic, self-indulgent. Now it seems unavoidable.

Sitting on the edge of my desk, I call Kerry Latrice Ahearn. Patrick is right; of course she's still there. She says she's busy packing, she's meeting Ronnie and an "advocate" in an hour and hopes to be in the shelter by tonight; she doesn't have time to talk. "I want to stop by, I can help you pack, Kerry."

"I don't need your fucking help."

"Let me come over anyway. We need to straighten things out."

There's a long silence. "Yeah. So come if you want."

I don't say, *I need to see what kind of mother you are, Kerry, see what I've made myself an accomplice of.* For better or worse, that's what I am. There's a child there, and I'm now responsible for his safety and well being, and I don't know enough.

It's rush hour in Green River. That's a joke, of course for anyone from a city. It means it takes four minutes to get through the center of town instead of three. Those mills still going—not many of the old factories in operation anymore—are letting out. Green River could be called a dying town, except that it's pretty well dead already. Most of the industrial jobs are gone. Farming is part-time, after-work

work. Some people have service jobs, some have jobs at the University, some at the few high-tech businesses miles away that started up in the eighties. The grand Victorian houses up in the hills, managers' houses, doctors' houses, bankers' houses, have stayed beautiful, fresh-painted, well-cared-for. But the real estate market remains weak. A house that might bring six hundred thousand plus in Newton goes for a hundred eighty tops.

Barbara's house is one of these, now divided for two families. It looks especially ordered and grand in the last of the sunlight, and I realize that it must have been sunny all day today, and the leaves at their peak and I didn't notice. Below, the owners and their children; above, Barbara and Julia. I park and walk up without ringing.

"Kerry?" No answer; I step in. I'm a little worried—what will I find?—but on first look, the late sun glowing out of the dark woods, the lighter floor boards glowing, plants catching the sunlight: here's Barbara's clear, no-nonsense spirit. From the bedroom I hear muffled noises I can't make out. For a moment, I imagine that Kerry is in there with some guy. In the corner of the living room, I see Andrew in a soiled disposable diaper, playing in dirt, dirt right on the floor, now I see the cracked clay pot, and the spider plant fallen, some of its roots exposed. "Andrew," I say, but there's nothing *to* say, and only now do I smell the odor of his shit, unusually sour and acrid, and I hold my breath and smile his way, head for the bedroom. "Kerry?"

I'm prepared to set her straight, get her to shape up, but she's barely in the world. She's sitting on the edge of an unmade bed, a pile of clothes next to her, and she's tossing these into her oversized, K-Mart back pack. It's like standing by a stream and throwing some dead love's things into the current. She's sobbing—by means of the limp, ineffectual gesture of her hand. The sound I heard is a moan, a keening. I can see she's a little wasted, wrecked—stoned or something—but just a little. Her eyes are bloodshot and their look diffused. I'm seeing serious depression; I'm hardly equipped.

"Kerry. Jesus, Kerry."

"Andrew okay in there?"

"No. Well, yes for awhile. He's done some damage. A plant."

"Yeah. I heard him," she says. "I'm sorry. He's a kid. Y'know?"

"Sure. It's nothing. A few minutes cleanup . . . and repotting."

"He's a little kid, that's all." She starts to cry, and I think, *This is theater. She's playing me for sympathy*, but I sit by her on the bed, and when I feel her crumple against me, I put my arm around her bony shoulders, and smell her nice sweet smell, the sweetness surprises me, and she crumples against me, and at that moment *I take her on.* I feel a tingling, a warmth, in my loins, but I let it be, I'm not ashamed of it. My whole life, when I've felt tender, when my heart opens, this happens, it comes with the territory.

"I can't even fit all these goddamn things . . . "

"I don't tell her, *You could if you did it neatly*. I ask, "You want me to help?"

"I can do it."

"Ahh, well, we can always use a big plastic bag if we need to."

My God. I've taken her on, for better or for worse, as if she were my child, or anyway my niece, and I say, "Kerry, please, I want to help, you've got a kid in there."

As if instructed, she gets down from the bed and stumbles barefoot into the living room, and she sits down by Andrew and takes him on her lap, and he nestles against her, smearing her clean, wrinkled blouse with wet dirt. She's crying, I guess, I can see her shoulders shaking, and now she stands and brushes off his hands and I notice black and blue marks along his thin thighs, and I wonder who made them, and isn't there a new mark on his cheek—or is that from before?

I look around the apartment to assess damage. Nothing much. One wall in the kitchen with crayon scribbles, and of course she hasn't straightened anything up, so there are books lying around on the floor, and all the kitchen drawers are pulled out or left open, and egg beater, screwdriver, ladles and spoons are strewn all over. But that *smell*. I follow my nose and find it, in the second bedroom, where Andrew's been sleeping. By his bed, the wall is smeared with shit. Finger painting. There's an open diaper with a loose shit on the floor.

Hopeless. Not the apartment, which will take me maybe two hours and then a wall to paint. No big deal. But Kerry. She's sitting cross-legged with Andrew in her lap, and she's kissing him and half-crying, half-singing to him, voice off-key and cracked with phlegm. *Hopeless.* I can't imagine she'll make it into the women's center or that having made it she'll be able to stay. We're talking serious chaos. I'm seeing chaos. I think for a moment of taking her back with me, but right away I see how impossible that is, dangerous for her, terrible for Jeremy, disastrous for me. I have a life and a job. *Hopeless.* I close my eyes. My grandfather is there for me as he always is at times like these. What can he do but murmur the old prayers? Are there words to say for a woman holding onto the edge of a cliff by her fingernails, and you know she's going to drop, it's only a question of time, and the little child who's holding on to her, what good can happen to him? I'm sure there are such words, but I don't know them.

I go to the closet where Barbara and Julia keep their records and find a CD of Brahms sonatas for cello and piano and put it on, as if the music could soothe her. I go through the house picking up books, collecting toys, working silently and trying to work in such a way that she doesn't feel it as a judgment on her. Working to pass the time while she gets things ready. And pretty soon she stops rocking Andrew. She goes into his bedroom to change him, I hear her talking to him.

I sweep up the dirt from the plant, find a bag of potting soil and some pots on the screened-in porch, and in a few minutes the dirt's gone and the plant is hanging from an exposed beam. You can't do much to hurt spider plants, I figure it'll be all right. The bedroom wall I'll save for another day. With another part of my head I think about taking Andrew for ice cream cones sometimes, taking Kerry to the movies, maybe bringing her down to the AFDC office—Aid to Families with Dependent Children—I'm sure she never followed through. I'll need to go with her, or an advocate from the women's center will, help her get welfare, child care vouchers, counseling, her G.E.D. Maybe if someone can hold her hand awhile, take her step by step. . . . I'm willing, if there's no one else. How peculiar: I do seem to be willing. Scrubbing crayon scribblings from the kitchen wall, I'm laughing at myself.

"Hey—what are you laughing at? You get off my back, will you?" Kerry calls out from the next room. But she sounds more in-the-world, angry because it's the way she is, she's angry by instinct, angry when she isn't helpless, in love or in despair.

"I'm not on your back, I swear," I say. "You want me to make some coffee for us?"

"If you can figure out their fucking machine," she says.

Driving up into the hills to home, I don't feel so altogether hopeless. I waited around until she took Andrew off to meet Ronnie Gordon. I wanted to say, *Please, take care of this place until you're out of here*, but I didn't. I set a time for her to call, told her I want to take them out for dinner. It's dark. Time to think of tonight's dinner for myself. I pull over at a bar and call Frank, invite myself over. Driving to his house, I think how strange, it's as if I'm acting in a kind of dream.

I don't pass a single car once I climb the secondary roads towards Frank's. Something's chewing at my gut. What? I scan. And now I "remember" what I've been working to keep out of consciousness—"*I'm going to ruin your life.*"

Nora hears my car and runs out barefoot, hoping to see Jeremy in the back seat, but she's nice about it, giving me a hug anyway and letting me take her hand on the walk over the blacktop to the door.

Frank's in the kitchen, sauteeing onions; the house smells of comfort. The onions and something else cooking and a heady improvisation off "Lush Life" by Sonny Rollins and the half-dozen candles and oil lamps that Nora always insists on warm the house and me. "Pour yourself a drink," Frank says.

"I need some advice," I begin, sipping my bourbon, though I hadn't known I was going to ask. "Now, don't tell me I should 'never have gotten started in the first place.' I know that. I want to talk about damage control."

"Okay. Sure. Cut up these carrots for me, will you? And sliver and flour that beef?"

So I do. Nora goes back to painting at her worktable nearby. I like feeling her in the kitchen with us. She has short, straight black hair and a beautiful but severe, thin face, almost an adult face; always I look at her as if it happened yesterday that Meg, her mother, took off to find herself at thirty-four; always I look at Nora as if she were nursing that wound, as if she'd built up incredibly complex defenses against the pain and it's all there in that adult look. And maybe it's not just my imagining.

I tell Frank about Boston, about Chuck Ahearn, Patrick Ahearn and the threat he's made. I brush over my visit with Kerry, my commitment to her. "How do you think he'll come after me? And what can I do about it?"

Frank nods, and thinks, and meantime, we busy ourselves with the sauté. He's got potato slices smeared with garlic, oregano, olive oil, soy sauce, roasting in the oven. *That's* what I've been smelling. Now he colors everything musky red with paprika and we're ready. Nora sets the table. "It's hard to figure out why he'd bother," Frank says. "What can he get out of it?"

We sit at the wooden table Frank built out of native oak planks—must weigh two hundred pounds, this table—and bow our heads, the three of us, and Nora says as she always says, in a singsong, "We're grateful for being here together and for our food. Amen."

"He probably thinks I can reach her," I continue. "And I suppose I can. I won't know—don't *want* to know—

where she's sheltered. *If* they take her in. But I expect to stay in touch. He spoke about the newspapers. What can he tell them?"

"Well, she's practically a child. Nineteen, you said? It could be embarrassing."

"What, Daddy?" Nora asks.

"You think Nancy would use it against me?"

"*Daddy?*" Nora says again. *"What?"*

"I think you'd better get her on your side," Frank says. I don't say anything, and Frank takes the silence to mean I won't call Nancy, so he presses. "And your boss, too." He turns to Nora, "There's this creep wants to get Dave in trouble. Dave's trying to help someone, a woman, a woman who gets beaten up by her husband. The husband's after Dave. You think anyone will believe he's a monster, this friend of ours?"

I say quietly to Nancy, "There's maybe going to be more fallout from sheltering the woman—sheltering Kerry."

We're sitting at a kids' table waiting for Jeremy's teacher to enter the classroom for our conference. It's late afternoon a couple of days after Patrick Ahearn came to see me. "The husband—" I tell her, trying to get it out quickly, before Jeremy's teacher appears—"the batterer—well, his brother is a lawyer and he's threatening me—not with legal action—well, maybe that, too, though I can't figure what he could sue about—but with lousy publicity. He may contact you. I want you to know in advance."

"What is all this?"

"What I said. Look. He wanted the woman's address. He's trying to squeeze me for it."

"And you *know* it? Why, David? I thought you said—"

"Actually, I don't know it. I *did* know it. Now she's living at Women in Transition. You know—*like you*—in transition. I *hope* she's in transition from that sicko. Look!" I snap, quarrelsome suddenly, "if I were a batterer, a dangerous batterer, a guy who might murder you, would you want me to find out where you'd gone?"

"Shhh. Why are you getting so defensive?" she says. "I simply asked. So she's with Stephanie Hirsh's organization?"

"I'd forgotten Stephanie was involved. That's right. The same one. I contacted Ronnie Gordon. She's living there now. I have no idea where. But the lawyer, the brother, figures I can find out."

"Well, actually, David, I wasn't going to mention it, but he called last night . . . . I told him I trusted you."

"What did he say? What do you mean, 'trusted'?"

Before Nancy can answer, Molly Hopkins walks in, her arms full of manila portfolios. I stand up and she waves me down again. "I'm sorry. I'll just be another minute." She takes one of the portfolios, stacks the rest on a table in the corner, and now she finds a notebook in her desk drawer and sits down at the low table that makes us all seem giants.

She's a soft, warm, blowsy woman with a couple of kids of her own. It's our first conference, but I've seen her at sings and parent meetings since Jeremy started school. "It's nice to see you folks," she says, with the folksy, unthreatening but authoritative speech that is shared by almost all the teachers at Jeremy's school. "Jeremy's one of my sweeties," she says, and *bang*, my heart opens to her right away. "He has a good time here. And he's grown a lot since last year. I used to sit with him sometimes in All-School last year. He seems so much older now. He's really good at taking initiative, following through, he's a real helper."

"He likes the reading this year," I say.

Nancy gives me a surprised look. "I thought it was science he especially liked," she says. "That's what he always talks about with us." Jesus, that's *it*, there's *one* Jeremy, but there are *two* Jeremy's, depends on whose house he's at.

And Molly picks up on this. "Of course, I know you've separated, but if I hadn't known from you, I think I'd know from Jeremy."

"What? You see him upset?" I say, jumping in, and I hear Nancy breathe and I know that particular breathing of hers, meaning, *There goes David again*. So fuck you, there I go!

"Not upset," Molly says, in the slow, steady speech of the school, "but *pulled*. I'd say pulled." She opens his art portfolio, and I see what she's saying. There's a picture of a child, a mother and a father. The child is in the middle, reaching out a hand towards the edges of the paper, where mother and where father stand, exactly the same height, though in fact I'm six inches taller than Nancy. The mother and the father stand frontally, hieratically, posing for the artist's eye. He's in shades of orange, she's in shades of blue. Arms stiff out, the child looks crucified between them.

Though I get it, it irritates me that she's psychologizing his work. I shrug it off. "Sure. Sure. Of course." I catch sight of the accordion partition that separates this room from the one next door, a wall that can be pulled back for assemblies. I'm reminded of something. I'm still here, listening, but I keep looking past her at the partition. It's like the one in my own school when I was a child.

Nancy just nods. This moment, we don't like one another much.

"And I see him," Molly goes on, "days he's making the transition, by himself a lot, a little blue, even a little quarrelsome. I've gotten so I can spot transitional days without his saying. And then I see the duffel bag and the soccer cleats."

Now *I* don't say anything. Nancy asks, "You think there's anything we should be doing?"

Molly Hopkins smiles and shakes her head. "That's just the way it is. I just want you to know what's going on. And there's one thing more." She leads us to the Comfort Corner of the room, a loft in which the kids can read, listen to tapes, work quietly. "This is why I asked you in." Under the loft there's a little cardboard room—walls of cardboard taped together, a bed, a dresser, a chair made of cardboard. And in the bed a clay figure. "That's Jeremy's. It's nicely done. But he keeps it in this private space, he doesn't show it or use it or share it—or break it up. And on transition days, he talks to the little figure in the bed."

"You think he needs help?" Nancy says.

"I think he's helping himself. Maybe he'd be able to talk with you about it. But don't get me wrong. Jeremy's not in trouble. He's handling it all quite well. I mean—he's sad, and he doesn't like living in two houses, and that makes perfect sense. But he's not in trouble."

We talk some more, talk about his math, his love of music. Now Molly excuses herself and we're left to walk out by ourselves. "Well," I say, "maybe you can talk to him. Or we could meet for dinner some night, we could talk to him together?"

"I'll talk to him. Then let's see."

"You said, just before Molly came in, you said you trusted me."

"That's what I told the lawyer. And I do. You don't have to worry. I know your bad points, and chasing after nineteen-year-old girls isn't one of them. But I have to say it again: I do wish you'd be careful. There's Jeremy. You said they were dangerous."

"I'll be careful. Let me know, will you, how the talk goes?"

I go home thinking, *the cost, the cost . . . best will in the world to do right by your child, and still . . . .* What sense can he make of it?

That accordion partition in Jeremy's classroom comes back to me. I was maybe six, seven, younger than Jeremy—first grade, second—I used to watch the accordion partition that served as a wall in my classroom. I was sure that one day the wall would accordion out of the way and the adult world would come out from the next room, where they'd hidden. *They*—my parents, my uncles, but more: the President of the United States, the principal, the police—would come forward and tell me and the children who didn't *already* know, "Look, we know you've been wondering about all the secrets, you've been trying to figure things out, you've thought everything was a little wrong. Well, it *was*. It was a test, a teaching, and now it's time for you to know the world, how it works, who pulls the strings and why they're pulled." And everything would be clear and good.

Now, blessedly, nothing terrible happens. I find a couple of calls from Gabriella on my answer machine, a message in the English office. I leave them unanswered. I spend a couple of late afternoons with a chain saw, cutting my cherry-picker load of logs into two-foot lengths, stacking the wood for winter.

One night, Chuck Ahearn calls. The ugly gravelly tone of his voice grates on me whatever he'd have to say. He says, "Mr. Rosen, you've got to understand my position. That's my son and nobody's gonna take him from me. I'm not nice like my brother, Mr. Rosen. I think you ought to give me the fucking number."

"I haven't got it."

"The telephone number. I think if you want to live very long, you hear me?"

"I'll give you the number, Chuck. It's an office number, that's all I've got. They can forward your message."

He hangs up on me. What about calling Gar? I remember his warning to Chuck that night. But I don't want anything to do with Gar. I won't be responsible for more violence.

On Thursday I get a note in my mailbox at school from Leonard Noble, so I stop by. He's dictating to his secretary, and he asks her to leave and pulls a couple of armchairs closer together, and we sit down. He pats my knee. He whispers. "I'd thought you were resigning from the Round Table. Are you still knight-errant for that poor young thing?"

"She's living at a shelter for battered women."

"Well, that's certainly to the good. If the fit hits the shan, that's the absolutely best possible place for her to be. You understand, I received a call."

"From Patrick Ahearn. That's the husband's brother."

"I want you to know, I don't take anything he said *seri-*

ously. Oh, I pretended to—I thought perhaps that would make him think he's *accomplished* something—and stop. But number *uno*, I doubt you've done anything untoward, you understand me?—and number *due*, I don't give a damn. There are female so-called students around here who would love to attack one of us for womanizing. But you've covered your ass beautifully, sending her off to a shelter run by *les femmes*. I just want you to know, you're in no trouble here."

"Do you expect him to do anything else?"

"Read the newspaper—the *Record*—tomorrow."

"Oh, my God."

He laughs, and using the laugh as cover sweeps me fondly, pat, pat, pat, out of his office. I'm relieved by his support, but it makes me uneasy. Like being respected and supported by some Nazi administrator in the thirties.

On Friday, the *Record* comes out with a small story on the front page of the second section. I sit reading it in the college cafeteria over coffee this morning. No picture of me, I'm unnamed. What's the news? Only that there's has been a report of a teacher at the community college keeping a young woman and her child away from her husband. The previous question of the possibility of rape, the suit against a women's shelter in Boston, are mentioned. Also unnamed, Leonard Noble (it must be he) explains that in fact I am protecting the woman from a savage husband.

Not so bad. No. Even if I *were* named, I wouldn't be hurt badly by a story like this. I tear off the page, fold it into my briefcase, head upstairs. The departmental secretary waves a memo at me. Kerry has just called, would I please call back?

"Someone just showed me the papers," Kerry says. "I didn't mean to make things tough on you."

"You haven't. Really. It's okay. What about you? How's the shelter going?"

"Yeah, well, it's pretty okay, you know? The other women know what's going on. They got me on welfare right away. They've got the legal stuff started. And it's great for Andrew. There's kids around. We gotta keep the place pretty clean. It pisses me off, the rules and everything. But it's okay."

"Listen," I say, surprising myself. "If you want to meet for lunch, there's a nice place near the center of town. Don't tell me where you are—I don't want to know—but is that feasible without a car?"

We meet at the Cornucopia. I say, "Hey, Andrew, come to Uncle Dave," and for the very first time, he comes to me, he sits on my lap of his own accord, though just for a few stiff seconds, and then he's down, back around the wooden table to his mother. She holds him and reads the menu. I realize he's clean, he doesn't smell. Looking up, she says, "What's this place? I don't get it. There's no hamburgers even."

"It's vegetarian."

"A hippie place!" she laughs.

"I haven't heard that word for a long, long time."

"Hey, I'm kidding," she says. "It's okay, it's okay, there's cheese. That's what Andrew eats. I'll have the chili. He won't eat much," she warns.

"I know what it's like, a little kid in a restaurant."

But he surprises us both by eating his cheese sandwich and going after his mother's bland chili.

A folk guitar plays over the speakers. There are posters tacked up on the otherwise bare walls, posters advertising folk performers, a musical group from Nicaragua, a concert of Indian dance. The old days, it would have been political posters. Now the politics is hidden, but it's the same people. Hippie?—not really, but young people's culture. Some of the children of the same people who used to be called *hippies*. I suggested the Cornucopia because it's a real community gathering place. The people who come here are like the people who work in the place, the same—young people mostly, not much money, mostly kind. They live out an ideology of kindness, openness, and while that's not much of an ideology, not much of what Gar would think of as an *analysis*, it might make this a good place for Kerry.

"I talked to the guy who handles the G.E.D. in this county. That's going to be *easy*. I mean. You probably think I'm real dumb, but I was actually good in high school—when I went. I could take the stupid G.E.D. right now, no prep, and pass it easy."

"I'm glad," I say. And I am, though I can sense something forced in this. She's being good, she's showing me how good she can be.

"I can get money for training, I can get money for day care. Did you know that?"

"Well, you sound great. I mean hopeful."

"Well, it's just me," she says, warning me off. "I'm not any goddamn different. You know, you give me a pain, the way you're always putting me down."

"Me!"

"I can read it in your looks. You think my cigarettes suck, you think it's depressing when I look at TV, you want me to be—I don't know—respectable and like Newton or Wellesley, my hair not messy. I'm getting a G.E.D.— okay. I'm not changing *everything*."

Suddenly, for the first time today, I notice her hair, it's cut, combed; I notice her clothes—just jeans, but washed, and a nice plaid shirt I guess she must have borrowed from somebody. She looks like she belongs in Cornucopia. And I see how pretty she can be. A little boyish now that her long hair has been trimmed, and with her narrow hips and no makeup. Her bruises are down to almost nothing. Her eyes look less crazy.

"Let me know," I say, happy to play the role she expects me to play, "if you need any help. I just think it's great, Kerry. I do."

She tilts the corner of her mouth in a wise-guy sneer, rolls her eyes, and pets Andrew's hair like mad to avoid looking at me. In almost an hour Andrew has only whined once or twice and hasn't cried at all. I make silly faces at him.

He makes Andrew-faces back at me.

My student Steve Rausch, same young man who came into my office when Patrick Ahearn was there, waves from across the room, comes over and leans a hand on the table and tells me he's sending out a first sheaf of poems and wonders which little magazines I'd suggest. I tell him and I introduce Steve and Kerry and Andrew, and I see how carefully he's not looking at Kerry, I see him catching her aslant, and I can feel him wonder about me and Kerry, and I think, Maybe he could be interested in her. Self-conscious, I grin and say, "Kerry's gonna be coming back to school next spring. Maybe some time this fall, maybe you can show her around."

"Sure," he says. Not the worst thing. Though right away I worry—maybe it is the worst thing; maybe she'd damage him, impede him.

"So," he says to Kerry, "what are you going to be doing?"

"I've been thinking maybe laboratory research," she says. I try to stay cool. I don't ask.

Embarrassed, I reach across the table and say, "Andrew, things are definitely looking up. Don't you think?"

Seven

Friday night I come home from teaching to find Gar Stone has called. I fast-forward through his message to make him sound like a chipmunk. Even in the squeak I can hear "Gabriella . . . Gabriella . . . ."

The next message, Gar again. I press *ERASE*. Erase, erase. I wish I'd never looked out that plate glass at the Museum of Modern Art and seen him strolling like some elegant *boulevardier* in the sculpture garden.

It's the deception that gets to me: not to let me know she'd been married to the son of a bitch. What else has she kept from me? When Gar comes to Boston, where does he sleep?

The phone rings while I'm making dinner, and I pick it up. "I'm back in Boston," Gar says. "I told you in my message." I don't answer. "I'm up here," he says, "for a couple of things. A real estate deal connected to some new Boston-artery construction, third harbor-tunnel stuff. And then I'm coming out your way to see Jenny, my kid, at school."

I grunt something.

"I catch you at a bad time?" Not waiting for an answer, he says, "Dave? I want to thank you for helping out with that crazy Ahearn." I'm still silent. "I've got things to tell you about that crazy fuck. My detective guy, Akavian, he's been on it."

I grunt.

"Hey, it was your idea. And you were right. So look," he says, "I'll be out your way tomorrow. Jenny's school's not fifteen miles away. From there I'm driving back to New York. Come on."

"You're a couple of fucking liars."

"I know I was dumb for a change. Come on. I'm asking as an old friend."

"You were married."

"Well, it's *about* Gabriella. That's why we need to talk. I'm trying to help her. *She* won't talk to me either. Oh, Christ, you're really pissed, aren't you?" Gar says. "I guess I hadn't realized. You know, it's funny—*everybody* turns out to be pissed at me. Gabriella, she won't return my calls. What the fuck are *you* so angry about? We didn't tell you we were married? What's the difference? You knew we were together in the old days."

"Yes, in the *old, old* days."

"So we kept a little something from you? So? Fuck you! What? Are you smitten? Are you smitten with Gabriella?"

"Smitten!"

"Jerked around then? Conned? Is that the feeling? Nobody's trying to snow you, Dave. Nobody gives that much of a shit about what you think, okay? Gabriella, she's one complicated woman. I've known her for a long time. She's not the young girl you knew."

"So she's angry, the way you beat up Chuck?"

"In a sense, yeah. But it's more complicated, it's a long story, it's our whole lives together. You know? She's got her reasons. And now—I guess I got her in some trouble."

"Maybe it's better if you don't come. I'm having a hard enough time. Chuck's brother—the lawyer—he's trying to make things bad for me."

"Yeah? Maybe I can help. I can get somebody to lean on him a little."

"That's all I need. You're really something."

"Ah, I don't mean like *that*. I've got political contacts up here. The legal community. That's all I mean, Dave, come on. Now please, okay?—meet me at Jenny's school. Old time's sake. My dear fellow—what have you got to lose?"

I hear something gradually happen to his voice. Gar has two voices, sometimes in the same rap—one, cultivated, elegant; one New-York-street-wise. He went to a good prep school, Horace Mann or Riverdale, he went to Columbia, but he likes to talk—I don't know—Bronx-Italian, Brooklyn-Jewish, Manhattan-Irish. Stillman's Gym. As he talks tonight I hear him modulating into genteel, as if genteel is going to woo me. Actually, it annoys me, reminds me of Leonard Noble. But it makes me feel his urgency. And what *have* I got to lose?

We meet at five o'clock at the athletic building at Jenny's school. It's a serious school, but what impresses everyone at first is the beauty and the size. It's bigger than a lot of private colleges, not to mention Green River Community College, and the labs, the field house, the theater, are perhaps as good as the ones at schools like Amherst and Williams. I know my way; I've been out here to see a play, and a couple of times to be at graduation ceremonies for children of friends.

We meet in the lobby and shake hands and head for the gym; our footsteps echo like mad. "She's at practice," he says. "We had lunch, I sat in on a couple of classes. I feel lousy and ashamed, I hardly get up here to spend any time with her. Tonight's her game against St. Paul's or Deerfield or somebody." In a moment our echoing voices blur into the music of the girls' voices and a whistle being blown. We sit in the stands above the court and watch two girls moving the ball down half court against a couple of defensive players; then the offensive players become defense and a new pair comes down with the ball.

It's not my game, basketball. I don't watch the play, just try to pick out Jenny before Gar tells me. Is it that tall girl? Or that real beauty? Now I see Gabriella's strong, broad mouth, the black hair she had in her early twenties; I nudge Gar. "That one?"

He nods. "Yeah. Lucky—she doesn't take after me."

I think about their other child. At the same moment Gar remembers, too. "The other one?—Sara—looked like both of us. Skinny kid. Wonderful, big eyes. Really, you'd have loved her."

I sigh and find I want to touch his arm. I stare at my fingers.

Jenny brings the ball down; she's smooth, she's got moves.

She waves and comes over. "We were taking it easy," she says instead of Hello. "You'll see tonight."

"This is Dave Rosen. A friend of your mother's, a friend of mine, hundreds of years we've known each other—right, Dave?"

"The sixties," I say. "Sixties, seventies." She looks like a child, slightly blurred in definition, and yet womanly, too, so much like her mother years back that I gawk at her and get embarrassed.

Jenny rolls up her eyes. "Oh, sure. The sixties, the seventies."

"You hear too much about the sixties?" I say.

"Oh, just *all* the time," she says, in the slightly affected voice of a watched adolescent.

It makes me feel protective; I want to make things comfortable for her—not, I decide, by continuing the joke but by taking seriously her complaint. "Well, you've got to understand, Jenny. It wasn't just youth; it was that, but for your Mom and Dad and me, it was supposed to be the start of a new world. You can't imagine how smug that made us."

"Speak for yourself," Gar says.

"*That's* one of the things we learned," I say. "To speak for ourselves. And I think maybe that part didn't get lost."

Now she looks at me.

I can tell she wants to get away and take a shower. But it's hard to stop. I want her approval, even her affection. Why? Well, I might have been this girl's stepfather. "I'd bet," I say to Jenny, "you speak pretty strongly for yourself."

"I try. Well . . . nice meeting you," she says.

"Nice meeting *you*," I say back.

Touching Gar's arm, she's gone. We watch her go, and the echo of gym voices hushes and it's just us and a couple of girls across the floor laughing about something, and a custodian comes in with a buffing machine. "I'm 'smitten'," I say, hand over heart, and we smile.

"Isn't she terrific? Best thing I've done, sending her here."

"And Gabriella thinks so?"

"Oh, sure. She agreed. But—you know—"

"She *had* to."

"I didn't twist her arm."

In my Accord I follow his Mercedes to a place that advertises, on a sign with letters like on a movie marquee, "Best Home Cookin'." I've eaten here some. Truckers and folks from the sixties. No New York power-lunches. "This is a place to have the soup and bread."

"How about the chicken stew?" Gar asks, looking at the menu.

"Lots of flour, not much chicken."

"How about the Jack Daniels?"

"Couldn't be better." We order drinks and soup. A young woman, soft face that reminds me of Kerry's, brings the drinks. Gar can't resist. He talks to her about the leaf watchers this fall, about where she lives, where she goes to dance. He does this, far as I can tell, just to see her take on a glow, laugh a little; he does it for the subtle sexual charge he's unaware of.

"So tell me—" Gar begins when the young woman leaves the table "—why's it *get* to you so much, that Gabriella wasn't ready to tell you about us? So fucking what? This upsets her."

"She asked you—"

"She feels bad, I guess. She likes you. And, listen, she asks after she's so hard to reach I almost give up. But I wanted to know, was there something I should bring out to give Jenny, and so I tried Gabriella once more, and she asks me to call you. Listen, why is she supposed to expose her whole life to you?"

I shrug my shrug. "No reason."

"No. No obligation. No! And while we're on the subject, why are you so fucking angry at *me*? Was I supposed to tell you about Gabriella and me when she didn't want me to? Why? And why do you sit there like a fucking stone wall in front of me?"

So I look into his face and tell him, "Oh. It's nothing new, Gar. It's just, I've thought of you for twenty some years as the worst of the sixties—narcissism posing as politics. And you're still the same."

"Nothing new, huh? Ahh, I guess I've always known. Back then, you *envied* me. You envied me, that's basically it."

"You think so? I don't think that's it. I keep remembering one particular march down Broadway, the time you trashed the bank. You remember?"

"Not specifically."

"We were marching down Broadway from Columbia, then across to Morningside Park to 'claim' it for the people of Harlem. Your people tossed plastic bags of paint at the bank. A couple of martyrs got beaten and dragged away to be chopped up into fuel for the next fire. You called it 'pulling the dialogue to the left.'"

"Sounds like me in the old days. I was such a wise ass."

"You snookered me into writing a letter of support to somebody—I think the Graduate Students Council at Columbia. It still aggravates me—I was conned."

"Yeah?" Gar grins. "Okay, you say so, I believe it. You can't tell me anything about me in those days I won't admit to. I was a real asshole. But, see, you must have wanted a guy like me to give you something. A little boost, a little panache? And then—well, then there's Gabriella, isn't that so? Here's what I think—Gabriella came to me, she stayed with me. That's it. That's what you've been holding onto all these years."

"You can think that." I want to *want* to keep my distance from Gar, to see him as con artist and bastard. Funny thing is, tonight it's hard. My anger is something I remember more than feel. Partly it's Jenny makes it hard to stay angry. And it's Sara, it's realizing that the loss of Sara is his loss too. I sip my whiskey.

"We need to talk," he says, and silently, for a couple of

minutes, sips his drink and looks around at the terrible poetic watercolor landscapes on the walls. In the corner the television is showing college football but thank God the sound's turned down. I'm not used to Gar silent. "Well," he says, finally, "now you know we were married. You know that."

"I *think* I know that."

"It's true. Gabriella's a good woman. She stuck it out with me for years when I was a royal creep. Yeah, we were married."

"And what don't I know?"

"I'm getting to that." He holds up his palms as if to ward off blows. "Now don't get pissed off. All right, Dave?"

I stare. "Oh, Jesus!" I say, and my mouth falls open. "You're *still* married! You're *still* married. Is that what you're saying?"

"No. Not exactly. Well, *yes*. I mean, only in name. In name! Sit down, Dave, for Christsakes. I mean, we haven't lived together for a long time. Years, I mean."

"But you're still married." I start to get up and get the hell away, except that now I'm too interested. The accordion partition of my childhood opens. The adults standing behind it reveal the Truth at last. Or maybe they just stand there laughing at me.

"We split up. I was fucking everything that moved at the time, that was part of it. She walked out on me, came up to Boston, when Sara was about four years old. We stayed in touch . . . and not just because of the kids. We still spent the occasional weekend, we went away one vacation with the kids together. She had Jenny and Sara with her, I gave her money, and I helped out with finances for Sojourner House. I had, let's say, a bad reputation in certain circles, so we kept it quiet. Gabriella also, I guess, never approved of me exactly. So we kept our relationship private. But we got along. We were about to get a legal divorce when the thing happened. In fact, at the time, I was kind of living with somebody else—I thought I was going to marry her. It didn't turn out that way. But see, we got along, me and Gabriella. This is the point. We're not married, we're married. We're a peculiar kind of team, and why exactly I don't know, I believe in her in some funny way."

"Gar, you're telling me you're still in love with Gabriella?"

"In love? *Love*? Shit, I don't know. They say that when a child dies, it usually kills a marriage. Well, ours was already *kaput*. But then, when Sara was killed, it's like Gabriella took her place. I mean, after the pills and the breakdown—"

"She had a breakdown?"

"Well, sure, she was hospitalized after the pills. You know about the pills?"

"She told me."

"She went kind of catatonic, into withdrawal, and Jenny and I kept up a kind of vigil, and she came out of it. Jenny was already living with me. Since then, I'm like Gabriella's brother, her old friend, her father, that's all. I like it that she needs me."

"And now she's not even talking to you."

"She's talking but she's not talking. After that shit with Ahearn—you know?"

"You did get pretty crazy."

"Yeah? Well, it turns out I was on target. And *you* were on target. You asked me to get Bill Akavian to do some digging? So he dug. Some files public, others not so public—juvenile. Akavian has ways. Turns out that Chuck Ahearn has been in trouble forever. Trouble? He *killed* a kid, stomped him to death when he was sixteen, kid had a knife. Ahearn went to reformatory for a couple of years. But it's the *last* few years that are interesting. He's been working for his father, I told you, but what Akavian dug up is a couple of drug charges: Ahearn released because of insufficient evidence, one, two, three times. And he asked around—the guy has a scary rep, let me tell you. No one wants to fuck with him. I mean violent. He's known to carry a gun. Akavian says that Patrick has his hands full. Keeps bailing his brother out of trouble. Partly it's family. But partly, Bill thinks, Chuck is useful to Patrick."

"Did you tell this to Gabriella?"

"I told you—she won't talk to me."

"What do you need from me? You want me to talk to her?"

"I figure she respects you, she likes you."

"*You* want *me* to intercede for you? That's funny."

"It is," Gar admits. "I agree. It is." Our soup comes. We don't talk. There's a lot I don't ask. Finally, he says, "Oh. I'd like it if she didn't know I asked you to help me out. I want to be back where I was with Gabriella. Jenny needs that, all right? I need it too."

We order another round of drinks, and we sit together without talking. There's a big sadness between us. Gar asks about Patrick Ahearn. After a few minutes he says, "The thing is, the board at Sojourner House asked her to step down—temporarily—as director. Asked her not to represent Sojourner House publicly. Something like that. It's a tough time for her."

I take it in. "Oh. Well, if it's like that—" I shrug.

"Thanks," Gar says simply.

Gar goes back to Jenny's game, I go back to Green River to have a drink and shoot a game of pool with Frank, and the whole drive I keep wondering what made my jaw feel this way. My teeth must have been clenched pretty hard. They're not clenched now.

I let Gabriella in.

Next day, Sunday, at the college library I look up Gar Stone in the *New York Times Index*, going back through the late eighties. I want to understand what he means by a "bad reputation." Fifteen minutes in the microfilm room and I understand.

Home again, I call Gabriella. It's all right, I tell her, it's all right, let's forget it. I know about your marriage, I know you're still legally married. You must have had your reasons. To keep off the topic, I ask about Sojourner House.

She tells me, yes, it's true, she's been asked to resign. The original lawsuit was embarrassing—it was dropped, yes, but still embarrassing. And now there's a second suit, for assaulting Chuck Ahearn. "But what the board resented most was that we used men, outsiders, to beat someone physically. 'Strong-arm tactics,' Gail called it."

"Well, she was after you for a long time, wasn't she?"

"That's right, I forgot, you were at the board meeting. The thing is, she wants the best for Sojourner House, for the women in the Sojourner community. I think she's disappointed in me."

"Is it because of Gar? Because Gar's involved?"

"What makes you say that?"

"I've been reading about his business dealings. The pair of luxury-apartment buildings he built under the old regulations, taking a huge tax break just under the wire. And now this mammoth project on the West Side. There's a big protest going on over how much low and moderate-income housing there'll be in those buildings. And the destruction of tenements to build the development."

"Gail knows about Gar. I told you that."

"But nobody else knows, and now I understand why. He's really something in New York. I mean he has a hell of a reputation. He's able to put pressure on the Housing Commission, he's able to bypass restrictions and hook into existing sewage disposal."

"A lot of it's his father, you understand. Gar's not as bad as they paint him."

"He said you weren't talking to him. He feels pretty bad."

"You know, after awhile, I always go back to talking to Gar. I know Gar. He can't stand not being on the right side. I've always been the *right side* for him. Otherwise, he'd feel he was no better than his father."

We talk about Gar, and that peters out and we talk about Gabriella. "You must feel sick," I say, "about leaving Sojourner House."

"No. No, actually I'm not. Relieved, mostly. I've been

wanting time to write about abuse. I need to step back and do that. I'm just sorry about how it happened."

"And you've got the money to live on?" I remember Gar again. "I guess you do." I tell her about meeting Jenny.

"I asked Gar to tell you we were married, were *still* married," Gabriella says. "But David, you understand—we aren't lovers. We haven't been for a long time."

"Oh, I know," I say, "Of course. I know." But only now do I really know. And in my mental video-phone I see Gabriella in her off-white silk blouse with the lace collar, I see her sitting with boxes all around her in that depressing little apartment she lives in like a skin of suffering.

So we talk like this on Sunday. And here I am, opening to her again. Then on Monday, she calls me and we talk about Jenny. Tuesday I call her, we talk about her book. Thursday, she asks would I like to visit her for the weekend. I can't, I tell her. Jeremy's coming back to me. But soon, I say. Soon.

Twice this week Kerry calls. When Sylvia Warner stops by to ask me about "that young woman and her little boy," I can tell her truthfully, "It seems to be going well for her. She's living in a good place." Standing in my kitchen, Sylvia closes her eyes in satisfaction, and she shakes her head. "We've both been praying, David. I know you're not a believer, Dave—"

"—But I *am*," I say. "I *am*."

On Friday, when I pick up Jeremy at school and we go out for ice cream, we meet Kerry and Andrew at Friendly's. She tells me about her preparation for the G.E.D. She ignores Jeremy, but she talks and talks to me in a nice voice, like, *Look how nice I can be.* She tells me she likes the shelter okay, tells me about a couple of the women she's met. Some woman named Sophie's okay. But she complains about one of the women. "I'm getting no goddamn sleep," she says. "This bitch—her kid cries at night and wakes everybody up and she doesn't give a shit. Then I can't get Andrew back to sleep and I'm wiped in the morning."

137

I'm a little bored, I've been seeing students half the day, but I nod thoughtfully, I play the uncle she needs me to be.

Jeremy and I drive home. The fall has had its second birth, when the oak leaves turn red. It always feels like a bonus, this second display. Look, I say to Jeremy, knowing he'll groan when I show him some final stubborn maple turning gold. In the back seat I know he's rolling his eyes, the way he does when I stop for a perennial garden in summer. "I know, I know," I say, "but don't we live in a beautiful place, honey? Don't we? Oh—I've made a meat sauce for spaghetti." I ask, "How would you like to visit Boston some weekend soon? I've got a friend I'd like you to get to know. You met her in New York. Gabriella Rossi, remember? How would you like that?"

"Fine, I guess. Can we see a game?" Sounds good to me. He asks about Kerry and I tell him she's that woman we're helping. "What do you think of her?" He thinks she's weird. We're home. Maple in the driveway's dropping her leaves to make a flaming yellow carpet under our wheels.

There's a car in our driveway, a red Camaro, not a car I recognize. Frank said he'd send someone over to fix my gutters and drainpipes before winter. But in a new Camaro?

I call "Hello?" as I walk in. "Hello?" Before I see anything I'm slammed against the wall, and I'm in Crazyland, everything is blurred, and even before I turn and see him, I know it's Chuck Ahearn, and I yell, "Jeremy, go! Run to the Warners'!" The words come out as an explosion, I have no idea what he's heard.

I turn, I see Jeremy standing in the doorway and I try to yell but I'm punched in the gut, I double up sick for breath, and Jeremy's screaming and I can't yell, can't speak. Now Jeremy's running and big Chuck with his pony tail flapping grabs him and shoves him inside the house and slams the door, and Jeremy's yelling and I reach for Chuck's shirt and Chuck turns, and his face is almost calm, deadpan, and I grunt "Leave him alone, please, you're scaring him, talk to *me*," and he takes aim with his fist, I can see it *coming* for god sakes, and I back up and jab out and keep my hands out, but that's a joke, it doesn't do a thing, his fist smashes through my hands and catches me in the jaw and I'm on the floor, trying to shake my head clear and I yell, "Chuck, talk to me!—Jeremy, get to the Warners'—Chuck, come on, let's talk. This has nothing to do with the boy. Come on, some big fighter, scaring a kid, talk to *me*. You want Kerry's telephone number? Is that what you want?"

Jeremy tries to get around him, Chuck grabs him with one hand and slaps him across the face and now I'm half crazy, I'm screaming, I make a rush at him and I'm smashed back against a table, and now Chuck has Jeremy by the shirt and he half-drags, half-carries him into the bathroom and slams the door. He can't lock it, but Jeremy stays put, and I'm flashing possibilities, the window of the bathroom is fixed, he can't open it to get out, maybe he can smash the glass but how—how fast enough?

And Chuck's back; before he can grab me again I get to my feet, bruised, dazed, buzzing like I'm on a drug, talking quietly now, talking, talking to calm him down, "Okay, you and me, Chuck, we'll work it out, I guess it's been hard on you, I'm sure we can work this thing out, don't ruin your life, it's not worth it, Chuck—"

He's not listening. He's got a tall brass candlestick in his hand, my family's old candlestick, and I think for the first-time, He's going to kill me, kill *us*. Because the candlestick weighs more than a hammer, one swing at my head from a guy like this, big as this, crazy, would cave in my skull, I open my hands and say, "You just tell me what you want, Chuck, and I'll do it."

"Yeah," he says. "You bet you will. You will."

"I will. What the hell, you just let me make sure my boy's okay, I'll tell you, I'll do whatever you want, okay? Let me get him out of here, no use scaring a kid, right? You want Kerry's number, I've got the number of the shelter, I'm sure you can get to talk to her in a few minutes. I'm sure she's ready to talk to you."

"You're full of shit." Chuck sits on the living room

sofa, my mother's old sofa made for a New York living room, not a big open-plan room like this with barn-board walls. He waves me into a chair. "My brother tried this the nice way, now you've got me, and if you want to come out of this alive, you bring that whore out here. I don't want shit to do with her, I want my kid. You want *your* kid? Then I want *my* kid."

"I get you—I'd get her out here, but she has no car. We can see her in town, all right? Three miles down the road, Green River."

"I want her here. We'll go get her if we have to. You call that whore. If I don't get my child, you don't get yours. You see how it is?"

"Maybe I couldn't see what you've been going through," I say. "Tell me the story. I want to hear your side. Your brother said I didn't know the real story. What's the real story? You tell me. Wait a minute," I say. "I've got an idea. Your brother's got some good sense, he's on your side. Let's call Patrick."

"You want the real story?" he says. "The real story is, you're going to get them out here, I'm going to take my little boy back."

"Don't you need to get him through the courts? What good if you take him and you're busted on breaking a restraining order? You can get a year in jail in Massachusetts. Think about it. I'm not saying you're wrong. Maybe you *ought* to take him. I don't know. Tell me the story."

"You want me to bust your head open?"

"Honest to God, I don't know her number." I hear myself whining, and I know that whining's wrong, cringing won't work, Chuck's the kind of guy sees a dog cringe he'd kick its head open. "I'll get to her. I'm not allowed to know the number. But I can call the women's center, Kerry'll get back to me." I go to the wall phone in the kitchen, I find the number and call. It's an emergency, I say. I need to reach Kerry Latrice. A volunteer says she'll try to get in touch. Is Ronnie Gordon around? Or Stephanie Hirsch? Really, this is an emergency. Neither of them are there, but the woman on the phone says she'll do her best. Please, I say. Please.

"You see I'm trying," I say. "Now can I go into the bathroom and comfort Jeremy? He must be awful scared."

"You sit down. You can call to him, tell him you're okay."

So I do, I yell, "Jeremy, we'll be okay, you hear? This man just wants to find his little boy. Don't worry. Just sit down on the floor of the closet in there. You hear me? Jeremy? *Jeremy?*"

"Uh huh."

"The closet."

"Okay. The closet."

There's no basement in this house; it's built on a crawl space. And the entrance to that crawl space is in the bathroom closet, and I'm praying Jeremy understands. You have to lift up a section of the plywood floor of the closet. I listen, but I hear nothing. "I understand," I say to Chuck. "You don't see yourself as an abuser—you see yourself as saving your child. Is that it? Tell me."

"Why doesn't she call?"

"She may not be home. Give her time."

"I'm taking Andrew out of there."

"Okay. Okay. I guess she's terrible for him?"

As Chuck talks he's slapping the candlestick against his palm for emphasis. "All she has to do is claim I abuse her—all she has to *do*—and goddamned Massachusetts keeps me away from my own kid. Somebody with a pussy, everybody bows down and nobody looks. I've seen that bitch with my own eyes twist his little fingers until he's screaming, I've seen her kick him off the bed when he comes in, middle of the night. My brother's a lawyer, he can't do a goddamned thing. *I* can. You understand me?"

"I understand you. But why like this? You can't stay on the run all your life."

"You don't think I can disappear? I've got my ways. You just get that woman out here or you're dead. And your fucking kid's dead. I don't play around. I'm like unstoppable, fucking unstoppable, you believe it, because I don't care, I mean, if I have to kill her, I'll kill her. I have to kill you, I'll kill you. The way they treat men nowadays, woman opens her mouth and the cops come down on him. I'm like *in the old days*, y'know what I'm saying? I'm no pussy licker, they're gonna have to kill me to stop me. I'm a one-man army. I'm like in the old days, I'm telling you. You and that big fucker thought you could stop me with a beating? Bull*shit* you can stop me."

"I wouldn't try to stop you. I'm not brave, I'm no fighter."

"You? You're a piece of shit like most of them these days. A piece of Jew shit. You think I'm gonna trust the courts? The judges are all pussy-whipped. You ought to hear my brother on the subject. A woman feels like kicking a man out and taking over a house, she just calls the cops and says he's beating her up, and he's *out* of there. What chance do I have in the courts these days? My brother says, not so long ago, a child was the father's property. The woman takes off, fuck her, she loses the child. Not now. Man loses everything *and* has to pay for losing besides."

I shake my head, as if agreeing that there's no justice for men these days. I hear noises from the bathroom. Chuck hears them, too. He gestures with his head. "It's just Jeremy walking around," I say. I call out, "Don't worry, Jeremy . . . . Chuck—listen, you want a beer? I think I've got one cold beer."

"I drank it."

"I've got a couple more in the pantry. You want a beer while you're waiting?"

"Sure."

Now I've got him talking. He follows me and says, "All the time I've been working for my father, I've been putting away a lot of money. For *him* I sell beer. You know that?"

I know but I don't say. "You distribute?"

"Yeah, for him I distribute beer. German beers, Irish. For myself I distribute other stuff. I don't mind telling you—I'll be out of here, I've got it arranged. I'll disappear real fine and permanent. Andrew and me will be a long way away."

The phone rings, I pick it up in the kitchen. Chuck's behind me.

"Kerry," I say. "Listen, something's come up, Kerry. Can you and Andrew get a taxi out here right away? I'll pay for the ride. Like, right away. We have to deal with something." And I hang up fast, before Chuck can listen in and find out that it's Frank, Frank Polidori, and Frank's asking, "You got troubles over there? Dave? What's happening? Dave?" I hang up and go into the pantry for a beer and from the tool shelf just above I take a utility knife, its pointed blade—a heavy razor blade—retracted, and slip it into my pocket. I pray to God he doesn't see. When I turn around, he's not there, I'm thinking, *Jeremy*, I call, "Chuck, here's your beer. *Chuck?*"

And yes, Chuck is heading for the bathroom. The candlestick's still in his hand. The phone rings again, and I take it in the living room and this time it *is* Kerry, and I say, "Kerry, I told you to take a taxi, I'm serious what I said to you a minute ago, I want you to come out here by taxi, and I'll pay for the ride, there's a guy out here you need to see, okay?" And she says, "What are you talking about?" And I say, "No, no—don't *worry* about the money, I'll pay when you get here." I hang up.

Now Chuck is banging on the bathroom door, because Jeremy's got the hook latched, and Chuck's yelling, "Open this fucking door!" And nothing happens and he pops the screw-eye with one thrust of his shoulders and I'm there and Jeremy's gone. He turns around and grabs me by the throat, "Where'd he go, that little fucker, where'd he go?"

"I don't know. Maybe the window? Listen, he's got nothing to do with this, I'm doing just what you asked, right?"

But anybody can see the window's a fixed pane and intact—he starts looking around and in the closet he finds the corner of the carpeting peeled back and looks at the plywood and kicks at it and says, "You! Open this. I want him.

Open this or I'll fucking kill you and burn this house down. You hear me?" I shrug, I bend down and pull upon the square of plywood and open the little space where the joists have been framed specially to give about thirty inches of space, and he says, "You get me a flashlight."

He grabs my arm and pulls it up behind my back and I lead him into the kitchen and take a flashlight off the wall and he smacks me on the chin with the back end and I know I'm bleeding and it scares me, afraid the blood will give him license for more, and he holds me up and half-drags me back to the bathroom, it's like when my father would tug me back to the scene of a crime—something I spilled, something I broke—and Chuck says, "You first, you get down there," and I do what he says, I wriggle down and I'm on my hands and knees on the polyethylene sheets we laid over the gravel, and I can't see a thing. It's damp; there's grit under my hands—gravel, fragments of dried cement. I feel a piece of wood: it's a two-foot section of two-by-six, and I grasp it.

Slowly my eyes begin to adjust. Chuck wriggles through the hole that's almost too small for him and blocks all the light down here but from the tiny slits where the foundation is vented; turning, I see Jeremy crouching by the cement block foundation for the fireplace and I think of Gabriella's daughter, Sara, whom I never knew, and my stomach turns over. Wildly, I wave Jeremy around to the other side where he can't be seen. I've got a few seconds while Chuck won't be able to see me without the flashlight. I think, he's so big he could never catch me down here! But suppose he really burned the house down. I know he would.

I'm holding the two-by-six in my left hand, the utility knife in my right, and with my thumb I push up the blade as far as it goes and I wait. I can hardly breathe, but I'm judging my chances, I'm no knife fighter, I need a lucky stroke to his throat or I'm dead. I get just one try—if I'm lucky—and there's no stepping back, it's not like dreams where you can play the same terror over and over until it comes out right.

His boots are down on the polyethylene, and his shoulders are squeezing through, and suddenly he stops. We must both be hearing the same thing, the sound of the front door opening, the creak of boards—footsteps. I hope to God it isn't Kerry, because I don't think for a minute he'll just take Andrew away. I'm afraid he'd take the kid and leave a slaughter and try to cover his tracks with a fire. I look up to where his bulk fills the hole hoping for a slice at his throat, but his shoulders and neck and head are still above the flooring, and I look at his legs, like small tree trunks, and I imagine under the chino cloth the great artery in the inner thigh and even if I could coldly kill I know I'd never find it.

He starts to lift himself and it comes to me, I make a rush at him and smash him hard as I can in the groin with the two-by-six, but the pants hold back some of the blow, he twists and kicks and I hit again, and now I'm after him with the blade, and I rip the pants and draw blood but it's nothing, and he raises himself, he mumbles down into the hole, "Oh, yes, I'll kill you, I'll kill you later," and now I hear a voice, Frank's voice, I can't get the words, and Chuck is shouting, and I hiss, "Jeremy, stay there," and quick, silent as I can be, the blood thumping in my chest, I lift myself up into the bathroom closet with blade open and in my left hand the piece of two-by-six.

The bathroom is to one side of the large living room, and I poke my head out enough to see to the front door, and there's Frank with a shotgun, standing ready, and Chuck walks past the swing and into the room, saying calmly to Frank, "What the hell *you* doing? My buddy and I have a little disagreement, what the hell you doing with a gun, you could hurt somebody—" and I yell "Watch him, Frank, he's crazy!" And Chuck keeps coming, palms spread wide but coming, and Frank says, "You better stay right there, you stop now!"—and suddenly Chuck dives I swear six feet through the air at Frank's legs and he's underneath the gun and the gun is up in the air and clatters over the floor and now I'm after him, and I think about using the knife but I just can't, I change hands and retract the blade and swing the board across his shoulders and he reaches out and grabs my ankle, and I'm down hard, he's got my arm behind my back and pain shrieks through my shoulder and he pulls me to my feet and Frank gets up to help but Chuck has a knife to my chest, I feel the point pricking me through my shirt, he's cutting into me, just a little, I can feel the wet, and crazy-stupid I think, *Goddamn, a new shirt*—

He has me around the neck and, walking backwards towards the door, he drags me with him, drags me out the door and down the walk, and Frank has the gun, he's out on the deck with the gun but it's useless, and I yell, "Get Jeremy, he's down in the crawl space—"

Chuck rips at my arm and jerks me past him so that the trees and the house spin around me and I'm sure my arm is going to snap but it doesn't, and he shoves me into his car and slams his fist into my jaw and now I don't know what's happening and we're moving, the car is backing down the driveway and swings around and peels rubber down the road towards Green River.

I stay sunk down in my seat, silent, not wanting to give him fuel for his rage; I keep my eyes open so I'll know where he's heading. The muffler rattles and growls. On the leg nearer me his pants are dark with blood, drying I think, the cut I made must have been nothing much. My own chest is sticking to my shirt, the blood drying. I slip my hand into my pocket—no utility knife. We head down the rough, patched road and skid onto the secondary, and I'm hoping he'll take me all the way into town, where maybe I can open the door and jump or at least yell, but he speeds up, slows down, speeds up, slows down, he's looking for something, and a mile further on he brakes hard and turns down an old logging road. Either he'll dump me or he'll kill me, and I don't have much hope he'll dump me. But maybe I can jump and get away in these woods, I know just where we are, there's a waterfall further on, we come here summers for a swim, maybe I can lead him towards the swamp below the falls and lose him, because I know the way across. And I'm wearing hiking boots but he's in fancy cowboy boots etched with swirls. But I reach for the door handle and at once the heel of his big hand cracks me across the throat and I'm gasping and tasting puke and the car lurches and bounces to a stop at a big log that somebody's set in the way.

"Now," he says, "you get on the phone to the women, tell them we want to meet Andrew and her in town. We just want to talk, you tell them. And you sound mellow and convincing. You really fucked up back there. You bring in this guy with a gun? Oh, listen!"

He's really crazy—call from the woods? But now I see the car phone. At the same time, at his feet I see some kind of ugly gun, machine pistol, assault rifle, whatever you call it, something unsleek and vicious. I sag down in the seat, my throat hurts, I figure I'm dead, what the hell, I close my eyes, I shake my head, "What's the use, Chuck? You're the one who fucked up. You think I can get Kerry to meet you anywhere now? Best thing you can do now is try to get away."

"I told you," he sighs, like a parent sighing over something bad a kid's done for the tenth time, "I'm not somebody you can stop. I *told* you, I'm like the old days. I can kill you. But *that's* not all. I'll kill your little Jew kid, I know where his mother lives. You don't think I'm gonna kill him if I don't get my kid back? Oh! Listen!" And he raises his palms and looks up to heaven as if to say, *How can I explain this to him?*—as if moved by some moral force, as if he were teaching me a sad but necessary lesson—and he clips me with a short snap of a punch into my cheekbone, and another, no windup at all but each one knocking my head back and blackness, lights in my head, a slap and I open my eyes and he says, "Now you call, all right?"

So I reach for the phone but he shakes his head. "Just dial. It's on speaker phone. Dial, you fuck."

I push buttons, I get information, I call the Center for Women in Transition. "Hello, it's David Rosen again. Who is this I'm speaking to?"

"It's Ronnie."

I can hear in her voice the anxiety that tells me she knows something of what's going on. "Ronnie . . . . Hi, Ronnie," I say. "I'm with Chuck Ahearn, he wants to meet with his wife, he wants to see Kerry and Andrew, he says he wants to talk with them."

"You can't talk?" she says.

"Sure, I can talk, I'm in his car, he's right here with me." At this, Chuck pounds me in the ear, so now all I can hear is a high ringing, but he's talking politely to Ronnie Gordon, and his face is calm and I hear him laugh, and I start to pick up words.

" . . . see what I'm saying? So there's no problem, okay?"

And Ronnie says, "Well, that's fine, I'm sure Kerry would be happy to meet with you, as long as the situation feels secure, and I'm wondering, perhaps down here at our offices—?"

But he's laughing, "Are you serious? You really think I'm going down there?"

My nose is stuffed, my ear is still ringing. I try to collect myself for a run.

"You let me talk to my wife on the phone, you just don't come between a man and his wife, we've had our troubles, but I think she'll see things my way, I think she'll come through for me."

Ronnie says, "Of course, I think that's a good start, I'll get her on the phone to you. Just a minute." Can the police trace a mobile phone? I'm thinking of Jeremy. As for me, I figure by the time they get out here they'll find me dead. This death: it's not the kind of death I'd imagined, giving me time to leave papers and instructions, time to think about God.

Chuck is waiting, and I think how terrible it is I don't even remember the last prayer a Jew is to say, and I think what a terrible Jew I've been, doing so little with this soul. I'm not thinking about what happens after I die but what I've been leaving undone with my soul like beautiful hi-tech equipment I've let sit around unused when it had such possibilities, and while Chuck is waiting I'm praying for Jeremy, but I think, No, that's wrong, that's not what I should be praying, and I say the *Shema*, I say in my head, *Shema Yisrael Adonoi elohenu, Adonoi echod. Hear O Israel, the Lord our God, the Lord is One.* And I say just that over and over in my head because it's all I know, and I hear Kerry's voice,

"Hello, Chuck," she says in her little-girl voice, the sweet, totally false voice she sometimes gets into. "I'm sure you don't mean bad, I'm sure you mean fine. I'd be happy to talk to you, you know I would, maybe we could meet in Green River, there's a place David knows, the Cornucopia. You want to meet Andrew and me there?"

Chuck just laughs, her ruse is so transparent, and I say to him, "I think you don't really expect to get Andrew. Do you? No. Not anymore. We're beyond that, aren't we?"

But Chuck wants to shut me up so he can talk, so he backhands me in the face. As I twist to avoid the blow, I feel something on my left side, my left thigh, and I know at once what it is—it's my utility knife, and I know what happened—when I couldn't get myself to use it back in the living room, I switched it into my left hand and unaware crammed it into my left hand pocket as I swung the two-by-six with my right hand. And so now I groan and double over to give myself a chance to slip it out, and the groaning makes Chuck lean forward towards the car telephone, and he's saying, "Now listen up, Kerry. You remember a place we went on vacation a couple of months back—don't say it, keep your mouth closed, just *Do you know?*"

"Sure, Chuck. I know."

"Remember where we went for a picnic? Remember? That's the place. I'll meet you and Andrew there in two days. Noon. You bring nobody else, and *don't worry*. You know me, baby. You remember what we did on that picnic? You remember? Noon, Sunday—will you do that?"

"Sure, Chuck."

"You *do* it."

"I'll do it, Chuck."

"You want me to send you money to rent a car?"

"I've got the money, honey."

And now I've got the utility knife in my left hand and I groan and twist and move it behind my back into my right. *Can I do this? Really? Am I doing this?*—but these are just words like a mantra to keep me from thinking while with no need for words my fingers press the blade forward and I use the full swing of my right arm to rip the blade deep as I can get it against his neck, into his thick-muscled neck, by the throat moving with his words and for an instant he doesn't *know*, the blood finds the slice before I've even turned to grab the door handle and before he turns to grab at me and I hear behind me a bellow and a roar so I know his windpipe's not cut, and I wait for the noise of the machine pistol and for the end of everything and I'm running for cover, through the trees now and down towards the swamp, still not turning to look, and now, behind a huge old maple, one of a line of sugar maples on what was once a road by a farm, I grab the tree bark and crouch down like a child playing a game and I hear a high-pitched howling and there's Chuck with his hands to his neck full of blood and his shirt soaked in blood and he rips off his shirt and ties it around his neck.

The blood isn't spurting, but it's oozing and dripping from the shirt onto his big chest, and he's got the gun and he doesn't see me and he must know he can't run with that wound and he's yelling, "Come here! Come here! You!"

"Use the phone!" I yell from behind the tree. "Tell them you're off Snowden Road!"

"What? What? What?"

"Off Snowden Road—tell them—a logging road to the waterfall!"

"What?"

"Throw the gun away. Throw the gun down and I'll come back."

For an instant he sees me. I get behind the tree—there's a noise like a chain saw and the branches and leaves crack and fall as he empties his gun into the woods. He's letting himself bleed, he's coming down into the trees, still shooting, and now I slip down to the ground and look for something to throw and find a rock and toss it a long way to make him think I'm somewhere else and I lie flat and bury myself under fallen leaves. If he comes this way, it's hopeless. I wait for footsteps or another blast from his gun but there's nothing—nothing for who knows how long—half a minute?—so I sit up and try to locate him.

There he is, down on one knee, no gun in his hand, trying to keep pressure on the wound. He looks like a fallen gladiator out of some Roman sculpture I must have seen. His chest is bloody, he looks as if he's meditating on something, and I run back, tree to tree, trying to see the gun. It's near him, and I wonder, Could this be a trick? But why would he imagine I'd come back? Why the fuck *am* I coming back? Let the bastard die! I hope he does die. I hope I can't do a thing for him; still, I find myself coming up through the trees, and I kick the gun out of the way and go after it and carry it back to the car, and he's howling again, and I yell, "Hello? Hello? Are you still there?"

"What's happening?" Ronnie asks. "Dave? Are you all right?"

"Get an ambulance down here. It's off Snowden Road up in the hills, you know the old waterfall? The logging road to the falls, the guy's dying, he may be past saving, he's bleeding to death, so get someone out here. I'll keep the phone line alive. If we get cut off, I don't know the number."

I'm out of the car and running back to Chuck Ahearn, who's on his knees now and dripping into the leaves, and I pull him up against me, my chest to his back, and put direct pressure on the slice, a lot of pressure, but the blood is running down my arms and all over my shirt. He's wriggling now, and I say to him, "Be still, goddamn you. You want to live, be still, I got to do this, you bleed much more, you're a dead man, can you hear me? Can you hear me?"

It seems he *can't* hear me. I'm slowing up the loss of blood, but I'm soaking, he's soaking, I know he's got just a few minutes and I know to do this, it's all I do know, I've got to keep up the pressure, and I hope it doesn't work, I hope he dies on me, but I keep up the pressure. I'm too far from the car to hear what's coming over the phone. Just noise. I'm getting tired, dizzy, I'm panting, wet from his blood and holding him up so the neck stays above the heart, I keep up the pressure, but it feels so long, and from far off I'm hearing a siren. I yell towards the phone, "I'm hearing a siren," but I'm sure the words are lost, and Chuck is so big it's almost impossible for me to keep him from sagging down. So big—like some bloodied warrior in *The Iliad*. I have to keep pressing my chest against his wet back and the weight is exhausting, and it feels slippery, horrible, but not just that—eerie and intimate—to be this close to him, smelling his sweat. His hair has come loose from whatever tied it; it's sopping up the blood. I'm covered with his hair. It's like some perverted *pietà*.

Now I'm hearing the vehicle jerking up the rough road, revving its engine, I hear the scream of its siren, unnecessary now, and I see the rescue vehicle from Green River and I start yelling, "Here! Here!" And I remove the hand I've kept pressed over the hand against the wound, I wave, and there are two men running, one holding a stretcher, one a medical kit, and I drop back and away and stagger to my feet and go slump against a tree while they work on him. They start some intravenous solution, I close my eyes.

Eight

For a few minutes that Friday afternoon, I rested against a tree, one of the trees that had protected me. I'll never be able to look at an autumn woods with aesthetic sadness again; I'll never think of it as a place where I used to "clean out my head" while smoking hash or tripping on mescaline. I'll remember the noise, the furious ripping of branches and the whoosh of leaves; tree trunks will be friends that kept me alive. I asked the policeman who stayed with me to tape the "crime scene"—another went along with Chuck in the ambulance—whether Jeremy was all right and could we go back home? Then I rested, eyes closed, until the ambulance went off, siren howling again, and the policeman from Green River had locked and sealed with police tape Chuck Ahearn's Camaro and turned to me and stood there waiting. Those few minutes I rested as I've never rested even maybe after making love. I held my soul in my two hands and promised to take care of it.

But already I was growing apprehensive. Because it felt so *good*. Driving back to my house with Officer Rivers, I saw myself a man in the company of men, and I felt that I'd done well and that he—they, the men—were *proud* of me, and that's when I winced, that's when my stomach began to turn over with nausea, as I remembered, as I remember now, the joy I felt, the satisfaction when I squeezed the utility knife and swung my arm and Chuck's blood filled the razor slice in his neck and I grabbed for the door handle—joy even if it would probably be the last thing I'd ever know. I understood what it meant to become your enemy.

Now my rest sagged into exhaustion, so that by the time Officer Rivers helped me from the car, I was barely able to walk down the brick path to the deck where Frank, Sylvia and Russell Warner, Jeremy, were waiting. My shoulder was aching, my neck was sore. I saw Sylvia stroking

Jeremy's shoulders, and I could see he scarcely knew it, and he said, "You're all bloody, Dad!" I said, "It's *his* blood." Getting past the disgust he's always felt for blood, even for a little scrape, he hugged me and said, "You killed him? You *killed* him?" And, Jesus, I wanted to soften his eagerness and Officer Rivers said, "Well, the man may live, but your Dad cut him up pretty good." He grinned and patted Jeremy's head and I felt I was the hero of a John Wayne western.

The Warners, Frank, seemed to know already. Someone must have called the house. I thanked Frank for thinking to bring the Warners over. Jeremy hugged me around the hips, and worrying about Nancy I said, "Careful, honey, you don't want to get that nice shirt all bloody"—though it wasn't a nice shirt anymore. It was torn and filthy.

He wasn't listening. I started to cry. Sylvia touched my cheek with her palm and Russell patted my arm and Frank disappeared and came back with a glass of bourbon. I drank up and kept sobbing, and Jeremy, as if he were the parent, said, "Dad, it's okay, Dad."

"You must have been so scared, honey. Under the house in the dark like that. You must have been so scared."

"It's okay Dad it's *okay*, Dad."

Later on, I washed, took some painkillers and drove Jeremy to his mom's and dropped him off at the door without talking, and I knew it *wasn't* okay and I went down to the police station in Green River to make a statement and answer questions, then up to the county hospital. There was a reporter there from the local paper, a TV newsperson, a woman with hair that looked like it was made of filaments of yellow plastic; I told them what happened. From the hospital I talked to Kerry, to Ronnie, to Frank.

It was clear from the first that Chuck was going to live. A few more minutes and he would have died. If he hadn't had a car phone, he'd be dead for sure. But once they'd stabilized him with a saline solution and sewed him up, he was in no danger. I wish he'd died, though I had to try to save him. I wish he'd died, but I sat in the anteroom waiting to make sure he'd live. After awhile I drove home, took more pills, fell into a deep, night-long sleep.

Now, alone in this house, days later, I still need music playing and too many lights. How distrustful and snobbish I've always been when people tell me about their "post-traumatic shock"—except after a war or a terrible loss, a loss like Gabriella's—but I suppose that *is* one way of labelling it when I fall into my bouts of weeping. What comes to the eyes behind my eyes is Jeremy: Jeremy dragged away, Jeremy underneath the house, crouching next to the foundation for the fireplace, Chuck's big legs closing off the light as they descend into the crawl space.

I call Jeremy two, three times a day. And so I have to talk to Nancy. Is he still dangerous, she asks, is it true he's out on bail? Suppose he comes here and finds Jeremy?

I don't tell her he warned me that afternoon he'd do that very thing. Probably rant. But I've notified the police. And every day, going to work and coming from work and in the middle of the day I drive down the street past their house. No point, really. The police have told me that Chuck is charged with assault with a deadly weapon and may be charged with kidnapping or attempted murder; he's out on bail because the family has agreed to put him in a psychiatric hospital for observation. Still, I watch the house.

On Wednesday I drive out to the woods by the waterfall. The Camaro is gone. The ground is trampled, I see where chunks have been removed from a couple of trees, cut out, I suppose, to show where bullets embedded themselves. I grow tired right away.

When I call Jeremy, when I drop in to say hello, he seems cool to me. It scares me. Molly, his teacher, calls and says, "He's doing all right in school, I thought you'd want to know. He's a kind of hero, you know . . . . We talked yesterday. Over lunch. That's what's prompted this call, David. He's proud of you one minute, angry the next—that you got involved in the first place."

"That's his mother's teaching."

"Maybe that's her *formulation*, but it's his own anger."

"I see."

"But as I say, the next minute—"

"He's proud."

"Of course. Well. You saved his life. Did you read the article in the *Globe*? We've all been following the story, you know." Molly laughs.

I know. More people than have ever read my articles now read articles *about* me. Gar calls. I get calls from friends I rarely see, friends who faded after Nancy and I split up. Barbara Johnson telephoned from Boulder. I'm a kind of hero in the women's community in Green River, so that I can't go to Cornucopia for lunch, can hardly walk through the halls at school without someone I don't know coming up to me.

Or *not* coming up—just looking at me strangely. I'm almost a hero, but I'm looked at as if I've stepped over some boundary, become one of those people seen after tragedy—car crash or serial killing—on the six o'clock news. My colleagues stop talking when I walk into the department lounge. Then they smile; they make some joke. When we pass in the hall, they drop their eyes. I spook them out. Leonard Noble called me in, congratulated me, made a joke about not knowing he had a street fighter on staff—and hasn't spoken to me since.

I have lunch today at Cornucopia with Ronnie Gordon. She waves me over, and I realize I've met her a number of times at parties, at political meetings. It's a small place, Green River and the hill towns. And it turns out Ronnie's the mother of one of Jeremy's soccer buddies. She's a single parent, and I like her bright eyes and her sense of fun and her lean, athletic body under the plaid shirt. She's not picture-pretty, but something's tough-beautiful about her face, and I start my imagining, the way I always do, until she tells me about her "partner," a colleague of mine at the community college—a young woman. But I like Ronnie right away, and I don't mind hearing from her that what I did was appreciated. "And you're a peaceful man," she says. "You remember, we were on that anti-war march together a few years ago? After the attack on Panama?"

And she names me as a defender of peace but I'm inside the moment in Chuck's car when he leaned forward to softsoap Kerry

. . . and I felt the terror and the joy waiting in my hand and I anticipated the sweet stroke deep into the neck flesh and the flesh opening and the blood filling the wound and then it *was* like that, *better*, the delicious wrath of my arm and my scream, and in my dream last night I saw the blood fill the car until we were drowning in blood. It wasn't Chuck—as on that afternoon Chuck himself wasn't Chuck but a phantom, a spectre, all the enemies of my life and of *our* life bleeding and feeding me with joy.

"You're one of the good people in the valley. I've looked at our books at Women in Transition, and you've always been a contributor, always been an ally. It makes me feel real good, you know? Kerry wants to see you and thank you, but she doesn't want to bug you. It must have been so terrible. In a way, you were experiencing what it means to be a battered woman. You know what I'm saying? It's good to feel there are peaceful men, you're a peaceful man . . . . Do you know what you want to order?"

On the way back to the college I have to pull my car over and throw up my good lunch.

All weekend and all week I've been waiting for the call from Nancy. She asks to meet me tonight in the Green River Cafe.

I get there early and sip my way through most of a double bourbon by the time Nancy gets there, in a flurry, telling me as she hangs up her coat how much design work she's been getting, how exciting that is, how satisfying, what a mixed blessing. "I never stop running. Thank goodness Jeremy is such an easy kid."

"He is. Has he been having nightmares?"

"Once." She takes up the glass of wine the waitress has placed in front of her. We're both silent. I'm waiting for her. "You don't know how it's been, though."

"How has it been?"

"We could have lost Jeremy. He could be dead."

I nod. It's true.

"Something could still happen."

I owe it to her not to contradict, not to get defensive, to let her talk. I just nod. It's true.

"You know I don't blame you. You maybe saved his life."

"I think maybe. Ahearn wasn't *out of control*, you know. That was the most frightening thing, that he was *in* control. If he killed, it wouldn't be in a rage. He *uses* rage, oh, but he's spookier than that."

"It must have been awful, wondering if he might decide to kill you."

"To kill *Jeremy*: that was the worst of course. That was the nightmare."

"*You did well.*"

"I feel okay about what I did. You know?"

"Well, of course."

"Still . . . I've been pretty depressed. I mean I get into bouts of crying. I guess . . . I've been feeling ashamed."

"Ashamed? Why? You don't feel you had the right?—"

"I *do*. I *had* to. It's not that. It's not what I *did*, Nancy." Now, over my empty glass, in the booth at the Green River *Cafe* for godsakes, with the TV over the bar barking about a football replay, I have to keep from weeping again and my shoulders are shaking, and from across the table Nancy puts her hands around my bowed neck and holds me in her cool hands, and I'm shaking my head, I don't know why I'm nearly crying, so stupid, but it's partly, I guess, that Nancy knows me for such a long time—I don't mind if she sees. I mind and I don't mind. "It's not what I did, it's how I *felt*."

"Oh, David. Don't expect so much of yourself. So you were afraid?"

"Yes, sure. God. I was terrified. But that's not it—" I hunch forward so nobody else can possibly hear "—it's that I *loved* it, that moment, nearly killing him, *trying* to kill him, it was such a goddamn joy. I've thought of doing therapy, but you know how I feel about that. I mean, I believe in it for everybody else."

"Well, you've always been an angry man."

I look at her. What do I say to that?

"Does that surprise you? Oh, David. Please! I know you pretend to be innocuous—"

"I wouldn't put it like that. *Innocuous!*—"

"—I'm sorry, I'm sorry. I'm putting it badly. You know—a gentle person. And whatever happened between us—you *are* a good man. I know that. I don't mean you're not. I just mean—the joy you say you felt—well, I'm simply not surprised. But look—so what? So *what*, David? Really, you expect yourself to be a saint! Don't you know the Church doesn't make a practice of naming Jewish saints?" She takes my hand. She squeezes my hand.

I try to laugh.

"And I don't blame you—I mean for what happened—*or* for what almost happened. Jeremy will get over it. And he's terribly proud of you." She sits back again. "But David—"

"You're still scared for him. I know. Of course."

"— David, please, I want you to let him to stay with me for awhile. All right? Will you do that? He has to go back to your house, I *want* him to, but I'd like it if—he didn't stay over. All right?"

"I expected you to say that."

She nods. "And are you upset? Just for awhile. Doesn't it seem reasonable? To let him feel a little secure?"

It *does* seem reasonable. I think of Gar asking Gabriella to keep Sara away from Sojourner House, and when it was too late for Sara, Gar asking Gabriella to let Jenny come live with him. It *seems* reasonable. Until Chuck Ahearn is put away for years. *If* he ever is. And even then—will Jeremy ever feel safe in our house—his and mine—again?

I shrug. My hands open up as if I'm offering her the whole world.

"If only you'd never taken that girl in!"

I see it slipping away, the way we've lived, Jeremy and I, bleeding away—our two weeks and two weeks, back and forth. I see joint custody slipping away, I see the very arrangement I would have fought through the courts—Jeremy part of Nancy's new family—hers for the asking now. She *is* asking; I can't refuse.

She keeps her hand on mine. She says, "You're going to see Jeremy as much as you want, David."

"Look, Nancy—tomorrow's Saturday. I'll talk it over with him tomorrow. Okay?"

You've always been an angry man, she said.

But no!—that was my father, my poor ignorant father, the man I never wanted to be. How he yelled! I locked the door to my room, and he slammed his fist against it, enough to crack the paint but not the wood—great restraint, really, because he could have busted that door easily—and I took a pillow or my own arm between my teeth and bit down and squeezed all my anger into a ball and stuck it away inside my throat. I swallowed his failure and his rage.

Now, I put Mahler's Sixth on the stereo to chase out demons. I stand at the entrance to Jeremy's bedroom and my eyes well up, and that gets me furious, that I *do* that to myself, it's such a set up. But still I just stand there and look at the slippers at the side of the bed, the Beatles poster, a seagull and whale mobile left over from Jeremy at five when we took him to the Cape and he threw up all over the whale-watch boat but still wanted that mobile.

I turn away.

I don't know if I'm going to be able to stand this.

Out of the blue, Gar calls. I tell him what's happened, I tell him about Jeremy. He says, "You want me to talk to your wife?"

"What good?" I say. "When I believe she's right. Of all people," I say, "you're equipped to understand Nancy."

"It's not the same thing."
"Thank God it's not the same thing."

Frank calls me, he calls me again when I say no the first time, to have dinner with him and Nora tonight. I'm lousy company, but I drive over with a *challah*. Holding the bumpy, soft bread in the paper bag, walking down the path to Frank's house, turning myself into someone who can speak to friends, I'm nudged by something, and it comes to me—the moment in the woods I regretted not taking good care of my soul. A *challah*—that's all my *shabbat* amounts to. That and Nora's "We're grateful for being here and for our food. Amen." I clear my throat and add, "Blessed art Thou, O Lord, who brings forth bread from the earth."

It's Nora's once-a-week turn to cook: she's made squash and onions, noodles with melted cheese. Kind of bland, but she's learning. I shake in the Tabasco. Turns out I'm glad I've come, even though I'm in for harassment tonight: I've told them about Jeremy.

Frank sits shaking his head. "I call it masochism," he says, his mouth full, half choking on his food to get it down so he can talk. "And Nancy! Nancy—I do think she's really worried—sure—but *also* really taking advantage. You know what I mean?"

"Why do you say *masochism*, Frank?"

"Yeah. Sure. Masochism. Masochism."

"You mean I'm letting her get away with it out of guilt? I'm paying myself back for the victory?"

"Victory. Some victory! You're alive. Jeremy's alive. That's a victory, it is!—but it's not like winning something. Well, I guess it *is* like winning something. But Dave!—"

"Sure. It depresses the hell out of me. He won't live with me for awhile."

"For awhile."

"But look—"

"Suppose the bastard came back? All right. Okay. But I'm asking, please, will you set appropriate fucking limits around this? Get your lawyer into the act. She wants something. Nancy. Wants to keep hold of Jeremy for now. I suggest getting her to sign a statement saying this is no precedent for custody."

"Okay. That's a good idea. I'll think about it." Frank must be seeing something in my face. He shuts up. We just eat.

Nora puts down her fork. "Dad? You mean Jeremy won't be living with Dave anymore at all? Daddy?"

"Just for now," I say.

"If he plays it smart, just for now," Frank says.

"That's terrible," she says. And Frank looks glum.

I know Frank's thinking about Nora, about himself and Nora, just as I always think of Jeremy whenever Frank hears from Meg again and starts to worry. Suppose Meg walks back in the way she walked out, finishes law school and walks in and wants Nora.

"How's the house over on Mill Race Road going?"

"We're really pumping to get them in by Thanksgiving. You want to come by in the morning, see where we've gotten? I'd like to show it to you."

"I'm going for a hike with Jeremy."

He nods. "Good luck, Dave," he says, so damned serious—none of his usual edge.

Later, when Frank's put Nora to bed, he waves at me to follow him down the stairs to the family room where we play pool. "You sit down," he says. He stands there half a minute not looking at me. Now he starts, "Dave, this is not negotiable. You listen. I'm giving you my shotgun. Not negotiable. Now, stop," he says, as he sees me getting up, "you stop! I know what you think about guns but shut up. I don't give a shit it makes you feel bad."

"Frank."

"You owe it to me as a friend. I don't want to see you lying dead or Jeremy lying dead and I'll think, 'Christ, I should have forced the issue.'"

"You don't get it. It's not ideological, it's just a pain in my guts. I've always felt the same. Vietnam days, the same. I just want out."

"But suppose you can't have *out*."

"I'd rather die than kill, Frank."

"Oh, cut out the melodrama. That's not the thing, kill or die. Would you rather pick up a gun or have Jeremy killed? That's the thing. Okay? No more talk." He goes into the storeroom. I can hear him unlock a drawer and he comes back with his big, double-barrelled twelve-gauged shotgun, the gun Russell Warner admires so much, the gun with the two beautiful black steel barrels, side by side.

I let him hand it to me. I open my hands and shrug as if the gun were a complex new computer and I was computer-illiterate, or as if to say, *Who? Me? I don't fly jet planes.* And he waves my gesture away like a cloud of mosquitos and says, "Shut up. I've loaded it with double-ought. Now, that's overkill, you don't need that. It's what the cops use. Double-ought. You can blast the shit out of an animal with this," he says. "*Or* a person."

"Godforbid," I say.

"Yeah, godforbid. I say so, too! But this is what I've got. So be careful, Dave. It'll go right through walls, double ought. What I wish I had is a pump gun. I wish I could convince you to go out and buy one. All you need is the sound—chk-chk—scare the shit out of anyone. But this is what I've got. And I won't let you out of here without it. So look—it's easy. You ever use one of these suckers?"

"You know I haven't."

He gives me a lesson: How to break, drop in the cartridges, close the gun, how to support the gun when you point and fire. Again. How to break and load, how to how to point and fire. You don't aim, you point. Okay? How to take the recoil. Now he watches me load. I slip the release lever to one side. My fingers are shaky; does it show? It interests me that I'm already lightheaded, almost dizzy. He makes me remove the cartridges, load again.

"The two triggers are separate. You pull one, you pull the other. Or you use two fingers. It's pretty easy."

Now he takes the gun and examines it and hands it back, looking straight into my eyes. I look back, I won't turn away, but I hate the look, and the gun is terror in my hands, the heft thickens my fingers into dumb things. The beautiful, oiled, tooled stock and shining black barrels seem like icons of a foreign cult. But I think, *It's better to take the damned thing and put it on a shelf and not start an argument.*

On the way to my car, Frank shows me how to cradle the shotgun, barrels down and out. At the car he hugs me, a brother, and the hug seals something, a ritual of terrible manhood. False pretenses, I think, but I say nothing. He means the best.

"So good luck tomorrow," he says solemnly. "With Jeremy. Good luck."

I nod my thanks.

It's our mountain, the mountain with the lookout tower at the top—the hike I took with Gabriella.

The first time I took him here for a hike, I had to help him up boulders. We never made it to the tower; I carried him on my shoulders for a final half mile, then found a mossy bank by the stream for our picnic and we splashed, roaring, in the swirling spring stream and went home to Nancy. Jeremy must have been four or, no, *five*, because before that I'd never have tried the hike, and after that I couldn't have lugged him on my shoulder so far—and we wouldn't have had his mother to come home to.

I remember the two of us peeing into the stream.

I remember the Great Boat Race, empties from boxed drinks with twigs stuck in for masts.

Now the hike is easier for him than it is for me. We both carry day packs with our lunch. Like a symbol—that we *share* the load; as if to say, this problem isn't just my burden. Uch! I hate symbols. I teach my students to avoid talking about symbols, lest the difficult world dissipate into abstractions. When I start thinking *Symbols* this morning, it means I'm trying to transmute grief and pain into lofty words.

We both know we're not here for a walk.

I find it hard to breathe when I look at my son. My heart

keeps turning over in my chest; that's where the pang is, physically, I mean—no metaphor. Not in my stomach but in my chest. I try singing. Jeremy and I like to sing when we're hiking. He knows the words to songs from a dozen Broadway musicals made into movies. We watch them on video and sing along. Now I sing "Climb Every Mountain" from *The Sound of Music* but camp it, knowing we both hate that one. False feeling; Jeremy joins in and we belt it out with a lot of quavers in our voices. It helps. It doesn't help. I see Gabriella's eyes, I think of Sara and Jenny.

We cross the stream the first time, and Jeremy climbs down the bank of the stream into the nearly dry stone bed and, crouching, gets inside the culvert and yells to make the echo, and it's like there's a ghost under my feet, and I call, "Jeremy? Let's move on out." And he crawls through and comes up the bank behind and grins and says, "Here I am!"

Of course it makes me remember the crawl space and I wonder if he's re-enacting his terrible descent that afternoon. I say, "I'm surprised you dare get into such a cramped place. After having to hide under the house like that? Pretty gutsy, I'd say."

He shrugs my shrug. "Yeah, it was awful, I guess. But it was just a few minutes. I'm okay." He stands arms akimbo in the middle of the path, seeing something in my face. "No. Dad. I *am*."

"I believe you."

"I was upset I guess. At first. Now—I don't know."

"It seems like a story, a movie? Is that it, honey? Something that happened to someone else?"

"No."

He says it flatly not to leave me an opening to continue. I wait for him and slowly he comes to me, kicking at the stones and gravel over the culvert. I bend down onto one knee and give him a hug, and he hugs back—but as if humoring me. "I was really scared for us," I say.

Now Jeremy picks up a stone and throws it as far as he can down the wooded hillside, and I can hear it hitting the leaves. "He was really crazy. God, he was crazy!" And he throws another stone.

I throw a stone of my own.

"Mom's mad at you."

"For getting involved with Kerry?"

"Uh huh. She says you weren't careful, you got to be careful."

My breath sticks in my chest with anger. Anger at Nancy, even though I know he's only using his Mom as an excuse. "Careful? I know. For awhile—well, your Mom and I think maybe it's better if you stay with her all the time. Just for awhile."

Jeremy shrugs. I'm throwing stones, doing my best to keep my voice easy.

"Just for awhile," I say again.

After a time, he says, "What about my room and everything?"

"I don't mean you can't come over. It's just you can't stay over. Just for awhile."

He takes this in. He scuffs the gravel with the toe of his boot. Usually I'd tell him to stop ruining the leather. Now I say nothing. He says, "Mom's getting married."

"I know."

Now Jeremy turns away. I want to touch his shoulders, but I'm afraid. "Jeremy? Honey?" I stand next to him and I say, "Are *you* mad?" He shrugs, I say, "Hit my hand. You want to sock my hand?" I open my hand for him to hit. He shrugs, he shakes his head, now, half-heartedly, he swings at my hand, then he swings again, whole-heartedly this time, and again, again, and now he's really into it, and he's sobbing and hitting and he yells, "What'd you have to spoil everything? You bum, you bum, you!" It's a comic slur we use together, but it's never been said like this. I put my arms around him and say, "Honey, I know, I know."

He shakes his head. "You *don't* know. I peed in my underpants. In the crawl space, Dad, I peed in my pants, and Frank knew!"

"Oh, anyone might have done that. It was so scary."

"I wish you'd killed him, because now he's alive and Mom says if he's that crazy he could do anything."

"But he's a person. We don't kill people, do we? Anyway, he's in a mental hospital. He'll stay there or he'll be in prison. He won't bother anyone."

"How do you know?"

"I don't know . . . . I love you honey. I'll protect you if I can. That's all."

"I love you, Daddy." He clings to me. "I don't *want* not to live together."

"We'll spend lots of time together. You understand?"

"I hate Peter. He's stupid."

"You don't."

"Why did you have to divorce Mom, anyway?"

"I don't know." I straighten up and resettle the little daypack. "You ever ask Mom that?—Come on. We're going to get hungry and we're only halfway there."

"Yes." He's hiking alongside me now, not walking or trudging but taking long strides in a steady rhythm the way I've showed him.

"And?"

"She says you didn't get along. That doesn't mean anything."

"No. Well, it means we stopped being kind to one another, stopped believing in one another. It wasn't just your Mom, you know. Both of us, we weren't such good friends anymore. But I think—" I'm about to say, *I think we're better friends now that we're not married*, but I'm afraid he'll ask why then we don't get back together. So I say instead, "I think your Mom loves Peter a lot now. A-lot-a-lot. Do you like Peter okay?"

"He's okay."

"Good. It's just for awhile, I promise," I say. "I mean, I promise to make sure you come back to your room and everything soon. I'll never let you stay just with your Mom, your Mom and Peter, not in the long run. We're talking a month, maybe two, just until the crazy guy is locked away."

"I thought you said—"

"He *is*. Well, he's in a hospital. We'll see."

Now we hike silently. Chuck is in these woods, hiding

behind trees. My eyes are constantly searching for places to take cover: a bolder, a giant pine. At the top, we come out into the open, and Chuck dissolves, we look out at the valley, the valley opens up inside me, interior space I haven't felt for awhile.

We put down our packs and climb the fire tower. The iron stairs hum and vibrate under our feet. I see Jeremy's hands tighten on the railing. He doesn't look down. *There's nothing safe in the world,* I tell Nancy in my mind. Jeremy knocks at the trap door. It's the same young ranger. I say, "Hello again."

The young man looks up from his computer and smiles, then goes back to work on something. A report—or is he the next Jack Kerouac? He's got topographical maps laid out on the desk. I line one up, north to north. "See?" I point, as I always do. There's our house, not much bigger than a fly across a room. Seen through the ranger's field glasses, I can see our front wall of glass, even the native-oak railing for the top deck I hoisted up last summer with block and tackle. "House always looks so nice down there," I say. Jeremy shrugs. "Come on! It's still your house, too, damn it. No crazy bastard is going to change that. Look—" I hand him the glasses. He looks, but he's not much into it.

The woods are much less fresh than they were when I was here with Gabriella. The colors are muted, everything seems burnished. I spot smoke a couple of hills over, and I ask the young man, "That's not a fire, is it?"

He glances up from his screen; surprised, he looks again. "It might be. Ten minutes ago it wasn't there." He takes the field glasses. "Yep. It's back of the stables. Might be nothing—some stupid guy burning off a field when he's not allowed. Thanks." And he's on the radio, and we wait around to see an emergency getting handled, but there's nothing much to see.

I lead Jeremy back down, not turning to look up at him, trying to make him feel I trust him, not catching him in the fear I know he's feeling on the trembling, ringing iron stairs.

We take a trail to a flat outcropping, private, sheltered by bushes and boulders, and spread out lunch. We can see all the way south to the Holyoke Range, all the way west to the Berkshires. "I sit up here with you and everything seems so peaceful."

But Jeremy's not listening. "Maybe," he says, "if you move into town, I mean sell the house and live in town, then it'll be okay, I mean safe. And then it'd be better anyway—easier getting to school, and getting back and forth between houses."

My house! I don't tell him what that would cost me, to leave that house. I nailed every shingle myself, I fixed every leak. Last summer, how I ached after I finally had the oak rail bolted in place. But I say, "Jeremy, you can't run. That man could still find me if he wanted. And anyway, honey, soon you and your Mom'll be living in *Peter's* house—"

"—Oh, yeah, I forgot."

"It'll be okay—a few months and everything will be back to normal."

Jeremy just shakes his head as if he didn't believe it, as if he'd never heard of *normal*. What's *normal*?

Nine

Gabriella calls. The message machine kicks in and then her voice, stumbling, on top of my greeting, "David? David? Are you there? Pick up?" and I pick up. "I'm here, I'm here."

"Oh. David . . ."

"Yes. Hi"—and then, like a teenager, I don't know what to say, and the silence gets filled up with feeling—a lot too quickly. But that's how it is, the air between us open and hurt and sad. She says, "I know from Gar. I'm sorry."

"What?" I'm stalling. I know what she means—not Chuck's rampage, not our near-murder, his near-death, his arrest—she means Jeremy and me.

"I'm sorry for you, David. Is it just temporary, you think?"

"I think." We listen down into the faint rasp, hiss of the hollow space between our phones. "You've been through a lot worse. A lot."

"I want to come to see you."

"When?" I say, calmly, and I reach into my jeans for my little leather book as if I were setting up a casual lunch date.

"Can I come out tonight?"

"Tonight?"

It's Saturday, I'm just home from dropping off Jeremy. Frank asked what about an early movie.

"Are you busy?" she asks. No, I say, not really, not really so busy, sure come, come, I'd love to see you. We say goodbye, goodbye then, and laugh at our own clumsiness; and before I hang up I sit holding the phone like a security blanket and my breathing deepens, it's like sipping wine, it's as if I'm breathing sadness but sadness feels better than not breathing, keeping off sadness by not breathing.

So I straighten up the house, though there's not much that needs straightening without Jeremy around. Dishes in the sink to wash, plants to water. I go through my music but it's no contest: it's Glenn Gould's recording of Bach's Preludes and Fugues, *The Well Tempered Clavier*. I sit in my big poppa reading chair and listen and begin *Middlemarch* again. First in college, then when I was a little older and more versed in Victorian culture, and now for the third time, when I understand more about marriages, compromises, failures.

I call Frank to tell him I'm not going to see him, but I forget to eat my dinner until Dorothea is nearly married to Casaubon and headlights sweep the ceiling of the living-room, so it's too late. I put down *Middlemarch*, quiet the music, and stepping into Sorrels wave from the front deck and meet Gabriella halfway down the brick walk.

We don't know what we are, sympathetic friends or lovers; we don't know how to greet each other. We settle on a hug.

Gabriella puts down her canvas bag and her laptop in the kitchen. She's wearing a puffy down parka that makes her look like a molting bird. It makes me smile, makes me feel protective, maternal. I help her off with her coat and go hang it up in the closet. We're both in clean jeans—a size or two larger than the ones we used to wear. I want to touch her soft, softly sculpted face, her dark curls. I let her be.

"I'd like to show you what I've written this week," she says. "I've been meaning to write this for a long time. I even have a contract, but I've had no time. I can use advice. It's on depression and abuse."

I shrug. "I'll be glad to look at it, but you're the expert."

She laughs.

I say, "Oh, I didn't mean it that way."

"I know, I know, I'm kidding."

"I know." I pour us both sherries and we sit at the kitchen table, Bach's precision of feeling in counterpoint to our muddiness. Not muddiness. Tentativeness, throat-clearing shakiness. "Thank you for coming. Really, Gabriella."

"Oh, that's so formal. You've always been a little like

that. I mean . . . serious." She doesn't take my hands, but she touches my fingertips. "David, I feel responsible—it was my foolish request in the first place—for what you've gone through out here. I dumped my problems on you. And now, Jeremy. Tell me—was he real upset? Of course, of *course* he was. How is he doing?"

"Oh, he'll be okay." Now she puts her hand over mine across the table, and I pretend to take it purely as sympathy—which maybe it *is*. And maybe because it's the tender touch of a woman after a drought of such tenderness, maybe it's knowing what she's been through, I don't know, but I let myself feel the pain in my heart and it's all I can do not to spoil everything by weeping. I can even feel a tinge of anger that Gabriella is *doing* this to me, giving me permission to cry, *unmanning* me. "He's had a couple of nightmares," I say. "You know."

"Thank God," she says, "nothing worse happened."

The meaning blossoms over the next moments of silence; I recognize more fully what all this means to her—it's not just a way of comforting me but a replaying of that afternoon at Sojourner House but with a different ending. Gabriella is mourning; it's *her* eyes brimming with tears. I pick up my dull-witted, narcissistic self from my chair and bend down beside Gabriella and put my arms around her. She leans to me. She leans to me and I know her eyes are closed as mine are, and we rock.

Very low, she says to me, "Something I never told you about the afternoon that I lost Sara. I stood near the top of the stairs, I told you that, and Sara ran up to me, and that's true, but there's one more thing. This man was screaming at us and I tried to mollify him, to speak calmly, matter-of-factly, but then—then I turned to run upstairs, away from the gun maybe?—I don't think so, I think it was to get to the phone or the buzzer, because I'd neglected to press the buzzer for the police. Actually, I must have pressed it, because the police were there so soon, but I couldn't remember, and I turned to run upstairs, that was stupid, I know better, and Sara saw me and ran. That's when he must have started shooting."

"Oh, Gabriella . . ." I'm stroking her back.

"And you—you came through," she says.

The music comes to an end.

"It could have been just the right thing," I say. "It's so random. Or—or it could have been *you* he shot and you'd be a dead hero. You know that. Don't you know that? Gabriella?"

"Show me the crawl space," she says.

So I get a flashlight and take her hand and lead her into the bathroom and lift the trap door into the crawl space and, stooping, shine the light down, and I look up to see Gabriella hunched over, curled up, trembling silently, and I sit beside her on the floor and hold her. She quiets and says crisply, in control, "Well, that's enough of that." As if she's been in deep water and now she comes to shore, she shakes herself off, stretches, and walks over to my reading chair and picks up *Middlemarch*, and for awhile we sit in the kitchen and talk about George Eliot's novel until she's able to dive in again. This need for new strength is so obvious that I touch her hand and say,

"Gabriella, it's okay. Shhh."

And she, she says, "Look—I do want to help. Maybe I can talk to Jeremy's mother."

"No. Thanks. No. What about you and Jenny? You want to go see her tomorrow?"

Gabriella laughs. I know what her laugh means: we each want to prescribe medicine for the other. Her laugh lets me prescribe another sherry, what the hell. This feels, all at once, so grown-up and sad and . . . deserved—not the pain, I don't mean that. I mean that just as musicians work so long and hard and finally can meet and simply play a duet, there's a thick, heady, rich quality to our talk that's distilled from the past twenty years of living since we were young adults and lovers. We've paid plenty for this talk.

Now she's tired, and I take Gabriella up to the bedroom and there's no question of making love. She gets ready for bed. "I'll stay up awhile," I say, so she'll understand that I'm not asking. I tuck her in and kiss her cheek and go up to my study.

I pretend to work. I fuss with papers, I send an E-Mail letter to my editor at the *Globe*. Tiptoeing downstairs, I stand at the doorway to the bedroom and watch Gabriella sleeping. It's nice. I go back to my study. From my big window I can see our mountain and the tiny fire tower etched against the pink glow of the night sky over Amherst.

Now I'm tired, and I undress in the bathroom and wear my once-in-a-blue-moon pajamas and slip into bed next to Gabriella like an old husband, I mean husband in a longtime marriage, and I'm grateful she's here, soothed she's here. It's as if not just warmth but a low-level humming is entering me from Gabriella.

It's when I close my eyes that my defenses go down. Bathed in that hum, my eyes closed, against my will I find myself eroticized, and I figure, Well, tough, that's *my* problem. It's still okay, even if I can't sleep, okay.

But now her fingers touch my shoulder, and she nestles against me, Gabriella, and opening my eyes I find she's turned. Tentatively, I reach my hand out to stroke her neck and her back and her hair, and she moans a little and burrows herself into me. I hold her against me, and she lifts her face to kiss me, oh, it's a long, long kiss, very sweet, and in my head I rehearse the words, *Are you sure, are you sure you want to?*—but I don't speak them, I share the spell with her, the dance of fingertips on our bodies. My fingers read her flesh like braille. I can read the years and the griefs.

I'm hard in the way I like, without urgency, hard but I can take my sweet time. It's like making love without being inside her. "Gabriella, Gabriella," I say, like love words, and lift her nightgown from around her hips and rest between her thighs, and suddenly she taps me and sits up, pulls her nightgown over her head and she's so *female* in the half-dark it takes my breath, and I take off my pajamas and we grin at each other and shake our heads in wonder and amusement, and she wraps her legs around me and I press myself into her and enter her softness, and it's not like home country, nor like something remembered and revisited, but my mouth opens with the strange depth of it, so strange the way flesh becomes—I don't know the words to say—a cave of music for a dance of a Sufi master, a dance to put the dancer in touch with the holy.

We make love, or we make *something* strange together, make love for a long time together, and it's like breathing-in warm wine, a time in which I feel hardly any need to come; my penis inside her is gesturing, signing, and my fingers, making speech, or making a language *for* speech. And maybe that's right, maybe that's what lovers do, invent a language for their bodies to speak, shape a linguistic community of two. Now I stop moving and touch her, and she wants me to move again, and now I feel her blooming, I listen down and down into the touch of tender flesh, as if there were something so far down to attend, and I feel her quickening against me, and when I think she's there—wherever—I begin to come inside her and I groan and try to shut up for Jeremy!—then remember that he's not around to hear and I let my groan become a roar, and I laugh at my own roaring, I wonder, is she coming, is she coming too, I think she really is, and I feel a kind of victory, we've made it through to this, well, God bless us . . .

I'm only half in this world, I fall asleep inside Gabriella and sometime later on she slips away and goes into the bathroom. Was she wearing something? Then did she know in advance? Like a college boy I'm embarrassed to ask.

So we sleep. Waking, surprised at being hard again, halfway till morning, I want to enter her again but I don't want to spoil things, don't want to be greedy—well, don't want to *seem* greedy, so I sink into her warmth and into sleep.

We wake and turn to each other. We kiss good morning and, surprised, make love. Coming, she laughs, laughs hard, and so I laugh. And we're quiet. The morning is saturated with peace. A gift—who is the giver? Outside, a gray day. Late fall gets sad in Massachusetts, when the richest colors are fallen to the ground, and on a gray day everything feels drab and chill and you know deep cold and icy roads are coming, and mornings when you have to shovel your way out to your car. You know *they're* coming, but this morning Gabriella and I, we're sheltered by this house and by each other. The fire in the wood stove has warmed the big livingroom and, upstairs, the bedroom where we lie around for an hour, *two*, the way I never do anymore, with a pot of coffee and a sour dough rye I've defrosted. A century ago, those months we were lovers, we'd spend Sundays like this, but we didn't savor it then, didn't see it as almost an art form. We didn't know to be grateful.

There's an erotic glow warming this room. We play—meaning flirt a little, tickle a little—in the big bed I built from two-by-sixes pegged together. This morning I see how beautiful Gabriella is, see as if for the first time. When we were lovers before, if you can say we were ever lovers, she was merely pretty, dark from her Italian father, the bones of her face sculpted by her Irish mother. I liked her broad mouth. Was she as pretty as, say, Andrea? What about Emily? But now, I sit cross legged on the bed, coffee cup in hand, looking at her without reservation or measurement or comparison, watching her at morning exercise in a lumpy sweat suit. We shower together. I scrub her back and her flanks, making love to her soft skin with soapy hands. She washes me, she even shampoos my hair, and I laugh and close my eyes and tumble down the waterfall.

Now I get up the courage to ask, "Gabriella, tell me—you wear a diaphragm?" She just doesn't answer. I don't ask again.

Back in bed, as we listen to Mozart, she says, "It's all *right*, David. After Sara, you see. After Sara, I had my tubes tied. You understand?"

Maybe it's my stupid question that destroys the morning, or maybe it was inevitable—as if we've been creating a field of energy between us that shields us from the empty places and the first inattention cracks the field and we tumble down—I feel the sudden distance between us now, and it's as if the distance is beyond my capacity to leap, and, as always, my whole life, I grow panicky at the empty space around me, inside me, I'm on a planet with no gravity to hold me, I'm imploding into my own empty center.

So I make a different sort of shield, of irony and distance, I contemplate, I analyze, I say, *Another secret.* Then: *Fool! What do you expect, fool?* I go out to split firewood, as men have done for so long to get back strength by using strength.

She looks so glum, sitting in my big chair with the Sunday *Times* and the *Globe.* So glum, and I think, *Do I have the strength for this?* Silently, we share sections of the paper.

She looks up. "What is it? It's something. What, David?"

"Nothing. It's nothing."

"David?"

"It's as if nothing happened to us. You know? Ordinary."

"I want you to understand," Gabriella says. "I can never, not with anyone, not ever again, not ever again be in what people call a 'romantic relationship.' It can never be the way it was when we were twenty. Not with anyone. I'll never be with you in that way."

When she says that, I'm in grad school again and she's gone off with Gar, gone off to live in his "political commune." It eats at my guts, and I say, "All right. That's fine." I pick up the *Book Review* and poke through it. We're both silent. Silent and silent. But finally I look up and say, "You keep all these secrets from me. How am I supposed to trust you? Even about Sara, you keep telling me different stories."

"I didn't think you'd throw that back at me."

"So now it's *my* problem for complaining."

"David, I've got something I want you to read."

You can always sucker a writer by getting him to read your prose. She goes upstairs and comes back with an envelope, addressed, not yet sealed.

"It's to my mother." She hands me the envelope. *Mrs. Sylvia Rossi.* Gabriella has written,

Dear Mother,

Jenny has made National Honors Society at school. We're very proud. It's hard to have her away, but I think the school is a very good one. Sara continues with piano, as you hoped she would. She closes her eyes when she plays the romantic passages in Chopin. She started out looking like her father, but now she looks more and more like me. Her eyebrows and her curly hair give away our Italian genes. I remember how you loved her when she was a baby. Too bad it's so hard for us to get to Florida and so hard for you to fly here.

All my love,
Gabriella

I look at her and can't speak.

"I can't do it to her. She's almost eighty. Sara was the beloved one, the grandchild she adored. *So.*"

"And you think you're writing for your mother's benefit?"

"You can be pretty cruel." She takes back the letter.

"You're telling me, I shouldn't worry about your lying to me because you even lie to your own mother?" And even while the words are being formed in my mouth I'm thinking, *What is it about me that I demand such honesty?*

She still says nothing. I feel like shit.

"All right. I know how bad it is for you. I know. I'm sorry I'm such a prig."

"Maybe I do want to bring her back for the minutes I write. I don't see what's crazy or wrong about that. All the time, I remember Sara dying, I mourn, I fill her memory with my grief, you understand?"

"And so you invent her living—"

"—I invent her living to remember her as joy— joy she was for me. She was so light, Sara. When she danced into a room— the Sara who could touch me with joy, she's gone. That's the child I need to bring back in memory or I'll dry up all the way. So I pretend—you're right, for *both* of us, my mother and myself. What's wrong with that?"

"Maybe nothing."

"There are times. I'll hear a funny noise and think for just a second, *Oh, that's Sara, fixing eggs for herself.* Or I think about telling her something that happened at Sojourner House. And then for just a moment—I mean, I'm not crazy—she comes back to me as she was, as joy. I'm sorry," Gabriella says, "I'm sorry, but I'm not an especially honest person. I don't care. It's not important to me."

"Don't you think you can trust me?"

"Sometimes you *are* a fool, Dave."

And I *feel* a fool. She *has* trusted me. I don't say anything. I stoke the woodstove till you can see the sheet metal glow. Sitting down again, I say, "Last night was something, wasn't it. And this morning."

"It's been fine, hasn't it?"

I nod, like an embarrassed adolescent.

Patrick Ahearn calls as we're washing and chopping vegetables for dinner. "I suppose you know this already. Chuck has left the hospital. Did anyone call you?"

"No. Oh, Christ!"

"No? He took off about noon. Now, you see how you've managed to escalate the problem? Here's an unstable young man, my brother needs help, there's no doubt about that, and now you've put yourself in danger, you've put him in danger. You've turned anger into real rage. And Mr. Rosen, when my brother gets enraged, he becomes—outrageous. Well, you already know that. Now he's broken the conditions for bail. Anyway, I'm sure you're not interested in the family's problems. I felt, legally, I needed to advise you of the situation so there are no recriminations later on."

"Have you heard from him?" I ask.

Behind me, at the sink, Gabriella asks, "David? What?"

"He knows better than to call me. I'd be forced to advise him to put himself under the jurisdiction of the court. I'd be forced to call the court to say I heard from him."

I'm getting angry. "Cut the phony words, Mr. Ahearn. Tell me what you *do* know. I consider the Ahearns responsible, this isn't a legal game, you *vouched* for this crazy bastard, now you tell me his rage is my fault?"

"Mr. Rosen, don't be snotty with me. I'm trying to be reasonable—"

"—When did he get out, did he have money? Does he have his car?—"

"His car? Of course not. He wasn't in a locked ward; he signed himself in as one of the conditions for bail. Now, I personally signed a restraining order, in case he should decide to leave, giving the hospital authority to hold him. Apparently, he slipped out past some negligent custodians, I have no idea. There was a visitor, apparently."

"What time?"

"Eleven this morning."

"And now it's five. Why the hell didn't you call before this?"

Ahearn doesn't answer. Gabriella says, "What time?"

Hand over the mouthpiece, I tell her, "At eleven this morning." I don't tell her I'm just as glad we didn't know. It was, a lot of it, so good a day, the bad stuff seems so insignificant now. Too good a day to spoil. Then I remember: Kerry. "Ahearn, you keep in touch with us. I assume you've called the police?"

"I've spoken to them on an hourly basis, Mr. Rosen."

"*Professor* Rosen," I say—and hang up.

That's the end of our peace this Sunday. Gabriella understands without asking. I say, "I'll get in touch with Kerry."

I call Women in Transition and explain; they'll try to find her. I call Nancy and leave a message to get back to me; I call the Green River Police. They hadn't been notified by the Boston Police—if Patrick ever really notified anyone. While I'm explaining to the police, I get a beep on Call Waiting. It's Kerry, and she's talking so fast I can't get a word in. She wants me to come pick her up, pick her up right away. I tell her to calm down, we've already called the police. "And Chuck doesn't know where you live."

"Oh, but you don't know Chuck. It'd be so fuckin' *easy* for him to pay off some taxi driver, pay him off with coke or something, you think it's a real big secret? The taxi drivers all know. He'll buddy up to some taxi driver and find us. He's gonna kill us. Or kill me and grab Andrew. Who the fuck knows. You want that?"

"What do you think? Kerry?"

"You don't *know* him. See, there's things I haven't told you. Please. Dave. Get me out of here. I've got to keep us safe."

"But he already *knows* where *I* live, remember? What's the good of coming here, Kerry?"

"Then where? I'm not sticking around to be killed. I'm taking a goddamn bus out of here if I have to. *You don't know Chuck,*" she says again.

"Just a minute." I put my hand over the mouthpiece and say, "she's terrified. Gabriella?"

"We can take her to Boston."

I nod. "Kerry? We can drive you to Boston." Then I have another idea—"Look, I'm not permitted to come into the shelter. Let's talk in the library. The children's room. There's a Sunday reading hour. You're in walking distance from there, aren't you? I'm with Gabriella Rossi. You get away from the house and meet us there with Andrew and we'll talk about our options. Don't worry, Kerry. Of *course* we won't desert you."

"What about the gun?" she says. "You still got the gun?"

I've kept Frank's shotgun. It's sitting, loaded, on top of a beam in the kitchen pantry. "I've got the gun. Now listen—Kerry, please—try to stay mellow with Andrew."

"Mellow!"

I call Peter's house and leave a message on his answering machine for Nancy. Another on Nancy's own machine. I warn her about Chuck. I know what those messages will cost me.

"Just a minute," Gabriella says, "one more call, David." I know she's calling Gar in New York, he's home—he says he'll get right on it. I'm annoyed that she turns to him—and what can Gar do? As we lock up and walk down the brick path, she squeezes my arm. She knows. I'm cradling the shotgun in the crook of my arm. This feels so ugly-primitive—man, woman, gun—it makes my stomach turn. With the gun covered with a coat on the floor in the back of the car, we drive out of the hills down to Green River, past the fire road I'll never see without remembering.

Everybody in Green River loves the library. How many of us are descendants of people who lived in New England when it was built? My grandparents were trying to survive pogroms in Kishnieff or Odessa. But so many of us want to attach ourselves to the calm, strong spirit we invent for this nineteenth century New England. It's an invention. I'm thinking of the loss of children back then. I'm thinking of the hard lives of the small farmers, of workers in the small mills just getting set up in the 1850's. The library is a white, classical revival building from the middle of the century, with trim beautifully articulated in a pale beige and fluted columns and a simple, elegant lintel over the portico. As we climb the steps, the library seems so out of keeping with our lives. Well, that's why we need that invented New England. Maybe that's why *they*—the people in Green River back then—themselves needed the classical order, simplicity—visual metaphors of the civilized.

It's good to come in out of the chill, gray day. We take off our parkas. Gabriella goes to tell the librarian that we're expecting a call, that it's an emergency. Returning, she whispers, "There's a story hour. I asked her to find *you* if there's a call. Easier to find a *man* here."

In the children's room, a young woman with Alice-in-Wonderland blonde hair is sitting in the midst of ten, fifteen, children and mothers. One father's there, seems to be checking out the mothers. The young woman is reading a story from a picture book. Some children are listening, some rocking, and some, like Andrew, are in another world, holding stuffed animals or rolling cars back and forth. But the woman reads on in sing-song. Andrew, sitting on Kerry's lap, is picking at a huge, stuffed, ragged children's-room bear. Gabriella sits down next to Kerry and I squeeze in next to Gabriella.

"You hear anything else?" Kerry asks. We shake our heads. "So what am I gonna do? What the hell am I supposed to do?"

A mother nearby smiles a fake smile, "Shhhh . . . " and Kerry gives her an ugly look—then throws up her hands. She rocks, rocking Andrew. Gabriella does something that surprises me. She puts her hand on Kerry's back and rubs in a great circle. She puts her arm around Kerry, while the young woman reads from the picture book a hip version of "Little Red Ridinghood."

. . . and the flowers were *so* pretty that Red couldn't help wanting to pick a bunch for her Granny. And the wolf left the path with Red and helped her find the luscious, red flowers she loved the best. "You know," Red told the wolf, "you have a terrible reputation."

"Oh, but I'm really awfully nice," Wolfie said. "Did you know that I've become a vegetarian? I'd *never* eat a grandma. Yuck!"

A child calls out, "Is it for true?" "We'll see," the librarian says—and goes on: "Well, I certainly *hope*

Kerry can't be quiet. She rocks Andrew the way Andrew rocks the bear, as if he were a comfort-object or an extension of herself, and watching them I think there are no good outcomes for this little kid, he's between a rock and a hard place—a father like that, a mother like Kerry. I can't imagine Kerry, she herself so incomplete, able to help him become what he might be, what he might have been, and seeing him in this circle of kids and mothers, I grieve for him as if I were at his grave.

you're not a grandma-eater," Red said, with her hands on her hips and a fierce look in her blue eyes. "My Grandma and I know karate, and we're not scared to use it."

When they got to Granny's house, they found the door open. "Granny, Granny, I've brought company for lunch," said Red. But Granny was nowhere to be found. Red and Wolfie ran from room to room; finally, there in the bedroom was Granny, very very sick. 'Oh, oh, oh, my tummy!' she groaned. Poor Grandma!

"We have to get her to the doctor," said Red.

"I think I can help," said the wolf, and he asked Red to please tie Granny to his back, and he rushed through the forest as fast as he could run, till he got to town. And the people were all very scared of the wolf, but he ran with Granny straight to the hospital. And by the time Red got there, the doctor had Granny safe in bed and soon she got all better, and the wolf and Red and her mommy and daddy and Granny had a great big party with carrot cake for the wolf.

Gabriella has her arm around Kerry, and she's whispering. I can't hear much of it, but I do hear, "Listen to me, Kerry. I *know* you're scared. I know how scared you are. I do." And now she must be telling Kerry about Sara, because Kerry's face changes and her mouth hollows out, and she says, "Oh, my God, no." And then something I can't hear and Gabriella says, "You don't have the luxury of panicking. You want it to happen to you, what happened to me? Do you? Do you hear me, Kerry?"

Kerry is shaking her head, crying, Gabriella squeezes her around the shoulders. "We'll stay with you, David and I."

"You don't know Chuck. He's *killed* people,"

A couple of women nearby hear this and look at Kerry and at one another. Kerry holds Andrew too tightly, and he squirms away and whines and she says, "Okay, okay, sorry."

"Killed people?" Gabriella says.

Kerry nods.

The librarian taps me on the shoulder. "Mr. Rosen? There's a phone call." I slip away.

Gar starts right in. "Dave? I just heard from Bill Akavian in Boston. Ahearn picked up a car a couple of hours ago, rental car, a Chrysler. So my guess is he's coming out. Otherwise he'd take a plane. How's about I come up there?"

"Nothing you can do," I say.

"Maybe I can kill the son of a bitch this time."

That's hard for me to swallow. Gar knows it. But I hear behind this tough-guy swagger a tenderness, and it's this I decide to answer. "Gar," I say, "I appreciate the way you care about Gabriella. I do."

"Maybe I'll come up anyway. Dave, listen, I'm gonna fly up—local airport—and have a car waiting, what the hell. No put down, Dave, I swear to God. I just want to be there. Keep the faith."

I shake my head. *Keep the faith*! Christ. Now it comes to me: Barbara Johnson's place. I find my pocket calendar and look up the date that Kerry went to Barbara's; sure enough, there's the number. I tell Gar, try us there first.

Back in the children's room, the long-haired story teller is leading the children and mothers in a song about caring and sharing. Kerry and Andrew and Gabriella and I slip away to confer between bookshelves.

"We can all go to Boston," I say, "but for how long? And why are you going to be safer in Boston? Listen— what about Barbara Johnson's? Doesn't that make sense? He'll probably be picked up, Chuck. Now you're settled here. What's the point of running?"

"Barbara Johnson's—okay, that's okay," Kerry says. "And Andrew knows the place. You've still got the shotgun?"

"In the car."

"That son of a bitch," she says.

We slip past the children, singing "Hello . . . Hello . . . Hello . . . " in Spanish and Swahili and French.

Ten

We drive Kerry back to the shelter to pick up her things. No secret now, the shelter, it's not far from Barbara's place—down this street, she points, and up that hill. I'm surprised how calm I am, how clear-headed. Way down in my belly is a low whine of fear but with it, the clarity I felt once in the seconds before a car crash; the shakes came later.

Kerry's twisted in her seat, turned away from Andrew, and Andrew begins to poke at her. Is he feeling how unavailable she is? Kid in a strange place, needing to be held. But she has nothing to give him. "I want choc-ate," he whines—"Mommy, choc-ate, Mommy . . . " on and on till even I want to bark at him. Kerry hides inside herself, twisting away, and he whines, and I try to soothe him by singing a silly song, and that flops. "Mommy . . . " and she turns like a dog you've bothered too much and yells, "You shut up, you fucking shut up!" And now he's crying, and she shoves at him, and I say, "Kerry, pick him up, come on, *now*." She says, "Oh, give me a break," but she picks him up and holds him, but she holds him so stiffly, as if she's a machine for holding, and he curls against this machine and I shut them out of my mind and turn to Gabriella.

"Old Gar—he's actually flying up to some local airport. He really loves you," I say to Gabriella.

"Well . . . I love Gar, too, you know?" she says. She takes my hand. She's comforting me, comforting herself, partly because of Andrew and Kerry in back.

We're the parents, up front, but now in the back Andrew is singing and playing with his mother's hair, and she's groaning, "Come on, hey, enough, sweetie, goddamnit." But she's all of a sudden softer. Kerry's wearing a beat-up navy wool sweater she must have picked up at the shelter. Her hair is ragged. She looks like a lot of the young, slightly depressed, spiritually deprived, vacant-eyed women around Green River now, children of working poor, pregnant in high school, married too young.

She gives me directions. Left at the church, right. Up the hill . . . . She takes out a cigarette; I look at her in the rear-view mirror and shake my head. "I'm a pill, I know, but please, I'd prefer you don't smoke in my car, okay?"

I see her roll her eyes. "For Chrissakes!" But she's grinning as she puts back the cigarette, and I'm a little embarrassed at my own cultural snobbery. Who has the right to talk about the spiritual deprivation of people he doesn't know and isn't part of?

Now her grin fades as we drive up the long street past empty mill buildings, workers' housing now cheap, renovated apartments for people on welfare, and curve up a hill towards the bigger houses where the mill managers once lived. I see her grow tense again, twist in her seat again, but now she's looking outside herself, she watches like a frightened animal, checks out cars, alleys between houses. "That gray Taurus," she says, "it wasn't there before, I think."

"Chuck's supposed to be driving a Chrysler . . . . That's what Gar told me. Kerry?—you said he killed people. What do you mean he killed people?"

"Yeah, well, he has." She breathes out, way out, letting air go as if she were a balloon. "He's killed people. Drug stuff." She shrugs. "I don't mean he's a *killer*. Not like he goes around *killing* people. But this one time I was there when a drug deal didn't go right and he figured he was being had—and maybe he was. I think he was. So he gets this pig-faced guy, Cuban or something, in the car, like they have to negotiate, and I'm driving, and they're rapping and laughing, and all of a sudden he takes out his gun, his pistol, and the guy says, 'What, are you fucking crazy?' And Chuck says in a nice voice, 'just a precaution.' And he says to the guy, 'I don't want you to see where we're going. You wear this. Wear it!' and hands him a couple of wool hats, you know, the stretch kind that seamen wear? And he makes the guy put them on and down over his eyes, one over the other. And the guy is starting to get real nervous and he's blabbing, and I look in the mirror and Chuck puts the gun against his teeth and shoots him through the fuckin' mouth! And I'm screaming and he smacks me and I start howling, and I pull the car over because I can't drive. He says, 'The hats didn't work worth shit. I tried to keep the car clean, but there's blood all over. Shit!' And he dumps out the guy's body and says, 'He was a piece of shit. I told you I don't fuck around.' So I have to help him scrub the blood with bleach all afternoon. I never told anyone. See what I mean about Chuck?"

I'm worried what Andrew is hearing, what he understands. But I want to find out. "Does Patrick know?"

"Patrick? Shit. Patrick knows. Just don't 'tell' him, you understand? Don't make him have to know he knows. Patrick is where the cash comes from for the deals Chuck takes care of. It's all cash, right? See, Chuck handles his father's beer distribution, and on the side . . . "

"— he handles his other distribution. He kind of told me."

"Right." Kerry says, "But see, you wouldn't understand about Chuck. Because Chuck can be really kind to people, no shit, really generous. Well look—I stayed with the son of a bitch, I kept going back to him. *You* think I'm some piece of shit, *you* think I'm one of these women who take any goddamn thing. Well . . . " She kind of laughs. "*I* don't know . . . Andrew, look at the wind, look at how the goddamn leaves are blowing." And she starts to cry and hugs him like a teddy bear again, and he's whining, and I'm looking for Chryslers, and Gabriella turns to Kerry and says quietly but firmly, "You can't do this. Kerry? Remember what I told you before? About falling to pieces? Kerry?"

"Yeah, yeah."

"You don't have the luxury," Gabriella says slowly and in great calm.

Kerry nods. I notice how when she's suffering, weepy—undefended—I like her a lot better, I even find a kind of beauty in her face.

"We're here," Kerry says. Gabriella pulls over. Kerry pushes Andrew into Gabriella's lap and walks fast up the steps of the porch and into the grand Victorian house—not so different from Sojourner House in Jamaica Plain—doctor's house, manager's house from the turn of the century. Toys are scattered over the part of the lawn behind the house that I can see. I take Gabriella's hand. In quick, horrible fantasy I see Kerry murdered and Gabriella and me raising this child.

It seems so long before Kerry comes back. Andrew sits quietly on Gabriella's lap until she tries to caress him, and then he squirms away and goes inside himself, inside his little body, and his eyelids stay open but his eyes close like a glass door. He's not here. Am I wrong to see him as irreparably damaged? I can see Gabriella wanting to caress him; she keeps her fingers just a little away from his shoulders. Now, barely touching, she sculpts his body. And finally, he eases back against her breasts.

Kerry rushes from the old house. God knows she's a Woman in Transition! She's carrying a duffel bag and back pack—maybe all her worldly possessions. I pop the trunk and she puts the bags in and we're off to Barbara's place. In my usual phony way I start sugaring her up, Hey, you're gonna be all right, the police know, the guy will be picked up. And look, I say, how far you've come these past few weeks, Kerry . . . but as I turn the corner I see in my rearview mirror a blue car follow, and still blabbing I try to check the markings, is it a Chrysler?—it could be.

I turn at the next corner, and the blue car turns, too. Okay, but I *know* these streets, I say to myself. "Hang on, folks," I call out, and take off like a shot, my little Honda, I turn into the alley behind the Congregational Church and hang a left at the next street and double back through the next alley, and the blue car's nowhere. The women are saying, "What? David? What's happening?"—and I say, "Nothing. Just paranoia. Just a car back there. Whoever it was, he must have thought I was crazy." I'm chuckling; we're back on the street we started, heading up the hill towards Barbara's place.

But now I get gut-scared, clammy with unease: he's behind us again. He must have found the shelter, followed us from the shelter, he must have figured I'd get back to my original course, and like a fool I did. But it feels outside day-logic, like a nightmare where you're driving or walking and there's an enemy in back of you, closing in. It's a big car. I can't outrun him; can I outmaneuver him? I scan my mental map of this part of Green River for alleys too narrow for a big car. He's closing all right. I can see his face in my mirror. It's Chuck, it's Chuck for sure, but he's cut off his hair, he looks like anybody.

We're a couple of blocks from Barbara's. I turn away from her place, jam down my foot and get a block ahead before he responds; we bounce over the broken pavement of an alley, and Andrew starts complaining, and Chuck's behind me, and suddenly I remember—fool!—this alley ends in a lot behind Skibiski Fuels, the heating oil distributor; and sometimes—often—the other way out is blocked with trucks. My neck muscles grow taut as if I were getting ready to force an opening, but Christ, there *is* no opening—two fuel trucks parked side by side—and I'm cursing myself—I've walled us in.

So I jam to a stop and swing around to face the car coming down at me, hoping to slip by before he can stop, but he fishtails the car to barricade the alley. Kerry's yelling something. Gabriella turns around and says very quietly again, "Now stop! Kerry? That's better."

"I'm not collapsing, just shut the fuck up!"

"Take a deep breath. That's better . . . . All right."

Now, for as much as a minute, nothing happens. We sit there in the car, and Kerry's whimpering, and Gabriella's patting her back, and it's as if this moment has been waiting for me my whole life and I'm not ready for it. I remember the last time, the time in the woods, the gun, the utility knife, the blood. I don't see him forgiving that.

Andrew is saying, "Mommy? Mommy? Mommy?"

"Shh, shh," she says. She starts singing to him, "The wheels on the bus go round and round . . . "

Now Chuck Ahearn steps out of the car, easy, mellow, smiling. He's wearing heavy exercise clothes—a sweatshirt with the logo of the Patriots, high-top sneakers. It's cold, there's a cold wind swirling papers and leaves in the alley. But Chuck grins—an old friend who's been playing a game with you. He holds his hands out, palms open, and as if this were a meeting of opposing captains, I get out to parley with him. "Kerry doesn't want to talk to you," I call out. The distance between us is maybe half a football field; a silence hangs in the air after I speak, as if the words were taking a long time to reach him. Finally, he answers, *"Not a problem."*

"She's got a restraining order," I call.

He walks towards me, slowly. "Not a problem," he says, his hands smoothing out the air. "Hey, if that's how she feels, it's a free country, know what I mean?"

I pretend to believe him, I let my shoulders slump, I open my own hands and shrug. "So what do you want? — You stay where you are. Hey, I said, *Stay where you are.*"

Now he's in field-goal range. "I just want my son," he says, as if we were calmly negotiating a deal. "You can understand that, you're a father, you're a dad, you want to keep your kid, right? I want my little boy. We're gonna get out of here, me and Andrew, and you won't have to deal with me again. Okay? Okay? Hey!" he yells—"Kerry? Come out here with that boy, come on, baby, it's Chuck, don't fucking treat me like your enemy. Come on out here, that asshole can't protect you. No need anyway," he soothes. "No *need*, it's Chuck, baby."

I've gotten a little ways from the car; can I get back, take up the gun, or maybe use the car as a weapon—drive the car into him? Each second makes it harder, but there's no single moment when I feel a surge in threat, enough to make me do something that terrible, so I keep trying to talk him back. He's so *big*—bigger than Gar. Once I had seats behind the bench at a Patriots game, the only time I've seen football since I was a kid. The men seen up close, not on television, they looked larger than life. Chuck looks like that.

He keeps walking towards the car, shaking his head and smiling as if we're playing some game. "You see, Dave? I told you I was unstoppable. Didn't I tell you? Now, I'm not after trouble, you just back off, come on, now —"

Gabriella calls to me: "Dave? Dave? Get in the car! Dave?"

Why don't I get in the car? Maybe because I'm scared of what I'd do with the car. Do to Chuck. But I'm backing up now, backing towards the car and Chuck is still, absolutely at rest—but now, now, he's half-flying through the air on top of me, and I'm down and flailing, it's hopeless, and there's screaming from the car, and my jaw is smashed, a fist, a boot?—and I'm seeing through water, and a blurred boot thuds into my chest and now *I'm* screaming, and it's dark and stars and I wake to a kick in the stomach, as if I've been ripped open, and I open my eye and turn to avoid another kick, and even in the midst of this moment of absolute attention, I'm feeling as if this has been waiting for me behind the partition, as if it's what I've been putting off, hiding from, this terror, and I know I'm going to die but I howl and roll away from another kick.

Half from a dream I hear a car door open and I turn my head to see Kerry standing by the car with the shotgun in her hands. She's pointing the gun at Chuck. I roll away, covered in mucous and blood, and shake my head half-clear.

Ever since Frank's lesson, the gun, sitting loaded on the beam in my pantry, has also been sitting in my inner geography, the way it must be when someone learns he has a cancer, and constantly sees with his inner eyes and locates in his inner skin the alien cells at their work. Wherever I walked in the house I felt it tugging at my inner skin. Sometimes, nighttimes, before I went to bed, I went downstairs to make sure the gun was still there, and as if it were some kind of satanic idol, I stood beneath it, staring at the scrolled tooling on the metal. Should I take it upstairs with me? I never could.

Now a frightened young girl in jeans is holding this gun,

big, double-barreled twelve-gauge shotgun, beautifully oiled walnut stock in the crook of her arm. I crawl to my feet and call, "Kerry . . . come on, Kerry," and I stumble back towards her, back towards the car figuring on pulling her with me, but she steps past me, waves me off, and lifts the gun to her shoulder. Gabriella calls out, "Kerry! Kerry, please!"

And Kerry takes aim and Gabriella is begging, "Please Kerry, you shoot him and they'll take your baby away, they'll take Andrew away, Kerry, please!"

Kerry leans her face down over the stock. Gabriella sinks back in the car. She's holding Andrew in her lap, rocking him, and now her face is like I never want to see her face again, a tragedy mask, but at the same time dead. Even through the closed window I can hear Andrew screaming for his mother. Gabriella doesn't look at him; she rocks him mechanically. All at once it mixes with the pain in my stomach, what this must be like for her. It's happening to me. I can't even distinguish between my own broken face and body and the pain I'm living as Gabriella.

I hold onto the car and watch Kerry.

Kerry takes aim and Chuck walks slowly towards her, I mean almost in slow motion, a step, a pause, a step, his hands outstretched. Finally she says, "Please take one more step, take just one more, oh please, Chuck."

He stops and says, "You let all these shitty people come between us? You don't have to worry about me, baby. The three of us get out of here, I've got money put away, okay? Fuck these people."

Kerry says, "See, my father used a gun like this on porcupines, Chuck. I told you. I remember skin and blood and guts splattered all over the fuckin' trees. God, I just decided, I decided I want to use this on you so bad. I'm going to try not to kill you. You see where I'm aiming? I'm going to blow your fuckin' testicles off. But the way shot spreads out, you can't tell. Please, take another step. Please, Chuck, don't stop. *Don't* get on your knees. Walk towards me, you son of a bitch. Maybe you'll get to me and get this gun away. You want to try, Chuck?"

"Hey, that's cool," he says. "I'm getting back in my car and I'm outa here, okay? I'll cut my losses. Okay?"

"Yeah, except I know you, maybe you got a gun *on* you, and I *bet* you got a big gun in that car, Chuck."

"Gun? What gun?—shit, I just got outa the crazy-hospital."

She walks *towards him* a few feet. I warn, "Kerry, no closer!" Just for an instant, I'm watching one of the nightmare fights of my childhood, fight between my mother and father, but this time it's not witch fingernails and slaps. This fight is going all the way. And I'm back, next to the chain link fence at the alley by Skibiski's. I realize, oh, I *want* her to do it, to pull the trigger. But I *can't* want that, can't be the person who wants that. "Please, Kerry?" I say.

She calls out without turning her head, "Dave, you stay here with me, okay?—but send Gabriella and Andrew out of here, okay? Tell Gabriella to get the police, okay?"

"Kerry, I heard you," Gabriella calls. "All right, I heard you. I'm going. Please. Don't do anything." And holding Andrew against her chest, she hurries out of the car but stops and again speaks coolly and precisely. "Kerry, please, listen: if you shoot him, listen to me, they'll take your child away. It's almost certain. And they'll put you away. Please." She runs, carrying Andrew, howling and squirming, down the alley to Skibiski Fuels.

"I'll get battery cables to tie him up, Kerry."

"You keep away, you fucking keep away from him!" she yells at me. "He'll grab you again for sure. Keep the fuck off."

So I feel stupid, bumbling, broken, not-a-man, but I stay—I stay as a witness, bloody witness, face-cuts streaming blood making it hard to see anything. But I'm a witness. In case she has to use the gun. But now I think, *Has* to? Christ—*wants* to, *aches* to—for if she's pretending about that, she's got me fooled. Her face is down low over the stock. If she shoots, she's going to rip up her cheek, but I don't want to spoil her concentration. Because Kerry is really concentrating.

"Oh, Chuck," she says. "Oh, please, don't you want to make a try for the gun? Shit. Then you better get down on your knees. Now. *Now*," she says, sounding fatigued, "by the time I count to three. One . . . " Her voice is getting crazy, not flat but up and down like a song.

He's down, down on his knees, he's grinning at her, he wags a finger at her. "You know what's in that gun, Kerry? It's probably light birdshot. And the gun will jerk and maybe you'll hit me with a couple of pellets and all that'll do is get me fucking *mad*. Kerry, you don't know shit about guns." But he's on his knees. "You don't know guns, Kerry, and you're freaked. I'd feel really a lot better if you get your finger off the trigger at least, stop pointing the damned thing, you're freaked."

At this, she leans further down over the gun. "Yeah, I am. Come on, please, Chuck."

"Oh, you wait," he says. "Oh, yes." In his inner eyes he's seeing, I'm sure, some ultimate revenge. Six months, a year, five years from now? . . . But he stays there, on his knees, and suddenly he bends forward and retches and a stream of vomit comes out. He wipes his mouth and mumbles, "That's the *pills*, that's the goddamn hospital, that's all."

"Kerry," I say, "you back off now. Wait for the cops. If you shoot him, you heard what Gabriella said, what's going to happen to Andrew?"

She steps back a couple of feet. "Okay," she says. "But I hope the fuck he gets up. Please, Chuck."

"You're crazy. You're the crazy one," he says. "You're the one belongs in the hospital."

I keep waiting for a cop. It seems half an hour since Gabriella left, but I check my watch and it's less than ten minutes. Finally I hear a siren. Kerry hears it and for a moment she must look away and slacken on the gun. I don't even see him make his move, but he's low and he's moving and I yell, "Kerry!" and just before he dives into her and tumbles her down, she tosses the gun away and it scrapes along the ground and I grab it. Just above her head Chuck stands and takes a big handgun from a holster under his sweatshirt and aims it at Kerry, but maybe out of the corner of his eye he sees the shotgun in my hands and as he swings his handgun towards me, Kerry makes a grab for it, and it clatters away from him over the pavement.

Now he's sees the shotgun in my hands, and he says "Fuckin birdshot!"—and I wait for maybe a whole second, more, I feel the heft of the big gun, steel cold against my finger, and I *see* he has no gun in his hand, I see that, and I know the cops are coming, I wait a second, no, *more*, and *now* I pull the trigger. Both triggers at once. I fire, and it's not birdshot.

It's the first time since I was a kid that I fired a weapon, and then it was a twenty-two in target practice at camp. Now there's a roar out of hell, a thunk and the recoil smashes into my shoulder. The sound echoes from the buildings; I expect to see blood and flesh splattered, but there's none; Chuck's jammed back hard against Skibiski's chain link fence and crumples. Now I see the blood.

Double-ought, Frank told me. *What the cops use.*

Cop car pulls up behind Chuck's car in the alley and the cop is on the car radio; now he has his gun drawn. On me. Kerry's face is bleeding and she's yelling something, and Chuck is holding his stomach, rocking himself, trying to get to his feet. I drop the shotgun and walk over to the cop car with my palms out like a Jesus. "Watch out," I say to the cop. "He may still have a gun." My ears are still buzzing from the shot. I'm dizzy. I keep retching but I can't puke up anything. The gun's explosion, what I felt as I pulled the trigger, maybe the bastard's death—all of it—it's more than I know what to do with. I'm soaked in my own blood and throbbing. I'm hardly in the world.

Gabriella carries Andrew, still crying, out of Skibiski's and Gabriella is murmuring "Oh my God, oh my God, oh my God . . ." and Kerry says, "Give him to me, shit, he's screaming for me." Chuck sinks down again, his body sags like a balloon, and I think how crazy-sick *brave* the guy is, how he keeps coming and keeps coming. God.

He's not coming now.

The cop tells me to spread my legs with my hands against the car. I feel his hands on me, and then he's gone. "Can I get up?" I ask. He doesn't answer. I turn to see him stooping by Chuck's body. "Is he dead?" I ask. He doesn't answer. He's chalking where the gun was, Chuck's gun that he's holding on a pencil; he borders the scene in yellow police tape from fence to car to the back of the building on the other side of the alley. Something about that makes me want to giggle. That it's so like a movie, I suppose. He goes back to his cruiser, I suppose to check on the ambulance and backup. I hear the radio squawking. Gabriella goes over to tell the cop what's going on, but he's saying, "Just wait. You please wait, ma'am?" Kerry's holding Andrew close, rocking him, walking him away from the scene.

I look at the taped area, police boundary, with shotgun, chalk outline of the handgun, and Chuck Ahearn stirring, twisting, silently, in spasm on the ground—it's the silence that's so strange—blood beginning to seep black now through his torn sweatshirt, through *his* boundaries. The tape marks the formal boundaries, conventional limits, of the real; the ***this***. There's a ludicrous, arbitrary, Alice-in-Wonderland quality to the tape, the reality it defines—then what about the limits of the body itself?—and I find myself giddy, wanting to laugh and have to force my face to stay straight. Over by my car Gabriella stands alone, wrapped in her own arms, stone-faced.

Now comes the howl of a siren. I fall down and down into the dark.

Gar is shaking his head, mournfully, so guru-like it irritates the shit out of me. He's leaning back in my big easy chair upholstered in threadbare blue velvet, the chair where, in a livingroom in New York, my poor father used to sit pissed-off throughout my childhood. It especially irritates me because I find myself wanting so much to rest in him, hand him the problem, which, he admits, yes, *is* a problem.

It's a problem, all right. Gar says, "Oh, sure, *this* guy is dangerous. No question. I mean, Chuck?—Chuck was, after all, an asshole. Dangerous, I know," he says, "oh, sure," gesturing towards me, my bruises. "But not over the long haul. But this Patrick Ahearn, he's cool. He might not do *anything*. You know? It might be enough for him just to make you sweat. It might . . .

"But see, there's no time limit on a thing like this. So you *keep* sweating and sweating. He could have you taken care of a year from now when he's on vacation in the Caribbean. For now—for *now*, you're safe. But in six months—yeah, he might set up a contract on you. We've got to think this through." For once Gar isn't manic, expansive, grinning. His eyes are narrowed, he's showing me Gar the shrewd businessman. It scares me, his seriousness.

At the top of my stomach there's a high-pitched pull—high-pitched, shrieking inside, there's a Yiddish word, for it, *shreck*, except a *shreck* is something that happens just for a long moment and this goes *on*; this kept me awake most of last night.

Patrick was very quiet over the phone yesterday, very much a lawyer dispassionately describing a business arrangement.

"Now, I want to reassure you, Mr. Rosen. You might think that this family might take some kind of vengeful action against you. You understand me? But actually, you're perhaps in no greater danger now than you were before you killed my brother. You have no reason to fear I'm going to take out a contract on your life. You understand what I'm saying?"

"You're threatening me is what you're saying."

"Not at all, not at all. No. The very opposite. I'm reassuring you that you're in no more danger of something terrible happening in your life than you were a couple of days ago. So don't worry. I don't want you to worry."

"I've recorded what you're saying."

"Well, I hope so. I do hope you *have*."

"Your brother had a gun to his wife's head. Your

brother almost stomped me to death." I manage to feel righteous when I say this, as if it were true about the gun. As if it weren't murder.

"Well, my brother had a terrible problem, Mr. Rosen. And you certainly didn't help, did you? But I've told you—I do understand what my poor brother was like."

I didn't tell him I knew about Chuck's distribution of drugs, about Patrick as money man and organizer. And I didn't say that after the blast of that shotgun, when I looked at Chuck, so out of it, his blood drenching his sweatshirt, I thought, from a kind of horrible aesthetic distance, how beautiful this body was, like a fine, large animal, and what a shame it was to damage it. I just said, "I'm really sorry. I know you cared about your brother."

"That's not good enough, is it, Mr. Rosen?"

I hung up. I sat in the study, throbbing under the codeine, and thought about Jeremy. I was going to have to give him up. I could see that. We can't live together. I remembered Jeremy in New York the afternoon we met Gar. After we left MOMA we took the subway down to the lower East Side and went on a walking tour of the streets where Grandfather lived when he came to America. I sat in my study with my hand against my bruised cheek and my head tilted to meet my hand, as if my hand could, like a mother or a lover, give me succor. And I realized that this was the precise way my grandfather sat, except that he also rocked his cheek in the cradle of his hand. I used to think of it as his mourning dance, but he sat like that so often, in grief over all the water under all the bridges, all the skin gone up in smoke. I wondered what my grandfather would say if he knew I'd killed a man. The *way* I killed him—the way: the gun fallen from his hand and the police about to come and one second, two, and then, thinking clearly, I pulled the trigger.

Killed? Oh, not just *killed*. For the past two days, since Chuck died on the operating table, I've been replaying the scene the way you replay a car accident, trying to make it come out differently this time. I've picked up the gun and called out to him and he's stopped, he's put down his gun, and I've stopped. Or I've shot him in the arm, in the leg, in the stomach. Or—not even that—I shoot him down the way I would have shot a rabid animal, dog or raccoon, as a job I had to do, something sad but necessary. But that wasn't how it felt. It's true, afterwards I felt for the beauty of this great animal. But when I pulled the trigger? There's no justification for what I felt when I pulled that trigger. I don't want to be that person.

The telephone has been ringing for two days, ever since the papers and television picked it up. I've been acquitted by the media. I'm cynical but relieved just the same. And as soon as that became apparent, as soon as I became officially a Protector and Kerry became a Valley Hero, the telephone has hardly stopped. I've left it on the answer machine. People mean well. Horseshit they do. Frank Polidori and Sylvia and Russell Warner, okay—they've called to comfort me, called as they'd call if someone died. Well, someone *did* die. But most of the others want to live out the excitement of a legitimate killing through me. Yesterday I went to speak to Leonard Noble. He offered me sherry and he grinned, grinned constantly. "Well! You'll just have to teach a course for us on American Violence, won't you!"

I didn't answer. He laughed. "Well, you know, David, I was only *kid*ding. But really, can you imagine what a *draw* such a course would be! *Violence: the American Experience.* With *you* as teacher? You know, you really ought to think about it."

I've gotten feelers from interview shows, two national afternoon talk shows, news shows. What they *say* they like is the college professor fending off the monster in defense of a mother and child. What they really delight in is a "justifiable" killing. Some writer called, wondering whether I'd thought about a TV docudrama. I told him to keep his damned writerly hands off. I didn't tell him I sit and shake and don't know why I'm shaking. I didn't tell him about the dreams. I'm afraid to fall into sleep because of the dreams.

Dreams of an endless chase in the dark, among cement staircases and overpasses, subway stations with no trains. No escape this time, and as I run, thickly, as if through a gluey atmosphere, I try to explain, words, words, words, and the figure behind me doesn't hear or doesn't understand or hears and understands but is indifferent, and now he's in front of me and now I've lost Jeremy, and I'm screaming, "Jeremy . . . Jeremy . . . Jeremy . . . ."

The woodstove is pumping heat into the cold house. We sit in my livingroom, Gar in my poppa chair, nodding and nodding to himself. I sit on the couch, Gabriella on a stiff-backed chair—it's the only place she's sat since we've been here. Kerry sits crosslegged on a big pillow right in front of the stove. Andrew's taking a nap upstairs. He's been clinging to his mother steadily; how much did he see? What did it mean to him? Kerry is staring at the old Ashley—just a curved steel box really—as if it were a fireplace, or a television. I caress her slumped shoulders with my eyes. She's someone else for me now. Ever since Chuck's death, I find myself touching her hand at the least excuse.

But for myself—I've conceded in advance, I've written it off, resigned myself, can't resign myself. Jeremy will live with his mother and I'll still worry, because who knows what Patrick Ahearn might do to me in revenge? If he knew me—and wanted to hurt me most terribly, and if he had no scruples—it wouldn't be *me* he'd have killed. I've given up in advance my own life, that's the least of it. Like my grandfather, like Gabriella but in advance, I'm mourning.

"Yes," Gar says, as if he'd been working it over in his mind. "Yes. We're going to have to go see Patrick Ahearn," he says.

"You're kidding." I know he's not kidding.

"You and me. You and me, Dave. We'll set up a meeting. Listen, we need to take the offensive. And you know how offensive I can get." He laughs, stops as if you flicked a light on and off again. "We have to take care of him before he takes care of you."

"You're not suggesting we kill him? You're not, are

you, Gar? Because understand—I'd rather leave the area, change my name, anything." At once I realize that Gar himself once went underground—went with Gabriella. Maybe I'll have to do the same. Disappear, with Gar's help, so that Patrick can't have me tracked down; if I'm not around, I don't think he'll hurt Jeremy.

Or maybe that's just what he'd do.

"What kind of a person do you think I am? *Kill*? No. Well, I mean I've got nothing profound against killing the son of a bitch, but I think we can do better. Here's my analysis. Chuck was family. Patrick's got a thing for family. So he *will* hurt you—if it's safe. The thing is to show him it's not in the least safe. The marines are landing, Dave."

Kerry looks up. "I hear Andrew." She goes upstairs.

"And that woman," Gar says under his breath, "is our landing craft. And our beachhead."

Gabriella shakes her head, and Gar raises his eyebrows. "What the hell," he says. "You never did approve of my metaphors." He looks at me. "We'll be okay. The police aren't pressing charges, you're not in some jail somewhere, we'll get through this thing."

I say, "Thanks, Gar. I mean for Steve Lerner. I can't believe how great you've been. You found me Lerner. And Lerner's been wonderful. Really, thanks." Steve Lerner is a local attorney, classmate at Harvard of Gar's head lawyer in Boston, John Goodwin. It was Lerner who got things smoothed out fast. Charges won't be pressed. I'm getting treated as a victim of crime, not a criminal. Gar paid.

Gar gets up and extends a formal hand to Gabriella, as if asking her for a dance. "Gabriella and I are going off to see Jenny at school for a few hours. *If* she can stand to be with me that long, a guy with . . . gendered metaphors. See, we're talking about murder and Gabriella worries about language."

"Language kills," she says, unsmiling. "You know it. Language lets people feel good about killing." She lets him lead her to the door.

Gabriella has been saying things like this for two days—when she says anything at all.

"Your job," Gar says, turning back to me, "is to talk to Kerry. You ask her for names. If you can't do it, I'll try. But please. Get names."

"Chuck's associates."

"Yeah. The guys he distributed to, the stores, the business people. Then I can get my guy on it. I can get Bill Akavian on it."

"I'll try, Gar. You leave Kerry alone, okay?"

Gar just grunts. Kerry comes downstairs with a sleepy Andrew. Gar and Gabriella bundle up against the near-winter day. Gabriella turns and gives me a hug, she holds me for a long time; unashamedly, I soak it up. Ever since I killed him, she's been so tender to me. But she goes through mood swings. Sometimes she won't look into my eyes, sits on the chair without talking. She massages oil of arnica into bruised muscles. I don't know that it does any good, but her fingers bring tears to my eyes. I'm a soldier who's done bestial things and comes home to be welcomed by wife and children as a hero.

Gar stayed at a hotel the last couple of nights near Jenny's school. I asked him to stay here but he wouldn't have it. Gabriella stayed with me. I couldn't make love, I wouldn't even start. It's the pain, of course, the constant headache, the bruised places. But not just the pain.

Gabriella goes off with Gar to see their daughter. That's good. It is, it's real good. I'm glad for her, I'm glad for them both. I'm ashamed that when I hear my broken door thud closed, I feel so heavy and frightened.

So. I've got a piece of cake for Andrew. I sit him between me and his mother and cut him forkfuls of cake and he lets me feed him, but that rankles Kerry. "You'll spoil him, he's not a fucking infant, he can feed himself, for Chrissakes."

I look at her, I wonder about her own mother, what it is she's passing on. But I don't start anything. "Kerry," I begin, "you gonna go back to Boston?"

"What for? My great family?"

"You must have friends."

"I guess. I'm making friends here. Shit, I'm part of a committee to help women get settled. That means *I'm* kind of settled. Everybody knows me around here. And there's . . . you." She tosses this off, toughly, so I know it means something. "I figure, Dave, I go to school, you could help. Right?"

"Of course I'll help. I'd like to. Get you started at the college. Kerry? I want to."

"I know you do. You're funny. I never had an uncle before. Jesus, you look like shit."

"Thanks."

"He fucked up your face good. It'll heal. The bastard."

I want to ask, does she know that the gun wasn't in his hand when I pulled the trigger? Does she care? Do we have an unstated pact about it? I know that in some way, the killing has bonded us.

"Listen," I say, clearing my throat, "I've got to talk to you about Patrick. You've got to understand the position we're in."

"Patrick! That cold prick. Your friend, Gar, he's got a big mouth, but he's telling the truth—Patrick's a dangerous prick."

"So please, Kerry. We've got to take care of this."

"Take care? Yeah?"

"Yeah, we've got to take care of this. Come on. You know goddamn well what I'm going to ask."

"Give me a break. You think I want him coming after me?"

"Kerry."

"Listen. The other day Gabriella got me pulled together. I don't think I'd have done shit it wasn't for Gabriella. But I'm nothing special, I'm just me. You understand? Don't think I'm not grateful," she says. "To Gabriella. And to you. Shit." She shakes her head. "The way you handled him? I couldn't believe it." She blurts a laugh.

"I didn't *handle* him. I killed him. You think I feel good about it?"

"Yeah? Even after he beat the living shit out of you?" She's silent; she wants me to know there's things she's not saying. "Well," she says, "you should have lived with him. I mean, he never tied you to a bed—you know what I mean? No. You *don't* know. You're so fucking naive. You are so *fucking naive!* I only wish it had been me blasted him. I wish to hell I hadn't turned my head."

"Oh, Kerry."

"Oh, Kerry, my ass."

"I'm not putting you down, Kerry. You were brave. You were. You saved my life. Taking him on like that. You must have been terrified. *I* was. Tell me—you spoke about your father shooting porcupines; was that true?"

She doesn't answer. She sighs. "I was such an asshole. I tell you to watch out and then I let him rush me like that."

"Well, he was so fast. I didn't even see him come at me."

"He *was*. He was a great athlete, Chuck. If he wasn't so fucking crazy he could have been famous or something."

I go behind her chair and bend down and put my cheek to hers. I had no idea I was about to do something so foolish. She doesn't misinterpret. I think she even likes this funny tenderness. She laughs. She guffaws.

"Oh, you, you're something else." She shakes her head. I can sense the bluster, all this frantic holding herself together. Kerry's tough *shtick*. What she needs is to fall apart just a little, sink into her sorrow. But I can't let her do that.

"Kerry," I say, "see, you've got to be brave again. Gar and I need names from you."

"Names . . ."

"Names. People."

"I told you, I'm not all that brave. It scares me. I've got a kid."

The kid is right now making a pattern out of cake crumbs on the table. I say, "*You've* got a kid? *I've* got a kid.

205

I'm just as scared. Hey! You think you're any safer, Andrew's any safer, than I am?" Suddenly, out of nowhere, I'm crying again, that's the way it's been these few days, I'm trying to talk and I'm furious at my own crying. Kerry looks up at me amazed. Her eyes deaden.

"Suppose he kills you," I say. "The Ahearn family will take Andrew if they want him. Patrick hates your guts. You want to see his family bring up Andrew? You've got no choice. You've got to stick with us or you may be dead, *we* may be dead." I see her eyes; or—I *don't* see them. "Kerry, no blanking out on me, c'mon, look at me, stop putzing around, *listen!*"

"Shut up, will you? Jesus Christ, I am listening. I hear you." She wanders the kitchen, pokes through the fridge and pours herself some juice. I keep silent, it's like a dance, it's her dance, and I watch her and pile up the cake crumbs with Andrew. She mumbles, "Anyway, I didn't say I wouldn't help. From a *distance*. Your friend talks about seeing Patrick? Fuck that. I don't want him knowing anything I tell you."

"Sure. *Sure.* You don't have to see anybody. I don't mean 'seeing.' Not 'seeing.' You won't be involved. I just need names. Chuck's contacts, people who know about Patrick and drugs and shit." I'm still standing next to her chair. I'm petting her hair, as if she were a beloved child. I don't know what I'm doing it for. She leans her head against my hand. It's crazy. Not sexual, then what? I've got no illusions about Kerry. I know about the empty place where a center should be.

"Names," she says. "Names is another story. Names. And look. Maybe . . . maybe I can like do better than just names. Okay?"

"What? Like what?"

"Well, I've got letters, Okay? To Chuck from people. I saved some letters just in case. Protection. I've got them with a friend in Boston. Scraps of paper from Patrick, notes about deals, about dealers, all sort of shit."

"Does Patrick know about this?"

"Not exactly. But he thinks I've maybe got something on them. That's why he's been wanting Andrew."

"You think?"

"Well, I think that's part of it. He wants Andrew so I'll have to shut up. Yeah, I think . . . . Names and evidence. Okay?"

I see Andrew crumbling cake crumbs like pollen over the kitchen floor. "Yeah, okay. Thanks," I say, and go for a pad.

Tonight it's the opposite of last night. Tonight I don't know how I could stand *not* making love with Gabriella. I drove Kerry and a silent Andrew to the shelter; I drive home and wait and listen for his car and want her back. When Gar pulls in the driveway, he walks ahead of her down the brick path and gives me a strange, thick look I can't understand. He looks at me and uses his eyes to gesture behind him to signify Gabriella: he can't talk, but needs to talk. He seems so solicitous of her, the way he cups her elbow and almost hands her over to me.

It's strange. But everything about Gabriella has been strange the past two days. After her initial anguish, she was calm and businesslike and I was glad not to have to worry about her, but it seemed overdone. Then she sank down inside herself; she sat in the straight-backed chair and didn't talk. Now, a darkness seems to emanate from her face.

The house is dark besides as I welcome her. It's warm because I've stuffed the stove again and again just to keep busy. I'm half-stoned on codeine. I say goodbye to Gar and he says, "We'll talk," and goes off to his hotel. I put my arms around Gabriella in the warm darkness, and the way she holds onto me I read as a message I need to read, and I take her hand and lead her upstairs. "You want some sherry?" I ask. She shakes her head. "How was it, the two of you seeing Jenny together?"

"She wonders why we can't get back together, Gar and I."

"And you?" I stop breathing.

"Me? Me, David? Oh, you know. I'm wondering if I want to be alive."

"Please, Gabriella. Oh, please."

"Don't worry," she says. "You know. I have obligations."

My belly's churning; I know what I'm going to say to her. All my adult life I've believed in the power of love—I mean *making* love, physical love—to heal and restore. It's a crazy thing to say to a woman who's just told you she maybe doesn't want to live, but I say it: "I want to make love with you." I say, "Is that all right?"

She nods, like someone half asleep might nod. "All right," she says. "Yes." Oh, it's too heavy, a ritual of love to exorcise demons. I say in the back of my mind, *This is too solemn, too solemn,* but it stays solemn. As I hold Gabriella, a line comes to me, "lovers, their arms round the griefs of the ages..."

The bedroom has drawn the heat from the stove downstairs. We undress in the light from the stairs, and, playing at being playful, I lift the cover and invite her in. "Step right this way, madame." She kisses my eyes. I can't remember the last time anyone did that. She looks just for a moment at some of my bruises, she runs her fingers over my chest and stomach. "David," she says. And I feel kind of grateful for my bruises, that they take her away from herself.

For a time we stay on the surface, holding one another, afraid to dive. We sculpt one another, warm flesh to warm flesh. And now we go through. I enter her body but it's not like *me* entering *her*, it's like both of us entering some other place. We go through. It's as if there's a curtain of air, or as if the molecules of air peel back, divide like the Red Sea, letting us through into another place, into the dark inside the dark. We make love in this dark in silence. What else do we make in the silence? It seems as if making love tonight becomes a kind of service. I don't know what we're serving. I could say God but that's not it exactly.

I wonder whether making love like this means entering the place my grandfather inhabited. I have the crazy notion that here in the dark we're consecrating her child, Sara, and maybe all the children caught in wars, in plagues of rage and emptiness, emptiness coated by ideologies. I'm a murderer myself, I'm filled with death, how can I calm the murderous world? But we're all there is, here in this pocket of darkness behind the world, to enact in a clumsy, tainted way a sort of ritual to make this darkness bloom.

But *does* it bloom? After love, Gabriella curls up, turned away from me and with that gesture I feel sure that all she could take from me tonight was a little comfort. I realize that the healing happened only inside my conception of Gabriella, and she herself is . . . something else. So now I stroke her back, but she says, "Don't, David. Oh. I'm so tired, I really am. So tired."

Eleven

Gar is dressed to the nines, whatever they are—in pin stripe and pearl-white shirt. I'm in professorial tweed jacket and the shirt and tie I use twice a year for special faculty functions. I'm out of place not wearing a suit; but the truth is, I don't even own one. We drive from Green River to Boston in my Honda, then switch to the Mercedes he leaves permanently in Boston. At a downtown garage we leave car and key with an attendant.

In the elevator Gar puts his big hands on my shoulders, as if he were squeezing me into one piece. "You okay, Dave?"

Bill Akavian has been waiting for us at the offices of Gar's attorneys on Court Street. "Everything's arranged," he tells Gar. Bill asks the receptionist to buzz John Parker Goodwin.

Goodwin is perfect. I'm used to lawyers in shiny suits and collars a little crooked; that's Green River. You can spot them any lunch hour talking cases together at the Cornucopia. Goodwin's suit was obviously made for him, a beautiful gray wool worsted. But a good suit—what does that take? Money, a good tailor. It's Goodwin's face and bearing that are special. They are above money but imply money, as do the low, indirect lighting and paneled walls. Billing goes to client but is rarely discussed. It's class Gar is buying for his various business deals in Boston.

John Parker Goodwin is lean and athletic, a man in his late forties like Gar and me, gray at the temples. I wonder about his rough edges. Does he have any? I wonder what he was like during the late sixties. I wonder if he ever smoked pot.

Gar asks him, "So what's the story with Ahearn?"

"We've told him we're interested, on behalf of our client, in a piece of land owned by one of Ahearn's clients.

We haven't used your name. By the way, Ahearn's 'client' happens to be his father."

"Oh, *good.*"

"He very much wants to unload the property. It's commercial. Near the new tunnel access. I've set the appointment for eleven."

Patrick Ahearn's offices are just a few blocks away, off Congress. We walk, Gar, me, Bill Akavian between us.

Why Akavian? "Just in case it gets nasty," Gar explained on the two-hour drive in to Boston. "Akavian's our insurance. Nothing's going to happen to us with Akavian as witness. Especially, I figure, with his police connections. So Bill will get us back out of Ahearn's offices." Gar held up a lecture-forefinger. "Not that Ahearn wants trouble in his own office, for Chrissakes. But I like the edge. By the way—it turns out that when Bill was on the police force he knew the Ahearns. Slightly. They're a Boston Police family. The grandfather, an uncle."

Now, walking against a cold city wind, he says, "Remember, this is all very low-keyed, Bill."

The way Bill nods in reply calms me. It's a nod from the world of men, that mysterious kingdom whose language I understand but always as translation, a second language, not my own speech.

Gar carries a leather attaché case, the leather heavy and glowing with a deep patina that makes me imagine he inherited it from his father. I'm envious of a case like that. He sees me looking at it. He pats the leather. "Them's our weapons, Dave." He sees something in my face. "Metaphor, just *metaphor,*" he laughs. He stops cold, middle of the sidewalk, and puts his hands on the lapels of my coat. "Let's get something straight, okay? *You did good.* Understand? You did what you had to do."

I did what I **didn't** *have to do.* The John-Wayne comraderie, especially in front of Akavian, makes me wince. I don't say anything; I go down into myself to where the sadness keeps me whole. My sadness, Gabriella's sadness, we're linked that way, and it's terrible to be linked that way. What kind of a beginning can that make? I hear Gabriella's words over and over: *I'm wondering again if I want to be alive.* Making love can't cure such wondering.

Patrick Ahearn is a partner in a small law firm in a fairly new office building. The offices of Gar's attorneys, Goodwin and the fifty others, are like the offices of a fine art publisher; Ahearn's offices, on the other hand, are brightly lit, expensively furnished in heavy white leather. Gar tells the receptionist, "Please announce us to Mr. Ahearn. We're clients of Mr. Goodwin. We have an appointment."

When Ahearn comes out to greet us, he surprises me by not appearing surprised. How cool—when there's no way he could have known. He simply says, "Please come in, gentlemen." It's only when we're seated and he's at his desk again with the door closed that he says, pointing to Bill, "Why is this gentleman in the room? You must be Garrison Stone. Am I right? But who's this man?"

"This is Bill Akavian," Gar says. "He's a private investigator."

"Must we bring a stranger into this discussion?"

Gar smiles, grins, shakes his head. "No. Not at all. Mr. Akavian will wait for us just outside."

As Akavian gets up to leave, he says casually, as if he hadn't planned to say it, "I remember your grandfather, Mr. Ahearn. When I was new on the force, a patrolman, he was just retiring. A very nice man."

"*Was* he?"

"A very decent man," Akavian says. "Everybody loved him. You look a lot like him around the eyes. I suppose you know that?"

"I'm afraid I remember snapshots better than I remember the old man."

"And I know your father. Mr. Ahearn was always very kind to us at Christmas. He's well liked. A decent man."

"Is he? I'm glad."

"I'll be sitting by your receptionist, Mr. Ahearn."

Patrick Ahearn waits for Akavian to be gone. And when he is, Ahearn says, "He thinks he knows my father? 'A decent man?'" He shakes his head. "He doesn't know my father." Ahearn seems to be speaking to us without posturing; again I'm surprised. "All my life," he says to Gar, not even looking at me, "I protected my brother Chuck. When we were kids, I *had* to. It became a habit. All my life. I've got three brothers. Our father never came down on the rest of us—not even on my mother—the way he came down on Chuck. I'm not going to talk about what it was like for Chuck."

Gar says, "I know you cared about your brother, Mr. Ahearn."

"I'll tell you . . . " Ahearn says. He doesn't tell us. He sits pondering. Finally, he says, in a dream-like voice that doesn't fit the office, the Italian suit, his rage, "It's something like bringing up a badly crippled child. I have a cousin doing that now. His whole life centers around that kid. And then suppose the child dies. It's something like that."

"I'm sorry," I say. "I'm really sorry for you and your family," I say, looking Patrick Ahearn in the eyes.

"And I told you, Mr. Rosen, that's just not good enough. You didn't have to kill my brother. I don't care what the police say, I don't care what the courts say."

"You weren't there," I say. "He would have killed me. If not right then," I add, "then another day. He would have killed his wife."

"So you've told me. But it does depend where you point your gun, doesn't it? You understand me? You didn't shoot him in the leg. You shot his chest away. We had to have a closed casket."

Now Gar leans forward. "I'm hoping I can help reconcile you two. We don't really need any more suffering, do we? The child, Mr. Ahearn, is being well taken care of. Whatever problems in the past—"

"The child is of no concern to the family, not anymore. No, we've passed that point long ago."

"All right," Gar goes on. "Now look here. If we can develop an amicable relationship, if we can put this behind us, I can imagine business dealings in the future. I'm based in New York, but I have interests in Boston. I think you know about me, don't you?"

Now Patrick Ahearn sits up and points a forefinger. "Don't try this on me, Mr. Stone. I may be a lot of things, but I'm not willing to be bribed into forgetting my brother. Yes, I know you. You just don't know the Ahearns yet. Now, you stop wasting my time. You got in here under false pretenses. We have nothing to discuss, and I'm busy."

Gar sighs a heavy, public sigh; he opens his attaché case and shoves a pile of xeroxes across the desk. "Patrick, I want you to look these over. We've done our homework, as you'll see. I've got a good organization, and we've been very lucky. Now, I'm not going to bullshit you. These documents, we've got the originals and copies in a number of different places. It's this way. If anything happens to Kerry Latrice or to David—or to the children, godforbid—my lawyers have instructions. It's all taken care of. You understand?"

Ahearn doesn't answer, he keeps his eyes on the documents; he fingers through them as if they were corporate by-laws or something; his face stays dead.

Gar doesn't say anything for a long time. I mean half a minute, more. Finally, he says, "But the flip side is, as long as they're safe, you're safe. No one intends to bother you or put you out of the distribution business.

"Now, I know you cared about your brother. I want you to realize what you're facing. When we get out of here you're going to ask yourself, 'Isn't there some way of doing damage without suffering repercussions?' I want you to understand—not only is the answer *No, fuck no, there's not*—it's incumbent upon you to *protect* these people. Not just not *hurt* them, you see what I'm saying?—*protect*. Because if anything happens to them, even if you're off on vacation, say, you've had it. Even an accident. Accidents can happen. But not to them. Am I telling you to play God?

In a manner of speaking, Patrick. And this is a life sentence."

"I want the two of you out of my office," Ahearn says. He looks down at the xeroxes and gathers them up.

"You can keep those if you want," Gar says.

But Ahearn pushes them back to Gar. He must have buzzed his receptionist; she comes in and we get up to join Bill Akavian in the waiting room.

When we're alone again, driving in Gar's Mercedes, Gar says, "I think we've got him. But don't fight me on this one—I still want you to get a permit to carry a handgun, Dave."

"No—No, I've got a kid."

"What's that got to do with it? You're afraid he'll play with the goddamn thing?"

"I don't want him to know me as a father who carries a gun. And I'd never be able to hide it. I'm no good at keeping secrets; if I tried, it would hurt us."

Gar shrugs. "Well, if it were *me*—" He pats his heart, and I realize it's not a gesture expressing feeling: he's got a small handgun inside his jacket.

That's when I realize that it *is* Gar, Gar, too, who's under threat. A life sentence. I put my hand on his shoulder and say, "Gar, thanks. Thank you."

"Come on, come on, Dave. We're comrades from way back."

"No—listen—you've probably saved my life. Or Kerry's life. Or Jeremy—saved Jeremy." I realize there's a lot I want to tell him, about how I've used him for years to be the man I'm not.

"Who knows, who knows?" Gar says. But he's grinning, as if it were the old days, I'm thinking of one particular morning, about 1968, lower Manhattan, six A.M., we blitzed a draft-induction center. While inductees were waiting, shivering outside for the doors to open, a few of us handed out cards telling guys how to keep from getting drafted, who to call, what to say, and Gar stood on the roof of a car and made a quick, arrogant, funny speech. Did it do any real good? It disrupted the process, maybe helped a few guys to stay out. Maybe it did nothing except make us feel good about ourselves. At least we got out again without being arrested.

Gar weaves through downtown Boston traffic like a cabbie. "Who knows, who knows?" he says again, a mantra.

I sit in Nancy's living room, late afternoon, in different negotiations. Jeremy has been asked to watch TV in Nancy's bedroom. I sit on the sofa, new sofa, sleek, stiff, leather sofa, goddamn bourgeois sofa, across from her big, scraggly old wingback, and tell her about Patrick and Gar. Our measure of safety. Our risks. She's wearing a mauve silk jacket—she must have come from a conference; I didn't know she even owned a fancy jacket. I think of Nancy in jeans. I suppose I still think of her as the girl she was when I met her, no older than Kerry.

I can see in her mouth how upset she is. Well, of course she is. I've put our child in danger. And there's the question of my face. "God, you look awful, David, I had no idea. Will those bruises go down?"

"Well, I hope so," I laugh.

"Frankly, I don't like it that Jeremy has to see you like that. For a son to see his father so . . . hurt. David? Does it hurt?"

I laugh again. It hurts all the time—not the bruises but my neck, my head. The pain is muted by medication.

Now her sympathy dries up. "It surprises you, doesn't it," she says, in this new grand manner she's developed, "that you could use a gun the way you did. It doesn't surprise me, David."

"I know. You've already told me what an angry son of a bitch I am."

"You're angry *now*. Oh, you want to see yourself as this decent, non-violent man. You know, that's what made it so hard to walk out on you, David. You're really an angry, controlling person. That's what I had to recognize. The whole marriage, you had me feeling guilty—not being an intellectual, not being political, not being competent with Jeremy. It took me months of therapy to sort this out."

"You think I bullied you."

"I wouldn't say 'bullied.' Well, yes," she says, thoughtful, "*bullied*, yes. But I certainly colluded. Well, you were older and wiser and so on."

"Now I'm just older."

"It's that *now you're not a threat*."

I'm waiting for her to get to the point. The point is, I suppose, she's got me nailed. No court order necessary. If she wants Jeremy to live with her and Peter, how can I say no? I'm hoping for days with him, that's all.

"I wish none of this had happened," Nancy says.

"Of course."

"He'll always have to know his father has killed someone. Of course, in some circles, you must be a hero."

She seems so cruel and bitter this afternoon, I can't figure out what she's doing. "It's not the kind of hero I want to be."

"I certainly hope not. Well, we're stuck with it, aren't we?" She sits brooding, and I don't disturb her. I hardly breathe, as if my breathing would set off an explosion and destroy me. She sits and sits and I wait and she knows I'm waiting and I think wants this obeisance from me, that I don't interrupt, don't say a thing. Finally she says, "Well. I want you to know I'm not taking Jeremy away from you. He'll be in danger wherever he lives from now on, that's the truth, isn't it?"

"I don't know, Nancy. I guess. Yes, I guess."

"That's what your friend Gar told me. He said it wouldn't matter. He was calling to reassure me, tell me you've taken care of the problem. Some reassurance!"

"I don't know," I say, surprised that Gar would have called her and not asked me. But not really surprised. I try to be honest—"It's possible Jeremy's more likely to be a target when he's with me. I don't know."

"Oh, you bastard," she says quietly. She won't look at me. But I see that the harsher her words, the lighter her sentence. "Please take care of him. Don't take chances. Promise me you won't take chances. And if anything changes, you'll let me know?"

"We're not enemies in this. I love him so much, Nancy."

"I *know* that!" she almost yells.

"Sure. We both do. I know, Nancy."

She reaches over and touches my face with her fingertips. "Uch. Davie, it must hurt." I go over to sit on the arm of her chair. I stroke her hair, as if *she* has the bruises. She doesn't prevent me.

It's gotten dark; I'm sitting with a football in my lap, sitting on Jeremy's bed in Nancy's house. I've rarely been in this other room of his. Different posters, different model planes. I'm almost afraid to look at his walls, as if I'll find there a different Jeremy. As Jeremy blabs a little uncomfortably, self-consciously, telling me what his friends say about the "shootout," not looking too hard at my bruised face, I wonder: might it really be better for him to stay in one household, one family: Nancy and Peter's? When his boundaries blur, when he's with his mother and me both for awhile, he's clumsy, self-conscious. But now, in his mother's house with me, and my face—my face looks like a boot ran over it, it's worse. I start rehearsing questions I can't ask—about what Jeremy wants—does he want to live in one household? He's too young, it's wrong. That's what parents are for.

I think about Russell and Sylvia Warner. On the way to Frank's tonight I have to bring them a pot of paperwhites in marble chips—something to say thank you for this past week. Sylvia changed my dressings, brought over tubes of cortisone cream and antibiotic ointment. I'm thinking about the Warners because they make me feel I have a separate life, they take me away from this room of Jeremy's in which I have no place.

Jeremy is describing posters and where he wants to hang them, and I'm nodding, but not listening, because I don't really get it, I don't get it—and finally I do. He's talking about *our* house, his room in our house.

"Anyway, I've got an idea, Dad. I want to paint the chest and the bed, maybe blue? And the walls? Do you realize everything's still white, like when I was a little kid? It's embarrassing when my friends come over."

"It is?"

"Steve's parents did wallpaper in his room. That would be okay."

"Okay, but no superheroes you'll get tired of in a week."

"Dad!"

"Okay," I say calmly. Joy hums in my pores. "We can go looking tomorrow. Tomorrow afternoon. Okay?"

"Frank," I say, "I've got something in the car for you. Will you come and take it?"

Jeremy runs into the house to find Nora. Frank and I watch him go. Frank doesn't say a word. He walks out to my car, leans in and pops the trunk, lifts out the shotgun and takes it into the garage. It was hard for me to carry it to the car; I sat in my kitchen, hands folded, and tried to make myself go into the pantry and couldn't. But neither could I leave it in my house, where it sat constantly inside my head. So now I close my eyes and try to feel it's gone, but it's not gone.

"Okay, David. Let's have a drink." He puts an arm around my shoulders, something he almost never does. I must look like hell. He shows me the new brick walk he and Nora worked on together.

"Why is she being so kind all of a sudden?" I ask this in a murmur to Frank while Nora and Jeremy are clearing the table. He blurts a laugh that is filled with distrust of women's motives, and that makes me defend Nancy. "Ahh, I trust her, Frank. I may not always *like* her, but she's got a lot of what once upon a time we used to call integrity. Maybe she just feels sorry for me. Hey, I saw *you* looking at my bruises and wincing—am I right? What she says is, I'm not a threat anymore. Anymore? See, I never experienced myself as threatening, but it's not my call. If somebody feels threatened, they feel threatened. What good is it if I declare my innocence? Well, now that she feels in control, she's being wonderful."

I expect Frank to shake his head as if I'm hopeless. And yes, that's just what he does. Now he motions to me to follow him, away from the kids. We take the garbage out to the garage. "What are you so fucking grateful for—that she doesn't cut your heart out? You're some threat, for Chrissakes. You won't even hold onto my gun. I can't stop thinking about that. Are you crazy? Some threat, you are. Please, do me a favor, take back the gun, keep it till next November. I don't need it. Please."

I shake my head; Frank sees something in my face that makes him put up his hands in surrender. I like it that he worries about me; I like it that he backs off when he sees I'm not to be budged.

We all head down to the family room to play pool—Frank and Nora against Jeremy and me. I grew up in the city and spent a lot of time in pool halls. I'm not spectacular, but I can run five, six balls. Nora is better than Jeremy. So it evens out.

I like to hear the balls click, I like to hear them rumble down the track from pockets to the end of the table. Just behind that door, probably in a locked shelf of a storage closet, is the double-barreled shotgun with the walnut stock. I keep seeing that gun, keep rehearsing, *Frank? Maybe I'll change my mind. Maybe I will hold onto that gun after all.* But I don't say it. I wish he'd ask again, but he doesn't.

It's good to see the kids together again. When we sat down to dinner, Nora said as she always says, "We're grateful for being here together and for our food. Amen." But then she added, "And especially for Jeremy being here." And she looked at him in her grown-up direct way. She's learned, in the absence of her mother, to mother herself. Maybe Jeremy is someone she can permit to be a child, as she can't permit herself. She teaches him, she listens to him. She's a year older, and for a girl her age that's like two years; yet she never lords it over him. Maybe they'll stay friends forever.

"You see that shot, Dad?"

"We got ourselves a team," I say, in the tough-guy New York street voice my father used with me when he felt close. A little like Gar's tough voice but older. That voice is metaphor for a style of urban being that had its heyday in the twenties and thirties, long gone, metaphor detached from its moorings; what can Jeremy make of it? My father talked in that voice when he'd take me down to Stillman's Gym to watch the fighters train. When I talk to Jeremy in that voice, I think I'm hungering for that old connection, fathering myself in Jeremy, as Nora mothers herself. "Okay, kid, let's see ya pop the ten ball."

Gar and I are strolling on the West Side of Manhattan, walking the long perimeter of the new city-in-the-city Gar will build. A couple of young guys from Gar's New York office walk together just behind us; at times Gar waves them over and points out something and one of them takes down notes. We walk on ahead. Gar is King of New York today, you can just tell, he owns the fucking city. His great, graying head and frame add to the effect, and today he wears a white silk muffler at the throat of his trench coat and a gorgeous Stetson—God knows who made him a cowboy! Well, he was always the king. That's how he was in 1968, his palace a seedy tenement cold-water flat on the lower East Side. Railroad flat turned political seraglio.

I suppose he grew up that way. Entitled. But not *old-money* entitled. His father taught him he had a right to a throne—but only if he asserted that right. Gar's children might be comfortable enough to sit on boards of museums. Gar himself still needs to build his city. And he delights in—you can see it by how expansive he becomes—the smart young men who wear good clothes so well and take notes so assiduously. He numbers ideas on his fingers. His hands shape an imaginary bridge that will link two buildings.

"A few years," he says, "there'll be a monorail right here, down along the river and over to Columbus Circle. I've been in consultations." As we stroll, he shapes the architectural spaces with his hands like air sculpture, wanting me to imagine little streets with shops like on Columbus Avenue, a city dream out of Jane Jacobs and Paul Goodman, with community centers and little parks, play areas with "people—trained people—to take care of kids and keep the equipment from turning to shit. And security gates and a security force so you don't have to become a fucking paranoid to live safe in the city." This last part is anything but Paul Goodman, who might have imagined community self-protection but never a private police force.

Still, he's selling it to me as if money had nothing to do with all this, as if we were still students at Columbia dreaming about the future.

"We used to believe," Gar says, his cupped palms holding this belief in front of us, "in the wisdom of a kind of collective, anarchic spirit. The way we said the words, '*the people*,' remember? Remember? '*The People*.' What I believe now, Dave, I believe that if you just leave things to 'the people,' leave things to happen, you'll get the lowest, the most savage outcomes, and it's the worst pricks who'll come out fine.

"But planning can do just as bad," he adds. "I know that. If these same pricks are the ones who own the future, plan the future, we wind up in a technological fascism—like in *Bladerunner* we were talking about. Yes. Sure. So it's got to be people like you and me and Gabriella if anything decent's gonna happen. And I do want to do something. Listen, I know what you think of me. Shit. You think I'm a vain son of a bitch. You use different words—you say 'narcissist.' Well, I'm saying, Okay, maybe I fucking *am* a vain son of a bitch. But I've got good dreams. I want to be known for generating and making concrete—hah!—literally concrete, okay?—good dreams. *Good* dreams."

And because I've gotten close to Gar, gotten to trust him in spite of his style, in spite of the aggression that's out front in him, hidden in me, I find myself opening to his dream, I do see it as good, good in his heart at least, not just a money-making thing.

He stops me and grabs onto my sleeve. "Listen, why don't you get out of the boonies, work with me on this. Would that interest you, Dave?"

"You're very kind. I feel you want the best for me. But I'm okay."

"What are you talking about? Who said you weren't okay?"

"I'm okay. I live where I live, I do the work I do—my teaching, my writing. You understand what I'm saying? I believe in it. It's my life. In that life, I'm a success. Not in New York, but in that life. I'm pretty useful. That's what I mean."

He throws up his hands. He laughs, he shakes his head as if to say, *How can you save this guy?* "Hey!" he says finally, "what profound shit! Who you got to prove it to? Not me, baby." He gives me a grin. "See what I'm saying?"

I wave him off, and he laughs again and looks into my face, eyebrows lifted. *No hard feelings.* So we go on.

We walk east now, away from his new city, from the Hudson around the Penn-Central railway yards east to Lincoln Center. "So you're gonna be meeting Gabriella for lunch?"

"Want to join us?"

He gestures with his eyes to speed up, get out of earshot of the men from his office. "Look, Dave. That's not how it is, you *capish*?" He removes his Stetson and brushes the brim with his hand. He plunks it back on his head and takes hold of my arm. "Dave, I'm not saying I haven't given it some thought, like going back to my original soul, you understand?—but the woman's not for me. She knows it and I know it. I love Gabriella. I do. But you think I want to live my life with a woman where I got to feel apologetic for the way I am all the time? Excuse me for breathing? Frankly, Dave, I like it when a woman thinks I'm the most glorious fucking star in the heavens. Gabriella? She's my Jiminy Cricket. Who wants to be married to Jiminy Cricket? You guys, you're the same, the two of you, the same—get me? A couple of pills sometimes, but the same. Listen, you wind up getting married—"

"—Married!—"

"I'm saying *if.* If. I promise to dance at your wedding."

"Our wedding." I'm laughing.

"We talked this morning, me and Gabriella. She said you were meeting for lunch. Well, I've got my bets down."

He gestures with his head. "Hey—see that guy over there? He's an undercover cop. Looks like a jerk tourist, right? That's the scam. He's like a magnet for muggers. The best. We talked one time. He's also at John Jay getting a Masters in Criminology. Hey—Dave. You want to come with me for a few minutes? There's a little gallery near the Frick, a painting I want to show you."

So we walk across town, cut through the park. The gallery is on a side street off Madison, and the painting is part of a show of American paintings from before the First World War by "The Eight." It's a John Sloan, a picture richly, roughly painted of three women hanging out laundry in a back yard and talking together. I've seen the painting in books. We stand and look at it awhile, then wander through the elegantly appointed rooms—more a private house than a gallery—of Pendergasts and Luks and Glaeckens and other Sloans. We come back to this one. "Best thing in the show," I say.

"Yeah, isn't it?" he says, proud as if he'd painted it. "It's fucking beautiful. I think it would be something to wake up to that painting every morning."

On the way out, he stops by the desk for a moment, then catches up to me outside.

"So," I say, half-kidding, amused by his playing art connoisseur, "why don't you just buy it?"

"I already bought it," he says. "That's why I brought you here."

"You *bought* it?"

"Well, prices are depressed a little. It's an investment."

I stand stock still on the corner of Madison and 71st. A beautiful, skinny woman in furs with a great furry sheepdog on leash crosses one way, a couple of well-dressed little girls accompanied by a nanny crosses the other.

"Well, I'm glad you like it," Gar says. He sticks his hands in his pockets, but I can see how pleased he is with himself. "Young woman I'm with now, a curator at the Guggenheim, she likes it, too."

In the sculpture garden at MOMA: near a Maillol woman, Gabriella walking with Jeremy; they're laughing together. He's teasing—that's his teasing face. Gabriella's face is animated, full of pleasure. I remember Gabriella's face in the car that afternoon, face of stone. I remember when she said her life was over, that she died when Sara died. I remember that she wanted it to be over. And I look at her face right now.

It's almost winter. Midtown Manhattan, dead leaves blowing. Not many people in the garden. A young woman sits by a reflecting pool. Jeremy and Gabriella are all bundled up. But even bundled, he starts twirling. Arms outstretched, he's twirling around the reflecting pool. I come out to the garden and wave, and Jeremy waves back like mad. "Can we eat?" he calls. Gabriella and I stand still and just look at one another. We're both scared.

Jeremy wraps his arms around my hips as if he's making a tackle. It's a disguise for affection he's a little embarrassed to show, especially in front of Gabriella. I squeeze his hand and won't let him wriggle away and I say, "Come on. Let's go eat."

So we eat, we talk with Jeremy. When he goes off to get dessert, instantly, like a tic, I imagine him kidnapped, by Patrick Ahearn or by some other crazy, imagine him gone forever. It's a momentary flash of helplessness. I don't pay too much attention. But I keep my eye on him.

Gabriella tells me that donations are up at Sojourner House. "Gail Kirkland and I had dinner last night.

Actually, we got a little drunk last night. Actually we cried together. I let her put her arms around me and—I must have been drunk—" Gabriella laughs "—I cried with her. We didn't talk a lot. But things are looking up. So—let's drink to Sojourner House."

We tap glasses of ginger ale. "So this means you'll be back as director?"

"I've never *not* been director, David. It means I'll be taking a public role again."

"I suppose you'll be busy all over the country."

She shakes her drink in her glass. "Oh, I'll be busy. I'm on the *Today Show* next week. There's so much work. But I want time to myself, too."

"Look—will you have time to see me? That's what I'm asking."

"I know what you're asking."

"No, you don't. It's not work, nothing to do with work. I mean, can we come together at all, middle of all this sorrow?"

"Oh, David."

"You mean, 'Oh, David' as in 'Oh, David, give me a break'?"

"Oh, David, *do* give me a break. I've got too much to think about right now. We have a conference of the National Coalition next month. You should see my schedule."

"It's important work. You think I don't understand?"

She takes in a breath and holds it. And holds it. I wait. "The other day," she says, finally, "a woman came in with a three-year old boy. The boy's mouth was lacerated on the inside with what she told Mary were cigarette burns. Mary asked, 'Your husband did that?' I mean, Mary was sympathetic but suspicious. The woman pulled open her blouse and Mary saw the same scars. There were some fresh lacerations. With gray ash embedded."

"—I understand. Enough. We've been through this."

"Most men hide the traces. They pretend to absolute uncontrollable rage, but they hit in unobtrusive places where bruises can't be seen. They pad the blow with a book or rolled towel so that the hurt is internal. They smash a hammer against the wall near their wife's head: a warning."

"Please. You're using these stories to keep me off."

"Oh, David. You think my stories have to do with *us*? You think I think we're that important?"

We sit with that a moment. "Okay. But tell me something. Are we maybe going to be together, you and I, you and I after all of this? Is that a possibility? Or are you going to feed yourself on horror stories the rest of your life? Come on! Is this a negotiation or is this an ending, Gabriella?"

"I've told you, David. I'm never going to be with a man. In the old way."

"I called you a nun—"

"I remember. Please, *please* will you stop calling me anything."

"You want me to stop calling you, period?"

"I don't mean that. I don't mean that." She folds her arms across her white blouse. This is turning out to be a business meeting. Suddenly my agenda is collapsing. I didn't know I had one, an agenda. A script. Under our talk I've been writing a play. *Play* is maybe not the word. It's something visual, a visual figure, a rising, complicating, culminating dance—maybe *dance* is the word. I wanted to celebrate. At this place in the drama or the dance I meant to recall the danger and the terror—*but look, see, the beginning of something good, I'm taking a chance. I've lived through a horrible initiation, and look, here I am with you.*

But I shake my head, wiping that script away. Gabriella raises her eyebrows, questioning. I shrug, I stay silent. She takes out her Weekly Planner and hunts through it like a prayer book. I can feel her wanting to fill the silence, I feel the power that gives me, so I say nothing.

She turns the pages of her planner.

"You told me I only pretended to myself that I'd died so that I didn't have to face the fact that I didn't die. I think that's true. But it's hard for me to be . . . what you want me to be: I mean, more than someone with work that has to be done. A lover? I find it hard to imagine. The mythology of love, David—"

"I'm not a fool, Gabriella."

"No, you're not. But you think I'm talking about illusions. I'm not. *Illusions*—really, that would be all right. It's much worse. The problem is, romantic love, the language of romantic love, disguises relationships of power and violence. Validates them. Look—" she takes a clipping out of her purse and passes it over. I roll my eyes. A man named Pinelli in Brooklyn, disregarding a restraining order, broke into an apartment where Claire Ruiz was staying with her two children. By the time the police arrived, the mother and baby were both dead of "multiple stab wounds." The clipping said that the victim and her "alleged" murderer were "romantically involved."

"You see? It's that language, David. 'Romantically involved.' You see what I'm saying? It becomes a *love story*. It's nineteenth-century opera. Love gone awry."

"What's that got to do with love?"

"Exactly. Just look at Chuck Ahearn and Kerry."

"You think everybody is like Chuck? Are you confusing me with Chuck?" But saying this, all of a sudden my heart rips through my body, I get dizzy, I can't say a thing. There's a long silence between us. In this silence I feel my own breath, and that brings me back. We're at MOMA.

"Are you all right?"

I don't answer.

"And Jenny," she says, "is my other priority. *Other* besides my work, I mean. The way Jeremy is yours. Of course he is. He has to be. And . . . . " She stops mid-sentence and sips her wine.

The silence feels promising. I say, "That goes without saying."

"It goes without saying," she says.

And it comes to me that—dear God—this *is* a drama, we're dancing a dance—just not the one I planned. And now, looking across at Gabriella's fine face, meeting her dark eyes, I wonder what it is we're making.

"Our lives are so complicated," she says.

"Oh, it's not going to be easy," I say, and I reach across to close her planner and take her hand. This begins to feel like courting.

"David," she says, finally, looking up into my eyes. "How are we going to manage?" She laughs.

It's so good to hear Gabriella laugh. I see my grandfather in the corner of the museum cafeteria. Okay, I lie, it's not my grandfather, it's another old man, hunched over his table as if he were covered by an invisible tallith. But I speak to him in my head, I say *Grandpa, Grandpa, I see the mourning in those drooping shoulders of yours, and let me say, it feels premature.* And he replies, eyebrows raised, looking at me with his deep-set eyes, *Nu? Just wait, then.*

You see? I say to the old man. He says, *So? Who said you shouldn't celebrate? If you can't celebrate, what do you have worth mourning? Ahhhh . . . but you always knew that. Why do you pretend you didn't know?*

Gabriella and I take hands under the table. "Are you okay?" she asks.

"You and me, we're both the walking wounded. I mean, you know—I get the shakes and have the same dreams. I imagine assassins. But I'm grateful. Let's not talk about all that."

"What about Kerry?" she asks.

"I'm keeping my fingers crossed. Right now, she's using me as an 'uncle.' Her word. She has people around her who support her. So she's straight. I'm afraid there'll come a time when she'll do damage to her life again. Psychoanalysts talk about a 'flight into health.' They mean when a patient 'decides' to seem really strong and healthy—but it's another defense. Or they talk about a 'transference cure.' Meaning, she wants my approval, so she acts as she's supposed to—but it won't last. Still, it's better than chaos, honey. And I'll do my best not to discard her. I'll be her Dutch uncle."

"You're such a snob, David," Gabriella laughs. "I want you to have more faith. I've seen it again and again, when you least expect it, people fool you. You can't give up on them. People come back. They make a life."

We hold hands like an old married couple on a good day and we watch Jeremy paying at the cash register. But I'm thinking, Sometimes you do give up on people, sometimes you have to.

I look into her eyes, and I see that she's there, Gabriella, she's full of her own light, the way Jeremy is full of his. She knows I'm looking and says, "So we come together in grief. It's going to be an odd life for us.

"Last night," she says, "just as I was entering sleep, Sara came to me, not as an eight-year-old but very young, a baby. But recognizably Sara. I felt her nursing from me, not from my breast but from my face, my cheek, so it was really kissing but I experienced it as nursing. I woke up in tears, but I felt very happy."

I don't say anything; I squeeze her hand.

"I told the board yesterday, I'm willing to stay on as director, but I want time to myself. Then I drove out to Crane's Beach. Nobody there in the winter. Just cold wind, sand blown across the road. But beautiful. I wrapped up and walked the shore, I watched seabirds. When the wind came up, I squirreled down into a hollow in the dunes, I covered my face with a yellow silk scarf, I felt the light through the silk and the wind and the sound of sand on silk."

"I think you're giving me a gift. Am I right? You're trying to tell me you're healing?"

"Well, yesterday, I tried to imagine I was healing, what it might be like to accept healing. Anyway, I want to give myself time, I want to write. I can spend some of the time with you, David."

"Well," I say, "and I can come to see you when I'm not with Jeremy. I can imagine possibilities."

Jeremy's back with ice cream. He pays it full attention, then asks, "Can we see that painting?"

"Which painting?"

"The one from last time."

"The Monet?" I guess.

He shrugs my shrug. We head upstairs. "That's it," he says, pointing.

The three of us stand in this bay of colored light. I look down into the sculpture garden. It was from here we first saw Gar—just three months ago. I turn back to the water lilies, and we lose ourselves inside the life glowing out of these canvases spread around us. All that light makes one big light and we can take it inside and warm ourselves. Jeremy narrows his eyes and opens his arms and puts his head back and *floats*. "Nice!" he says. He's pushing; it's where he *wants* to be. But I think he gets there, too, a place that doesn't need Monet in order to pulse with light.